I0818905

villa COCO

ALSO BY ANDREW SEAN GREER

Less Is Lost

Less

The Impossible Lives of Greta Wells

The Story of a Marriage

The Confessions of Max Tivoli

The Path of Minor Planets

How It Was for Me

ANDREW SEAN GREER

villa COCO

—a novel—

DOUBLEDAY NEW YORK

FIRST DOUBLEDAY HARDCOVER EDITION 2026

Published by Doubleday, a division of Penguin Random House LLC,
1745 Broadway, New York, NY 10019.

Book design by Casey Hampton

Library of Congress Cataloging-in-Publication Data
Names: Greer, Andrew Sean, author
Title: Villa Coco : a novel / Andrew Sean Greer.
Description: First Doubleday hardcover edition. | New York: Doubleday, 2026.
Identifiers: LCCN 2025036495 (print) | LCCN 2025036496 (ebook) |
ISBN 9780385551977 (hardcover) | ISBN 9798217008124 (trade paperback) |
ISBN 9780385551984 (ebook) | ISBN 9780385552783 (open market)
Subjects: LCGFT: Fiction | Novels
Classification: LCC PS3557.R3987 V55 2026 (print) | LCC PS3557.R3987 (ebook)
LC record available at https://lccn.loc.gov/2025036495
LC ebook record available at https://lccn.loc.gov/2025036496

penguinrandomhouse.com | doubleday.com

Printed in the United States of America

3rd Printing

The author would like to thank Lee Boudreaux, Lynn Nesbit, Claire Conrad, Mina Hamedi, Maya Guthrie, Maya Pasic, Laura Cherkas, Aliza Wong, Daniel Handler, Laure Thorel, Doug Hamilton, Michael Field, MacDowell, the American Academy in Rome, and especially everyone at the Santa Maddalena Foundation. In memory of Rosina, Alice, Carlotta, *Giuditta, *Paride, *Giulietta, *Quo, and most of all, Max Rabino.

For
Enrico Rotelli
and
Beatrice Monti della Corte von Rezzori,
my baronessa

The trick to life is knowing what you want.

—PRINCESS MARIA AUGUSTA

part
I

The little Tuscan train station, brown shutters against yellow paint, seemed so fanciful you might unwrap it and find it was chocolate. The departures and arrivals sign had half its bulbs burnt out, so all our young man could discern was a cuneiform description of the current train strike, and while he looked for and could not find a living person, he did find a statue labeled *San Drogo*. The saint wore a floppy hat and seemed overburdened with a crosier, a scythe, and a sleeping lamb, as if he were carrying the shopping for another, more important saint. Our young man himself was overburdened with books, luggage, gin, fish oil, and doubt. He had followed the telegram's nonsensical instructions all the way from the Eastern Seaboard to Florence, whose domes and spires he glimpsed only briefly before boarding a tin-can train into the Tuscan hills, and now stood in the hot wind of a late-September day. For a long time it was only himself, San Drogo, and an olive tree whose roots were breaking through its planter. Though in his later travels, on sea and shore, he would become accustomed to the sensation of foreign air, this first arrival in Italy would be minted forever in his memory.

Here is the telegram:

GIOVEDÌ COME BY 5:15 TRAIN FLORENCE TO S. DROGO GAZELLE WILL BE WAITING BRING GIN FOR PRINCESS & FISH OIL FOR FAINA

He had made his way to the Florence train station; he had taken the 5:15; he had brought gin for whatever princess might desire it and fish oil for anyone named Faina. He looked around for this "gazelle" supposedly waiting for him, though, as the range of the gazelle does not extend to Europe, he was dubious.

A car arrived: a beat-up old creature trailing a veil of dust like a warthog bride. It stopped in the middle of the parking lot and for a long time did nothing; Saint Drogo, with all his shopping, seemed more active. The electric sign flashed something in Sumerian. Then the car door opened and out popped a person so lean and small our young man thought it might be an adolescent. But it was an elderly man.

"JOE!" the man shouted, waving. His head was lightly feathered in gray, accompanied by a raptor's beak and fervid stare; his movements were equally birdlike, jerky, startling.

Our young man's name was not Joe.

Halting bits of a foreign language were tossed toward him, like gym class balls our young man was unable to catch. "Giovedì" was the one word he picked up: JOE-VE-DEE. From this and the telegram, he realized someone had misunderstood his name for the Italian for "Thursday." Then again, an American might be called anything. As might a man in a train station.

"Gazelle?" our young man asked.

The man nodded. He did not smile. Gazelle's name seemed to suit him, as he bounded up to take the bag, threw it into the car as if furious with it, then gestured for our young man to jump in, talking the whole time in guttural dot-dash language that did not at all remind one of the fluid, musical Italian heard in foreign films. The only understandable word was a peculiar one: "MITSU!" he would shout, "BITCHY!" Then he would point at the car and smile proudly. Our young man came to understand it was a Mitsubishi. He clutched his duffel to his chest. The Mitsu-bitchy awakened in surprise. It started, stalled, then started again. A shout from the driver. Then, with a leap over a rock pile, they were off. Our young man sighed to be in a place, at last, where he could take life seriously.

I call him "our young man" because the sight of him—all gangly, double-jointed limbs, waves of filbert hair, and a raised-eyebrow expression of both innocence and arrogance—is so much more like a soulless marionette, an unenchanted Pinocchio, than a twenty-one-year-old American near the end of the millennium, that I can hardly bring myself to write of him in the first person. I'm sure an elderly toad, if magically presented with his younger tadpole form, would sooner eat it up than recognize the creature as any version of himself. So it goes with time.

Because of course the truth is "our young man" was me.

"There's a place in Italy in need of someone. Why don't you look into that?"

These were the words of my college adviser upon our final meeting and the only actual advice he ever gave; the rest of our meetings, infrequent as they were, consisted of heavy sighs at my choice in major (Archives and Record Management) and at my amorous choice in gender (my own). A dedicated engineer and committed womanizer, he clearly considered both choices personal failures. He wiped his forehead with a handkerchief and looked sadly into my eyes. It is unlikely this "place in Italy" had occurred to him unaided; he must have canvassed his colleagues for some way to save his poor, gay, bookish charge. He produced an ad clipped from the paper, which he tossed to me across the table with the regret of an executor producing a meager inheritance:

> ADJUTANT DESIRED for owner of modest country house. Collection of books, objects, art such as a Picasso to be cataloged before Christmas. Duties: dictation, pruning, shopping, hunting martens. Italian desired. Stipend, travel, board, and room. Tuscany, Italy. Write to: Baronessa.

An address in a town called San Drogo was provided. I looked up at my adviser and asked what an adjutant was.

"It's a military term," he explained, loudly closing a book as a sign that our time was finished. "From adiutor in the Roman army. It means assistant."

Looking back at the paper, I asked what a marten was.

"It's a weasel-like mammal with partially retractile claws," he told me, "and Picasso is a painter goodbye." He stood up, offering his hand and wishing me good fortune in all my future endeavors. My time in this college backwater was over; I was being thrown into the vast ocean of the world.

I had not considered Italy; then again, I had not considered anything. My mind in college was, shall we say, elsewhere. Let me try to make a funny story out of something hard: It was a time of pandemonium. Freedom had come for men such as myself—sex and romance released all at once as if by a drag Pandora—and oh, the party it was! Yet I was ill-prepared for a carnival of flesh. Here I was, as inexperienced as the Amish (no teenage stolen kisses, no prom night fumblings, nothing), suddenly let into the circus tent to join the sword-swallowing, sleight-of-hand, and juggling of partners. The ensuing burlesque lasted for three and a half years, and I ended up the equivalent of the escape artist trapped in his own device (in reality: handcuffed by a boyfriend to a radiator). My roommate (handy with a lock) gave me a note from the school saying I was currently failing two classes for lack of attendance. It was the splash of cold water I needed; I closed down the carnival just in time, sent away the clowns, and managed to graduate. But it had been a narrow escape, and I vowed: No more men for a while. No more chaos. I would cuff myself instead to intellectual pursuits and the neat methodology upon which I had heretofore relied. The bloodless precision of the archivist's life.

My parents approved; both trained in classical physics, they were glad to see me return to the Newtonian world from that quantum realm of terrifying entanglement and sex. For them, life was an equation, and now that I knew one variable (myself), I could solve for the unknown: my fate. Graduate school? Librarian? Closet specialist, so to speak? They would provide the round-trip ticket with a return at Christmas. Their only expectation of me: "It is time, Son, to take life seriously."

What could be more serious than Europe?

I wrote to the address on the advertisement, giving my credentials. I did not mention the very many ways in which I was ill-suited. I sent my application off and began my wait.

What was he like, in those days, our young man—me? Charming, inquisitive, organized, focused, and true, loyal to my friends and kind to animals—that's how I would have described myself back then. A Boy Scout of a man; a flower of American youth; a mensch. But that is not what I was at all. Looking back, I see a carefully reared and protected young man, cosseted as a Pekingese, insufferable, officious, a cable-knit sweater over a cable-knit heart, who had managed to surmount all distractions and complete the course readings and ace the last tests—but was in no way prepared for the crucial final exam of Real Life.

I am too harsh on myself. I am certain I was no more or less irritating than any other good American son of the century, unweathered by experience and unwise to the world. Whatever attributes one found in me were simply, as in the Pekingese, part of the breed. I was still young enough for my qualities to change, like a fresco as the artist reconsiders the position of a saint, but the moment was coming when they would be set forever.

As I went to sleep that night in my dormitory sardine tin (what twins have ever slept in a twin bed?), my mind was on the Baronessa, the marten, the Picasso, as strange-sounding as some novel from another time, another language and tradition. I felt as if I were on a boat headed into unknown waters. Was it adventure I craved? To meet a challenge to my very way of being? Something other than the phantomless folklore of suburban boyhood, or the make-believe importance of college rituals, neither of which I could believe in anymore? But, having never had any real challenge or adventure, how did I know I wanted it? Could it really be what my parents advised: to take life seriously? I did not know. As a boy, I used to lie awake and watch the crossed squares of light that would manifest suddenly and glide across my bedroom walls and ceiling. I did the same that night. And, just as they had long ago, they enchanted me, even though I knew they were mere headlight projections from ordinary cars of my ordinary world, for they seemed like heralds from some unknown destiny.

And, indeed, I later received the telegram with an arrival date and my instructions.

> GIOVEDÌ COME BY 5:15 TRAIN FLORENCE TO S. DROGO GAZELLE WILL BE WAITING BRING GIN FOR PRINCESS & FISH OIL FOR FAINA

The advertisement had mentioned a "modest country house," and this I took to be the winking language of the very rich, and expected (as one does when one knows nothing) an extravagant mansion perched on a hill. Perhaps I imagined it would be pink. Our journey from the train station, however, was not uphill but down, serpentining beside a river until we crossed it on a stone bridge and entered a dirt lane marked not by the iron gates of a villa but by a cardboard sign with a marker drawing of a boar. Farther along, the lane was met by another, and at this intersection sat an elderly woman in a red chair, shouting at us as we passed. Additional narrow lanes, each more treacherous than the last, and darker, deeper into that oak forest of banished fairies and bitter enchantments that children fear. We plunged through mud, then rose at last between two olive groves with trees arrayed in rows like men-at-arms, their silvery foliage fluttering, tattered, in the early-autumn sun. There was the raw smell of wild mint. An alphabet-block set of hives was stacked beyond, and from it came a muttering of bees. I saw no turrets, no castle walls, no clock towers. But where else would a baronessa live?

I was determined to avoid the clichés Americans expect of Italy—though these turned out, of course, to be the very images that had fed my decision. Stomping grapes for wine, sun-drying tomatoes on a roof, dancing the tarantella; who knows what idiotic fantasies I had picked up? What was certain was that I would not fall for some black-haired, half-shaved stranger leaning on a pitchfork before an olive grove. And so I took my vow, like a monk's, that for this period, I would enter the cloister of my work, my mind, and tend the garden there. The row of cypresses made me smile; what I needed was not romance and chaos but order.

For the whole journey, this Gazelle man kept up a series of barks in his language. I could not tell if they were directed at me, the road, or perhaps at his private god. He had been spry taking my bag, but up close I could see he was quite old for luggage duty, probably past sixty, though if one could look past his sun-lined skin, his smell of cigarettes and manure, and his one gold tooth, he had the profile of an old-style movie star. He had probably been a lady-killer in his youth, this Gazelle. Perhaps still was.

We met one car along the road coming toward us—a lizard-green Fiat—driven by a man with features blurred by sun reflections, and neither he nor Gazelle could decide how to pass on the narrow road, dodging back and forth as they approached each other, until the lizard decided simply to bolt along the edge, and as it passed I caught the eye of the young driver: blond, bespectacled, bewildered. He seemed to be fleeing the wilderness we now were entering, and his mouth was open as if to give mute warning—but in a cloud of dust, he and his car were gone.

"ECCO!" Gazelle barked, and we came to a sudden stop. The car shivered and died. We were not anywhere different from where we had been before. To our right, the olive trees rose up a sunny hillside. To our left: a two-story, ivy-covered wall. Nothing before us but more road, leading back into that terrible forest. Where was the house? The honk of the horn startled me. But what startled me more was when a portion of the wall began to move, swinging out on hinges to reveal a dark room within, crowded with baskets, and out of this darkness walked a woman . . .

"You're Giovedì?" she asked. Her sandals scraped along the dusty path. The late-September day was bright and hot as midsummer, but there was the scent of burning leaves and a sensation, in the shadows, of the first hint of autumn.

She was older than I was, but what exact age I was too young to guess, for she walked with the slim elegance I associated with a queen or prime minister, yet her style I thought of as youthful: tank top, dark denim overalls, gold hoop earrings. Her face was narrow, with a wide forehead and chin. Her eyes were large and half closed in the bright sunlight. She wore her kinky hair natural, and the light caught the gold in its spirals, lighting it briefly from within like a Venetian chandelier. She seemed aware of the effect and put a hand to her hair, tossing it as she smiled. She seemed like someone who knew many things that I did not.

"Yes," I said. "No," I said. "I mean—"

"I'm Estelle." She held out her hand and I shook it. "You're here too early."

My mind scrabbled at her words, looking for a handhold. She spoke with an accent I could not place. "But I . . . I . . . the telegram said—"

This Estelle produced an elastic band and, both hands behind her head, began the difficult act of pulling all her loose Afro into it. "Yes yes, you're fine. But Coco, she sent the telegram without consulting me. You see, the rooms aren't ready."

I wondered who this "Coco" was and somehow understood there was no place for me to stay, and my face must have conveyed it because she laughed and put one hand on my arm. "I mean in the villa! For your list. The rooms aren't ready."

"Not ready?" Panic twitched within me.

Back to taming her hair. "Don't worry, she will find things to occupy you."

I could see that what I had taken for a stone wall was in fact the plain, flat side of a building, studded with windows whose iron bars were equally twined with ivy. Along its length I could now make out three doors: a large double door camouflaged (and presumably made unusable) by greenery, the small door through which Estelle had appeared, and a wooden gate painted precisely the deep green of the ivy. On that gate hung a dark bronze knocker in the shape of a foot, and poking out above it, one could see the green aigrettes of a bamboo grove. How strange to find bamboo in Italy; I wondered what maniac had planted it. Along the wall also were two stone benches, and I saw, in the shadow of each bench, a number of huddled black kittens, staring bright-eyed up at me. Across the road was another wall, this one built to the height of the olive grove, which it supported. In the wall was a low green door that I assumed led inside the hill to some cool, dark chamber. And above, hanging down over the cliff of the wall: an herb garden fragrant with rosemary, thyme, sage, and others whose leaves I could not yet identify. A basket lay on the road below these with a pair of shears inside. I saw a dog race by on the dark path down the hill, a flash of white fur.

"But . . . I understand I'm to complete a catalog by Christmas. And I don't even know what I am cataloging—"

She was finishing with her hair; perhaps she did it automatically, because her hands seemed engaged with the task without involving the rest of her. "You'll have it done in no time. And don't worry about this heat wave, things will cool off any day now! That's how it goes around here."

"You work here?"

Estelle released her hands to her sides; her hair, compressed, had gone from gold to bronze. "Oh no! I'm a kind of . . . eh, neighbor. A friend of the house."

"I'm sorry for asking . . . you're French?"

"I'm Italian," she said, then smiled. "And Algerian. A long story." She looked behind her to where the door had closed, hiding itself once again within the ivy of the wall. "You'll stay in the house with her. I live just down the road. I know this all must seem so strange to you, an esteemed archivist. You're probably used to regularity. Things aren't exactly like that here."

"Oh, I'm not . . ." I was going to say "esteemed," but something made me stop. Was this some terrible comedy of misunderstandings?

"Let's get you into the house," she said. She shouted at Gazelle, who had begun to smoke on the roadside. She said quite a deal in Italian, then turned to me. "Oh yes! We call it Villa Coco."

Estelle reopened the door and gestured for me to enter the house, and I saw that this "hidden" door led, in fact, to the kitchen. It was of two parts: before us, up a few steps, was the kitchen proper, laid out in a U shape with a sink to the left, an old white-enameled stove in the center, and a cutting board set into the counter at the right. Canisters were crowded on shelves, straw wiskets hung on hooks, tarnished silver platters were mounted one above the other on the walls, books huddled together, painted ceramic bowls overflowed with fruit and vegetables, and as if the decorator imagined this might not be enough, the wall behind the stove was tiled in black-and-white op-art trapezoids. The second part was the dining area, as free of clutter as the first was crammed. A long table of dark, polished wood stood before an enormous fireplace, on whose mantel sat two crudely done brass cupids in an erotic position, and around the table were arranged tall chairs with white linen covers tied over the cushions. At the center of the table sat an ornate blue-and-white-speckled fruit bowl from which rose a similarly mottled candelabra of sculpted cherubs, and above it all hung two great concentric metal rings, each with half a dozen lamps, such as one sees in an Orthodox church. It startled me: this combination of the coarse and the sublime.

"Ah, here they are," said Estelle, picking up a set of keys from the deranged confusion of a countertop. "I've been looking for these for days."

"So . . . this is the kitchen?"

"The cook's not here right now," Estelle said. "She has a headache." I could well understand why. "Her husband, the handyman, is somewhere. Do you want to meet Coco?"

"Who's Coco?"

"Lisabetta. I call her Coco. She'll be down soon."

"Lisabetta?"

Her eyes brightened with amusement. "The Baronessa!"

I noticed now that beside us, at the entrance and still two steps below the kitchen, was another humble door. Estelle examined my face more carefully, then lifted the latch. The door opened onto what looked like a dimly lit chapel. I gestured for her to go before me.

She waved her hand. "Oh, I'm not going in. I'm heading home. Don't worry. If there's a crisis, I live just up the road, you turn left at Signora Guicciardini. The lady who sits in the chair and yells at cars."

"She's always there?"

"You'll be all right, Giovedì."

"Oh, there's been a misunderstanding. My name's not Giovedì. It's—"

"Of course," she interrupted, shaking her head. "Who would be named Giovedì? But Coco thought it was funny. She always has a nickname for people at first. Gazelle's name isn't Gazelle."

"I wondered . . ."

"It's CHA-zel," Estelle said, scraping her throat at the first syllable. "He's from Lebanon. You'll know she likes you when she uses your real name."

"She doesn't like . . . Ghazel?"

"She'll like you! Thank God you're handsome."

She let me pass before her into the dimness of the room before closing the door and sealing me in alone, and I wondered if this was all a terrible mistake.

I had entered a realm much cooler than the heat of the kitchen or the dusty road, with a humid, vegetal smell. What I took to be a chapel seemed now to be an entrance hall, and I understood the two ironbound doors to my left were ones I had seen from outside, now long overgrown with ivy. Facing the unused entrance doors and perhaps four strides away was the most striking aspect of the room: a wrought-iron staircase that crossed the wall diagonally, from upper left to lower right like a filigree sash across a bosom, hugging the wall until arriving at the cool stone floor. The space's only windows flanked the entrance doors and stretched up to the ceiling, but, being also overgrown with ivy and barred with iron, they let in only a fluttering, greenish light, and as these were the only windows in a large room crowded with objects, it took me a moment to apprehend that I was in a hall of treasures.

Beside me and on the wall opposite were shelves and vitrines in metal, glass, and wood, not one like another, and each held a pirate's trove—amphorae and terra-cotta goddesses, brass oil lamps and red lacquerware bowls, cloth dolls and wooden shoes, the marble bust of a soldier and a purplish stone carving the size of a thumb—crowded without any obvious sense of order, material or chronological or otherwise. It looked both like the British Museum and like a child's bedroom, filled with beloved trash and treasures. My heart dropped to the floor as I considered how I would ever tackle cataloging this hoard. Nowhere was there visible this Picasso mentioned in the ad, not that I could have identified one. Above the display cases, on the whitewashed walls were hung three enormous paintings done in a dark and modern style that disguised, in the dim light, their subjects; there seemed to be nudity, but perhaps it was fruit. From great brass urns burst stalks of bamboo so tall they brushed the ceiling, and in the middle of the room sat an elaborately carved walnut desk with a worn pink velvet bar at the bottom, perhaps for kneeling in prayer. It must have been very old. On the desk sat a sculpture of a boat in bronze. It caught my attention; from everything in the room, this was the one object picked out for display. There seemed to be a plaque with something written—

"Koo-koo!" came a voice from above.

I wondered if this was the cook. From outside, I could hear birds arguing with one another.

"Hello?" I said, then tried my only Italian: "Buon giorno?"

There arrived, long before the personage herself, like the scent that heralds a storm's arrival, a cloud of dense Italian language flowing down the stairs. The staircase was built so that anyone descending was hidden from view, coming into sight only gradually, and so first only a white cotton slipper appeared, followed by another, then by the lacy hem of a white garment. Step after step to the rhythm of this endless language until the hypnotic effect was spoiled by the arrival of two fawn pugs tumbling down the stairs. Now a papery hand, gripping the iron railing. The garment revealed itself to be an empire-waisted gown of eyelet lace. And then at last her face appeared in profile, talking away to empty air—perhaps to the pugs, perhaps to Estelle, perhaps just to a world sure to be listening—a gaunt and imperious face topped by fine white hair, intricately curled; a pointed nose and an underbite; and lofty, cunning, creased green eyes, which now, as she pulled wide a fold of her garment, turned to look at me:

"Koo-koo!"

I was utterly confused and, assuming she mistook me for someone else, foolishly spoke: "I'm your new archivist." I added, awkwardly: "Baronessa." For this could be no one but herself.

The Baronessa stopped on the staircase and, while the pugs continued their plunge to the lower depths, leaned forward into the lorgnette of her curiosity. "Eh?"

"Your new archivist." I cleared my throat. "Giovedì."

A sharp rebuke: "You're not blond!"

"I . . . Well, that's a matter of—"

With a curl of her lip: "And you're American!"

"I'm from Washington, DC."

This seemed to stun her like a stab to the chest. "Estelle!" she hissed, then continued down the stairs, waving her hand. Her accent was peculiar, and untraceable. Hardly Italian, somehow not European at all, or at least not from a country still on a contemporary map. Later, I would discover that her words, rather than sticking firmly to the language at hand, as one dines on the dish the waiter has set down, instead seemed to pick from everybody's plate. I also found it impossible to guess her age; she had the pale, chartaceous skin of the elderly and hair as white as a snowy owl, but spoke in a manner both suave and crude that did not match my conception of the antique. Was she one hundred? Seventy? A withered forty-five? "You're no use to me. You'll have to go on the next train. Estelle!"

My chest was flooding in panic. "But I've . . . I've come all the way from—"

She raised her head. "Estelle!"

"She's gone home."

"Do you see a [Italian word]? I left it somewhere."

"A . . . a ba . . ."

"A bastone! A *cane*, in your American language. It has a horse's head. The mouth opens to hold a pair of gloves. I suffer from a vertigo and I need this terrible cane. I am really only comfortable at sea. Estelle!" By now she had arrived at my level, and I realized how small and delicate she was. I stepped forward to offer her my arm and she glared at this insult to her vigor. "You will go home on the next train."

My heart was a rabbit trembling in my chest. I could not go home on the next train; that would mean going home on the next plane, back to my parents and their anxiety and their judgment. I closed my eyes and winced, thinking of my mother's critical gaze and angled diacritical brows, her suggestion I go into laboratory work; I thought of graduate school; I thought of the disastrous temptations and distractions of the circus. Each fate seemed to bring its own handcuffs. Then I remembered something in Sumerian.

"I'm sorry . . . Baronessa . . . but there is no next train," I said haltingly. "There's a strike."

She squinted and leaned toward me with her right ear. "Eh?"

Loudly: "I said there's a train strike."

"[Italian word!]" she said, throwing her arm up. "Then that's even worse, because my friend Pippa comes today, and if she does not come by train she must glide here on witchcraft. She is very amusing. Always wears her hair up with an artificial flower. She's done it since we were twelve. She is Saxe-Coburg and Gotha. Her aunts and uncles were kings and queens."

This fact resonated in the chambers of my mind with bits of history as old as her collection, unreconcilable with the present day. "Baronessa—"

"You will call me Lisabetta. It's from Boccaccio. She is the one who keeps her lover's severed head in a pot of basil. I would love to do that, but life does not provide every opportunity. Or you will call me Coco. This I leave you to decide." I could not imagine calling this imposing woman anything of the kind. She gestured with her free hand and began a precarious walk across the stone floor. "Come with me. We have to find Nimali the cook. Estelle has abandoned us."

I informed her that Estelle had said she would return later.

She leaned her head back with a hearty "HO HO HO!" This crude laughter surprised me in someone so haughty and fragile. "Nimali!" she began to shout. "Nimali! Koo-koo!"

I informed her that Estelle had said the cook had a headache.

"Nonsense. I don't have a headache and I am ninety-two."

It seemed to me a strange way to diagnose others. "Ninety-two? You look wonderful."

Her expression was that of someone at the top of a high mountain, looking down on the poor creatures just beginning the ascent.

"Baronessa," I said, "I wanted to ask about my position—"

"Eh?"

"I have a question about the position of adjutant—"

"Eh?"

"My job!"

"This is of no concern. If not the train, I have heard tell there is also an omnibus. I am going down to the pool. Since you must for the moment remain, maybe you can bring that basket. And of course you should go for a swim."

I told her I had not unpacked my swim trunks, as I had just arrived.

"Oh, go without," she said, waving away my worries. "It's more satisfying to swim in the nude. Are you concerned about this old lady seeing something? Don't concern yourself. I am completely blind!"

She stepped close to a painting and, with a delicate pinch of her forefinger and thumb, removed a single hair. A brisk smile at me.

She was not blind in the least.

We did not make it to the pool. Like a child restless in the company of adults, the day provided its own diversion.

I was very worried about her turning me away so summarily. So I tried all my charms; I carried the basket as she desired and listened to her speech, in which I would grasp a subject only to find it had slipped away from me and we were on to something else: "It's a shame you don't know Italian or you could have talked to the station manager. These train strikes are an annoyance, but they're sporting. There's always one train that gets through. I know my chickens, and my friend Pippa, she'll grab it. Speaking of chickens, we must deal with our sworn enemy, the marten."

The Baronessa led me through the kitchen, where we found her bastone propped near the stove; the handle was carved into an elongated horse's head, and she demonstrated its spring-loaded jaw ("You see, I'm not a liar!"). We passed from the dining area into a room whose windows were completely shuttered, giving me little sense of it except a glimpse of low couches at the far end and a set of paintings, and I found myself caught up in another sheaf of bamboo, set precisely in my path, then banged my knee on a wicker table. The Baronessa did not seem to notice; she maneuvered the obstacle course easily, talking all the while: "Pippa once found me in Kandahar by donkey cart. All the donkeys were busy, but one happened to have her husband's name, and the driver had to admit it was God's will. I am taken by a whim to visit the little bathroom over there . . ."

She swung open an enormous door and we were bathed in sunlight; before us was an arcade with a potted orange tree and, beyond it, a courtyard of paved stones set into the grass. We stepped outside and the pugs followed us. Every wall seemed to be covered with green vines of wisteria. The Baronessa gestured with her bastone at a small stone building across the courtyard; a door was set in its wall, half hidden by the wisteria. I wondered how to deal with this woman, whether to flatter or coax her or boss her around. But the elderly lady, more spry than I imagined, had already vanished inside.

Another voice, this time distinctly male: "Signore!"

I turned and found that beside me stood a tall, mustached man in a T-shirt and shorts. He had a proud and cautious demeanor and a protruding lower lip, which gave the sense he doubted that what you were saying was true. Later I would learn he was the cook's husband; they were both from Sri Lanka, and his name was Vinsanda. The Baronessa, unable to untie this simple Sinhalese knot, called him Vinsanto, the name of a Tuscan dessert wine. He said a single word in Italian, but he was not addressing the Baronessa. He said it to me.

"[Italian word]."

"Scusi?" I asked. I had picked this up from an Italian movie.

Vinsanda blinked his eyes, then repeated the word. It sounded like "matzoh" but couldn't possibly be. He gestured gracefully to a space outside the courtyard that I understood to be a garage. More Italian followed, but simple words, repeated, in the way one speaks to a dog. He stepped away and, with another gesture for a canine, waved for me to accompany him, which I did, looking back at the courtyard, where I saw my duffel had been delivered. The pugs were circling it as if it were an idol. I worried they would "mark" it; alas, there was nothing I could do but abandon my duffel, and the Baronessa, for what might lie within the garage.

A manhole, it turned out, the cover of which had been removed and set to one side. All around, the items typical to a garage crowded the walls—saws, screwdrivers, glass jars of nuts or bolts or screws, broken windows, broken chairs—along with items atypical to a garage, such as a bronze nude sculpture facing the wall. I walked forward to examine it—but Vinsanda clapped to regain my attention, pointing toward the hole. "Pozzo," he said, this time quite clearly.

"Pozzo," I repeated.

"Piano," he said, or so it seemed.

A pause. I heard him repeat: "Pozzo piano." It seemed to be a complete sentence.

I repeated these phonemes and he nodded. Then he walked out of the garage and up a set of stairs into an apartment above, where he closed the door. Apparently, having communicated this sentence, he had wiped his hands of the whole affair. I approached the pozzo. A smell assaulted me, and instantly I understood Italian.

I heard a voice from the courtyard: "Koo-koo!"

It seemed the entire complex worked on some antique septic system, perhaps even one of Roman invention. However ancient, this was not the kind of work I had come to perform, but it seemed Vinsanda felt it was not his kind, either. If I solved it, perhaps it might win me a chance to stay—but did I want to stay on these terms? Did I want to stay at all? I felt alarm at either option: to be thrown back into the churning ocean of possibilities or else to remain in a place disappointed that I was neither British nor blond nor bathing in the nude . . .

"Koo-koo!" The voice was coming closer. The pugs appeared at the garage door and stopped, staring at me. I looked into the pozzo, but it kept its own counsel. I heard her voice: "Has the American left?"

Without thinking, I shouted: "I'm here!"

Slowly, the Baronessa came into view in her white dress. "Aha! Are you interested in auto parts?"

"No, there was a man here who said—" and here I swallowed and searched my soul for strength. "Pozzo piano."

"Really? Pozzo piano?"

"I think that's what he said."

"The pozzo is slow?"

"I think it's overflowed."

"Pieno," she said very firmly. "Full. Pieno."

"I know this isn't the kind of thing—"

I felt a sharp pain on my arm; she had hit me with the horse head of her cane. "Oh, I love solving house problems! I need you to search in my basket for the little red book. There are two men who can help us with this. One, unfortunately," she said, holding out a hand, "is in Napoli."

I was not yet a student of Italian geography. "That's far, isn't it?"

She presented her other hand. “The other is dead.”

She stood, hands outspread, in a pose very similar to that of San Drogo.

“Then let’s call Napoli.”

“As you say. Find for me the little red book full of numbers. Find for me Cicciano. It will be in the old part. Luciano Cicciano.”

The red book (which was not little) turned up in her crowded basket. I sat on a white metal bench going through it, slightly annoyed that I had been pulled into a matter at such a far remove from my job description, and yet eager to prove myself worthy. The book seemed to be arranged, as she warned me, in an “old” section, crammed with names and numbers, many crossed out, and a newer one, starting over again at A, with room still to spare. I was reminded of adjoining church graveyards.

“Luciano Cicciano. Here it is.”

“Now find for me the little green thing.”

“What is that?”

“It is a telephone you can walk with.”

“A cordless phone?”

“You can make it sing if you press a button on its base.”

Surprisingly technical knowledge for a woman who was born twenty-five years or so after Bell’s invention, but accurate. Once I found the base in the living room, we heard the cordless phone ringing; of course it was in her basket. We returned to the living room and sat on the white sofa below an old painting of a woman in clogs. There followed a fumbling with the phone and the book, a few false starts, and then a rapid conversation in what I thought was a very stern tone. Through the open door into the courtyard I could see my duffel, still upright on the paving stones; it was possible I saw a stain on one corner. The Baronessa sighed. It sounded to me like bad news, but she returned the phone to the basket and turned to me with a nod.

"Bonne fortune! Well, a kind of fortune. His cousin took the truck on a trip to Montepulciano. That isn't really far at all, but we have to wait until he's finished his coffee. In Montepulciano, that could take a while. And involve grappa. We don't want a drunkard dealing with the pozzo."

"Maybe we should stop using the tank until he comes."

"You are a strict young man! I am glad I used the facilities or I would become a criminal in your mind!"

"I just meant—"

"You know," she went on, suddenly wistful with her hands in her lap, "queens have visited this house. Mick Jagger once came. There have been Nobel Prize winners and movie stars. This might be the most glamorous shit in Southern Europe."

I was shocked to hear this word come out of her elegant mouth.

She went on: "It will be sad to see it go." She explained that every ten years or so, these ancient repositories had to be emptied by a professional. "But I must let go of many things."

"I hope he comes before your friend gets here."

"Eh?"

"I hope the driver comes before your friend arrives."

I watched as her grin emerged like an animal from a long hibernation. "What a wonderful idea!"

It took a little more fumbling to find the green thing again, a little more Italian, followed by a second call in French, and yet a third, once again in Italian. A gasp of happiness came from the old woman. She tossed the green thing into the basket and clapped her hands. I could have been seated beside a child.

"We have solved two problems at once," she announced. "Pippa will arrive with the septic man."

And that is exactly how it happened. An hour later, lumbering down the narrow dirt road, arrived an enormous vehicle with a hose looped on its hood, like an elephant on its way to a temple, driven by a sour-looking young man with curly black hair, and in the passenger seat could be seen, seated precisely like a queen upon that elephant, an elderly woman with a yellow silk chrysanthemum in her hair. Pippa. Or, rather, Principessa Giuseppina Maria Augusta Raffaella of Saxe-Coburg and Gotha. It took both the driver and Vinsanda to help her descend. Though she was dressed in loose harem pants, tunic, and striped pink scarf (looking to my mind like one of my mother's bridge partners), I could not help finding a resemblance to the elderly Queen Victoria. Her great-great-aunt, it turned out. But, as Vinsanda led the princess immediately to her room, I was not to meet her until dinner. There were, after all, more important matters:

"Did you bring the gin?" the Baronessa asked me as we watched the truck maneuver its way into the yard; this was done through the green gate in the wall, and it was a very tight fit.

"The gin?"

She looked instantly irritated. "I told the man in the telegram specifically to add a part about the gin. For Pippa."

"Oh yes!" BRING GIN FOR PRINCESS & FISH OIL FOR FAINA. In my hasty preparations, I had in fact purchased a fifth of Bombay at the Duty-Free. I retrieved my duffel and returned with the gin and the fish oil. She plucked the gin from my hand and said the fish oil was for later, adding: "How lovely for a young man to be nicely dressed for dinner."

She turned to me with a grin and seemed not at all as grand as before; she looked much more like the little old lady she truly was. Good-spirited, hard of hearing, a bit wobbly getting up from a chair; as innocent as the chickens clucking down the hill. And yet I was not fooled. Shall I admit it?

She terrified me.

Dinner was very late for American tastes: eight thirty. I took the Baronessa's comment to mean I was to wear my best clothes; of course I had packed only one jacket and tie, and that only because I imagined life with a "Baronessa" would entail at least one night of fine dining. I had not imagined I would be expected to dress to celebrate a septic tank. I was told my room was opposite hers ("with the animals," she added unhelpfully), then was left to discover what this might mean. I took my duffel up the stairway I had first seen her descend and found myself in an upper hallway painted its entire length with vines, leaves, and flowers; here and there, I noticed small birds or insects. I also noticed at least five open doorways, any of which, I thought, might be her room or mine—until I looked into the first one, seeing a boudoir done in pink, with two tubs set into the floor and an enormous Japanese print showing, in vivid anatomical detail, a woman at her bath. I took note that this must be the Baronessa's quarters and found, in the room opposite, a painting of a lion attacking a sheep: the animals. I set my bag inside, closed the door, and lay down for a moment on the surprisingly lumpy bed.

My memory of that day has the overwhelming blur of a border crossing, where the onslaught of unknown languages, scents, tastes, habits, and customs causes one to pick those details necessary for survival—visa requirements, currency exchange, common phrases—so that the amusing or decorative—the station clock, the officer's mustache, the dusty false flowers in the window box—are often forgotten. Or, at least, held in suspension, waiting to be useful. And it was only later that I made out the framed ex-voto paintings (one man saved from drowning, another from industrial mangling, a third from fire, all by the intervention of a rather Dietrich-like Mary); the stenciled roses near the ceiling; beside the bed, an antique photograph of a handsome, serious, and somehow familiar young man in wire glasses; the magnolia leaves outside my window tilting back and forth like hands drying themselves in the sun: the details that would become my life's companions until Christmas. If I managed to stay.

When I came downstairs, the two elderly women were already seated at the dining table with a chair between them. They were chatting in English, presumably their preferred language when together. The chandelier above was lit, as was the candelabra, with its base of fruit and sculpted cherubs. Pippa was staring at an ice-filled glass, which she held with a perplexed expression. I assumed it was the gin I had brought. She had changed for dinner—meaning, she had changed her flower. It was now a red silk chrysanthemum. The rest was all flowing robes and harem pants and scarves, at least two. The Baronessa was in a long blue quilted jacket and wore a pendant in gold Arabic script. I now see them as bohemian elegance, but back then, to me, they looked like a pair of lesbian hippies. Then again: What did I know of dining with aristocracy? My experience extended only to my parents' "fancy" dinners, to which my mother wore a cream silk blouse and pearls, my father a cardigan, and salmon mousse was unmolded in the shape of a fish, to the oohs and ahs of the guests—the height of 1980s suburban sophistication.

"You look very comme il faut," the Baronessa said sternly.

I looked down at my navy blazer, chinos, and yellow tie, very pleased. "In a good way?"

She paused. "A tie seems extreme for a weeknight." My hand moved automatically to my tie, but she went on: "Now sit right here," patting the chair between them. "We need a man to separate our femininity. Giovedì, this is my friend Pippa."

I greeted Pippa and, glancing up at me from her glass, she looked even more perplexed. Perhaps this was as exotic an experience for her as it was for me.

I took the seat between the two ladies, and now we were three, all in a row, facing the kitchen, where I at last got a look at Nimali, the cook. She was a short, sturdy, fortyish woman with a prominent nose, large Cleopatra eyes, and black hair pulled into a braid that fell to the small of her back. She wore a brightly flowered housedress such as my grandmother used to wear, which tied in the back, and she stood with two hands firmly planted on the cutting board, staring at us with pursed lips. Her eyes met mine. She looked at the old women, then back at me and shrugged: sympathy toward this new arrival, this American, who was, like herself, a mere servant here. I marveled at how many of the people I had met had come from afar—Ghazel, Estelle, Nimali, and Vinsanda—and it made me curious about the world my employer had created.

"We were talking about Pippa's family," the Baronessa was saying. "Princess Margaret is her cousin, and Pippa didn't know she was once my guest! What a nuisance. Someone called us ahead of time and said to put a bottle of whiskey in front of her, *plop!*, like that at the table. She drank from it the whole time. And it was lunch. I remember we had linguine alle vongole."

"Buone!" cried Pippa.

"Buone!" replied the Baronessa, adding that the clams had come straight from the Adriatic. These cries of "buone!" and "buono!" and so on were a particular affectation of conversation at Villa Coco; later, I was to realize it was an aspect of Italian conversation in general. It meant "delicious," referring to the food just mentioned, and it did not matter if the talk was of a death in the family, a crisis of the heart, or the *Titanic* disaster—if one noted that the penultimate dish served to the ill-fated passengers had been foie gras, the very mention of the delicacy would bring cries of "buono!"

"You know this story, Lisabetta. That I once . . . had the princess's *mother*," Pippa remarked. Her voice startled me, both rough and smooth—like a bottle of whiskey set in front of a princess. Her accent was startlingly British. I was slow to understand that the princess's mother would be the Queen of England. "And she admired . . . *something of mine*. That spelled *disaster*! You know if the Queen admires . . . *something of yours* . . . of course you have to *give* it to her. Usually it's a bowl. A serving spoon. Just my luck . . . that she took a liking to my *sofa*."

The Baronessa said that of course she knew this story!

But Pippa went on: "Naturally I could not *give* it to her! It was . . . *Gustavian*!"

I laughed as if I understood a thing she was saying.

Pippa lifted one beringed finger in the air. "So I had one of my masterstrokes!"

She turned to me and I blinked in expectation.

"I had it *copied*!" she said grandly. "Copied by an infamous falsario . . . a *counterfeiter*. I sent the copy to the Queen . . . and *kept* my *own*. I'm sure she never knew the difference."

The Baronessa winked and stated that the princess was an inspiration to others.

"Maybe she was testing you."

I was the one who said this, and both women turned to stare at me. I could see the petals shivering in Pippa's hair.

"I am certain you are saying *something very interesting*, young man," she told me in her clipped accent, "and that we would grow to become *friends*, but I am afraid I only understand . . . the King's English." She gave me a warm smile and put her hand on mine as she spoke very carefully. "The American dialect . . . Is. Beyond. Me."

Imagine the effect on an arrogant young American, who has never bothered to learn a single word outside his language, a nightingale who thought he spoke in the sharp, clear language of all birds, only to awaken inside a cage of cockatoos. I sat there absolutely still as Nimali set down a soup beside the princess and began to ladle it into her bowl. A silence held the room in suspension. I saw the Baronessa's eyes go to Pippa and then to me.

"Then I will translate!" she announced.

The rest of the dinner was as absurd an event as I have ever attended. I would ask the princess a question, for instance, "Where did you last travel?" and then, like a food taster passing an approved dish to the king, the Baronessa would lean politely and repeat my question to her friend, who listened intently: "Pippa, he's asking about your time in Zanzibar." Then the ridiculous process would be reversed—even though I made it clear I could understand the princess perfectly—"Tell him I found great love and great disappointment," and the Baronessa would turn to me, light flashing on her pendant, and say: "Pippa says she found great love and great disappointment." This had the effect of doubling the experience for everyone but Pippa. Nimali stood with a platter of roast pork, her eyes wide in alarm; even someone who spoke no English could understand the absurd back-and-forthing, like a hostage negotiation.

Eventually they wandered into their own conversation, leaving me behind. The Baronessa related the entire story of the pozzo, which surprised me, as it seemed as inappropriate a topic as I could imagine. "I know you are an early riser, so perhaps you can inaugurate it!" the Baronessa offered, and Pippa seemed to take this as a great honor. Then their talk became more intimate; of course they had forgotten I was there.

"He's very handsome," Pippa said, specifically looking away from me. "But what will you do with an *American*?"

The Baronessa said Americans could be taught.

"They can be taught to speak English, even *be* English, perhaps," Pippa replied, "but not to be *Italian*."

My employer agreed that this was so and said I was called Giovedì. Like a girl Friday. "My man Thursday!" she said with delight. "He is here to . . . count the spoons, as you suggested. But my bedroom and other rooms are not ready. We await Oscar."

"Ah yes!" Pippa said mysteriously. "And has the . . . other gentleman approved?"

"Giovedì has a degree in archives," the Baronessa said, and this seemed to settle whatever strange matter they were talking about.

I pretended to be occupied with my wine, which was remarkably sour, and began to enter my own thoughts, my discomfort at being treated like a servant by this houseguest, when I heard a new direction of the conversation: "And, Lisabetta, speaking of great loves, what about yours? Have you made contact?"

I did not lift my gaze. I could hear my employer shuffling restlessly beside me.

Pippa: "You told me you would try Venice—"

"In Venice, it may be I have met some success," the Baronessa announced. "But there are serious obstacles. And there is some urgency."

Pippa leaned across the table with a fork in her hand. "Do not give up, Lisabetta! We must *act* while we are *young*!"

I am afraid to say I snorted a little at this remark. The table looked at me while I struggled seriously with my salad. I caught the cook's eye. Then I saw a mouse run across the kitchen counter. Nobody else seemed to notice.

The Baronessa changed the subject to one of local tragedy: a woman in the nearby town of Rignano had been discovered dead in her own home, a woman approaching the age of our two ladies, cut down, as the Baronessa said, in the "prime of her life" as owner of a restaurant where she made her own tiramisù—

A cry from Pippa: "Buono!"

"How do you like my friend Pippa?"

We were on the stairs to the upper hall, which the Baronessa took briskly for a person her age. Pippa had gone into a bedroom in some lower quadrant, and we were left alone.

"I . . ." I grasped for a phrase that would not seem too rude: "I can't say what I think."

She looked at me shrewdly. "She's a terrible snob! But she has the most creative and persuasive schemes. You *will* have to learn Italian."

"I will?"

She continued her march up the stairs. "Three things. The first is to learn to dress for dinner. There is a place we will visit in Rignano, called La Formica, which has what you need. I visit it every week or so. The second is to learn Italian. In the house you may speak American, but in the car it is to be Italian. In macchina, italiano! The third is to learn history and culture so we may speak at the dinner table. I will give you some books and you will visit Firenze and other towns. Clothes, Italian, and culture. You must promise these things."

"So I'm going to stay?"

We stood before her doorway and she looked hard into my eyes but did not answer me directly. "I have one kindness to ask of you," she said. "Please do not put a hat on the bed. It brings destruction and death."

This catastrophism startled me. My only response was that I did not have a hat.

"Also, never drive down the hill. The road is washed away and we will fall to our death and that is not how I plan to go."

I said I had no intention of doing so. I was not aware I was to drive at all.

"Then we're safe," she said. A smile. "Something I am now remembering is that we have *two* pozzi. But something I am not remembering is *where*."

I said, "There must be another manhole somewhere."

"No matter," she said, looking at the vines painted down the hallway. "Someday, someday . . . it will find *us*."

Her eyebrows rose dramatically.

"Buona notte," she said before closing her door.

The last I recall of that evening is undressing and putting myself to bed. I did not entirely fit, head to toe, because of the ornate decorations of doves at the foot, so I lay diagonally, and even the hard lumps of the mattress could not prevent me from feeling peace and contentment. I had opened the window to the night; it had no screen, but I felt protected by its iron bars, which were embellished with ivy. From beyond those bars I heard the whispering of bamboo in the night breeze. Words of Italian buzzed in my brain, all nonsense, but something like the sensations of the stomach digesting new foods; perhaps already the language was being assimilated into my being, and I would awaken with supreme fluency. I might even know how to dress for dinner. From beside the bed, the young man in the antique photo looked down: lean-faced with slightly parted lips and a sense of vulnerability in his eyes. When I imagined away the musketeer whiskers, he seemed almost contemporary, and I could picture a man staring at me that way from across a crowded bar. I reminded myself of my vow. No entanglements, not even with dead men in photographs. And then I recognized him: he was the spitting image of the man in the lizard-green Fiat we had passed on our way in. And yet the photograph was surely fifty years old or more. Another mystery.

That was when I turned to the window and saw, bracing itself against the iron bars, a monster from my deepest fears: cat-sized, with a dark belly and snow-white throat, a tense shaggy tail, an apricot nose, and small rounded ears, the creature bared its sharp teeth and stared at me with eyes like drops of black poison. It all happened too fast to notice retractile claws. I screamed. Nobody came. I screamed again. Nobody came. The creature flicked its tail brazenly and flew off into the night. I screamed even after it was gone, closed the window, and locked it. Nobody came. I was shaking with terror. This, I would later realize, was our sworn enemy: the marten.

I screamed again.

Nobody came.

I awoke too early, blaming the time difference between the East Coast and Florence, got myself out of bed, and with a cautious hand opened the window; it was creature-free, festooned with ivy, spangled in sunlight, but smelled a bit like cat urine. The room was supplied with a shabby yellow robe, and though it was too short for me and clashed with my light blue pajamas, I felt like a baron myself walking down to the kitchen and making coffee. Not a soul was awake to see my failures with the coffeepot, and I emerged into the courtyard with my final success.

Free now of pugs, baronessas, and septic problems, I was able to enjoy the dimensions of the outdoor space. It was bordered on two sides by the house itself—the veranda in which I now stood, enjoying my coffee, and a high stone wall to my left. The side to my right was occupied by a small stone building (I knew the garage to be on the lower level), from whose upper story came the sound of a radio playing what I took to be Southeast Asian music (I assumed this to be the home of Nimali and Vinsanda), connected to the main house by a narrow stone arch. The fourth side—there was no fourth side; it was a panorama of the Tuscan hills behind a mulberry tree. Within the quadrangle thus delineated sat a thick stone table, like a sacrificial altar, and four wrought-iron chairs. In the middle of the table sat a bowl of purple petunias, so dark they were nearly black. It was only when I was turning back to the arcade that I noticed, set at the corner of the villa, a small marble column, carved down its length with at least a dozen names: Hector, Claudius, Lucrezia, Barone, and so on. The names were in red, and a few were marked with asterisks.

"Buon. Giorno," came a voice from behind me. I was so startled I nearly dropped my coffee.

It was the princess, who sat at a marble table with a pot of coffee, bread, and jam; she had been hidden by a garland of ivy. She had changed her flower from last night for a pink one; an expression of optimism, I thought. I noticed she wore light blue pajamas with a yellow robe. Somehow, I had managed to dress like a princess.

She took no notice of our identical apparel. "I," she said.

"Am. Leaving." She pronounced each word very clearly for the idiot before her. "Train. Station."

I nodded as would an idiot.

"Tell. Lisabetta. Thank. You."

Another nod.

Then she stood and produced a small envelope. "This. For you. Until we meet again."

She placed the envelope in my hand and made her gracious way into the house. Hypnotized, I put the envelope in the robe's pocket. Soon Vinsanda appeared from the villa, like an actor directed to balance the scene, carrying two old-fashioned suitcases with leather straps. He looked hungover or simply weary from this world. To me, this American in a small robe in the courtyard, he said nothing. In a moment, I heard a car engine start and stutter its way up the road. I decided not to embarrass myself further, drank my coffee, and went back upstairs. I found a bathroom that, perhaps to compensate for its lack of windows, was completely wallpapered with small medieval beasts, and I began to run myself a bath (there was no shower). Apparently I was to bathe with a jug. Only when removing my robe did I remember the envelope. I pulled it out and opened it; somehow I had expected either a confession of love or an apology for taking me for a servant. Instead: a stack of Italian lira notes.

I had been tipped.

"Koo-koo!"

It was almost eleven when the Baronessa appeared on her balcony overlooking the courtyard, clutching a book. She seemed to be wearing an enormous blue linen blouse over a white cotton skirt, perhaps a salute to the heat wave. All around, the world was still humming as if it were high summer, and pots of geraniums bloomed around her so that the Baronessa floated on a purple cloud, in which tiny bees were darting. To my surprise, her first question was about the bed in my room.

"It's fine," I said, straining to look up at her from the courtyard. "Thank you. But last night—"

"It isn't grumeleux? Full of . . ." And here she cupped her free hand and tapped it across the railing.

I could not guess what she was trying to say. "Mice?" I asked.

She sighed. "Not mice. Little hard parts that interrupt the sleep."

"Lumpy! Well, to be honest—"

She hit the railing with her fist, surprising some bees from the folds of their flowers. "I suspected. It is very old. I'll have a woman come in and fix it. I should have done that before, but I hadn't thought about it. Where's Pippa?"

"The princess is gone. Vinsanda drove her to the station." I took a deep breath of indignation before I told her I believed the princess had given me a servant's tip—

"She is a nuisance," the Baronessa said with a wave of her hand, and began walking toward what I realized must be the top of an external staircase, hidden behind the wall. "But a genius. My friend Oscar will be here shortly, thanks God. An artist of some talent and a delizia. Everything I do is for him. And my cousin Giacomo . . ." She disappeared from view, then emerged near me at the bottom still talking: ". . . papers I don't understand. Do you have the fish oil?"

I wondered what part of her monologue I had missed that we had arrived at fish oil. I told her I would grab it from the kitchen where I had delivered it, and when I returned she nodded with satisfaction.

"My young cousin Giacomo, related in too complex a way

to interest you," she said, returning somehow to the earlier topic as she walked across the courtyard. "Estelle calls him Giacomo-Giacomo. How do I explain? I do not know the word in English. You know when you climb up a very tall mountain, as I used to do in my seventies, and you reach the top, and your legs they go . . ." She made a very convincing attempt at making them quiver, which alarmed me, as she was leaning on her cane. "We call this Giacomo-Giacomo!"

I shook my head in confusion.

She repeated the demonstration. "Giacomo-Giacomo!" She seemed to be amusing herself.

"Giacomo-Giacomo," I said.

"What is the phrase in English?"

"I have no idea."

"Anyway, Giacomo-Giacomo, he will be by sometime next month. He is the only relative I speak to. He is from Vicenza and possibly works in publishing, and when he visits he brings Asiago cheese, which I remember from my childhood. He once lived with me, but I was unable to corrupt him." She laughed. "And we may have Estelle. I have brought you a hat to wear and a book." She handed me a straw hat and a worn hardcover along with the basket of her belongings. "It is on how to prune roses. This is very important to get right, as we have a number of roses to get wrong."

I thanked her, as this was indeed in the job description, though not what I expected to be my main duty. I put on the hat (slightly too small) and opened the book to illustrations of the flowers in bud and bloom. It seemed to be from the nineteenth century. It also seemed to be in Italian, of which I informed my employer.

She raised a finger gravely. "You promised you would learn."

I sputtered with a response. It seemed my transformation from "too American" was meant to be instant.

I thought it was time to change topics to one burning in my mind: "Baronessa," I said, as firmly as I could and trying to keep up with her as she descended, cane in hand, the stone steps behind Vinsanda's apartment, to a little opening in which some white clothes hung on a line. There was a twitter of birds in a nearby rosemary bush, whose fragrance filled the air. "We should talk about the catalog. Time is very limited, and if I am to be thorough—"

"Eh?"

"I said time is limited."

With her cane she pushed a hanging shirt out of her way. "Limited? I am barely in my nineties—"

"You said your deadline was Christmas."

"Only if you learn Italian! And learn to—"

"I will need to know what to include, the date, the provenance—"

"Eh?"

"If you please, what am I compiling this inventory for?"

She stopped her brisk walk and stood regarding me as she might a piece of furniture that had suddenly begun to talk. I wondered if she was deciding how much to trust me. And then she said something very mysterious:

"I have put something in motion from which there will soon be no returning."

I waited. Two birds made a racket in the eaves. We stood in a silence that added no more to my understanding.

I said, "We keep being distracted by things like the pozzo. And the roses."

She laughed and began walking again. "It is beneath you?"

"I am not," I said carefully, "trained for these."

"Who is? No no, we must take what comes, you and I. Hiring you was a necessity." Then she added, with a sly smile: "Crusoe had his Friday. You are my man Thursday."

I sputtered in frustration, seeing my days lost to roses and chaos. "But the catalog—"

"The rooms are not yet ready. We must wait until Oscar. Ah!"

From the vicinity of the garage there arrived a small dog, white, hairy, and merrily covered in leaves and brambles. Its muzzle was, for some reason, stained a bright shade of blue. The Baronessa clapped her hands. "High spirits! Dirty and not at all ashamed of himself!"

The creature ran toward her immediately, contorting itself in delight until its frantic attentions came my way. Through its filthy hair I could see two black eyes looking at me with adoration.

"You have met Pushkin and Gorky," she explained, referring to the two ridiculous fawn-colored pugs who followed her nearly everywhere, "but not the other member of the household. He sometimes goes on naughty adventures and I worry. I once had a dog who was attacked by a wild boar. Survived, but she always left the dining room if there was pork." She scratched the head of the little white dog, who writhed in delight. "This is Cesare, who has a heart—how shall I say?—too soon made glad. You will feed him at night."

I bristled at this new duty imposed upon me but stifled my reaction. I asked why the poor dog's face was blue.

"Ah! He found a ballpoint pen and could not resist it." From this, I perceived Cesare had eaten it. A sigh came from the Baronessa: "I understand the temptation! Do you know what? He lived nine years in a kennel before a tartufiere rescued him! A truffle hunter who gave him to me. Nine years! Everything was new to him—balls, toys, trees, rocks—he had to learn how to do everything!" Her gaze went to me with a mischievous smile. "Perhaps you have something in common . . ."

I wondered if I had heard her wrong, but she went on:

"As for the rest of my dogs, they are all here," she said, gesturing to the marble column marked with names still in sight in the courtyard behind us. "The asterisks are all the ones that were *not* pugs. My little elephants' graveyard."

I told her it was quite beautiful.

"You know that elephants really do bury their dead. They will bury other creatures, too. I met a game warden in Kenya who fell asleep in a hollow and awoke to find two elephants covering him with twigs." I recognized the flutter of a smile. "One must always keep an eye open."

A sudden vision came to me.

"I saw an animal last night!"

Her voice rang with hope: "A spider?"

This confused me. "No, not a spider, the . . . the . . ." I searched my memory, then emerged in triumph: "The marten!"

She let out a little yelp. "The faina!"

Ah—so this was what the fish oil was for. "Faina" would not prove to be another houseguest. "Outside my bedroom window!"

"I would have screamed for someone to come!" she said. I did not admit that I had done exactly that, and someone coming had been my fondest wish. She went on to explain that the creature had taken three of the chickens. At first they thought it was a fox, which would have been easy to avert as it would not climb a wall and one could merely patch holes in the fence. But the stone marten was different; lithe and agile, it could get through any barrier, even a roof. They were like snakes, the Baronessa said, but snakes with wings. They seemed to be able to fly. So she had consulted Ghazel. "Can you understand Gazelle when he talks?"

I looked from her to the book in my hands. There were

so many incomprehensible things in Villa Coco. "I'm afraid I can't."

A faint sigh. "I just thought, perhaps, since none of the rest of us can . . ."

"You can't understand him?"

She put both hands on her cane and stared at some weeds as one stares at party crashers. "He first came to Italy as a monk. From Lebanon. He knew no Italian, but of course there was the vow of silence. And the rest was all Latin. So he got along just fine. But he fell in love with a girl over the garden wall, and the monks threw him out. He learned just enough Italian to get the girl pregnant, which couldn't have been much. And he never learned another word!" With a quick gesture she plucked some weeds from a potted geranium and tossed them on the ground. "I don't know how we communicate," she added. "But somehow it comes through! My friend Oscar says talking to Gazelle is like speaking to someone in a dream. Ah, here he is!"

We had slowly gone farther down the hill into the forest of bamboo I had glimpsed the day before peeking out above that gate. The smooth green stalks were a great contrast to the native trees around us and gave this part of the forest a strange formality. My employer informed me that she had planted them herself. In a little clearing, beside a chicken-wire enclosure, stood Ghazel, fists on his hips, staring at a crowd of six or seven chickens.

"Gazelle! La faina!" the Baronessa began in the tone of a tennis player announcing the score before a serve.

Ghazel, completely unstartled by our arrival, turned, gesturing with his hands to make a globe, and said the following: "FAINA! INTRAPPOLARE!"

The Baronessa whispered: "He wants to trap the thing."

Ghazel tapped his chest. "FACCIO! IO!"

"He'll do it himself."

"OLIO! PESCHE!"

"He's asking for peach oil," the Baronessa said, furrowing her brow, "but we understand he means the fish oil. Hand it over quickly, Giovedì."

I gave her the bottle that had traveled across the Atlantic and wondered why I had gone to the trouble when such a thing must be easily found nearby. She presented it to Ghazel, and he thrust it into his pocket without a glance at me. I had a notion it would never be used. He pointed to the chicken coop extravagantly.

A loud whisper from the Baronessa: "Ah, he has more to say!" She was as excited as a medium in a séance.

Ghazel spread his arms wide. "PROTEGGERE! POLI!"

"He wants to protect the chickens. He said poles, but I'm sure he means chickens. Isn't that sweet. Go on!"

Now, his palms flat, he seemed to be miming being trapped in a room. "MURO! CANE!"

She paused thoughtfully at this translation, a finger to her chin, then turned brightly to me. "What a wonderful idea! He wants to make a wall of dogs!" She asked him a question in Italian.

He repeated himself excitedly. "DI CANE! DI CANE!"

Her bright expression fell in disappointment. "Ah, no, I'm mistaken. Not dogs. Di canne. It's always an issue of the double consonant with Gazelle. Di canne. Bamboo!"

"DI CANNE!"

"A wall of bamboo. Well, that's more sensible. Though the other did have some afflatus. A divine inspiration." She spoke some more to the wiry old man, and he replied in kind. "Ah, he's going to start tomorrow. You and Vinsanto will help him. Please keep an eye on Gazelle. His inspirations don't always work out. Once the chickens got fleas, and his solution was to nail their feet to a board and spray them with pesticide. It killed the fleas. And the chickens, too, of course. Let us go and practice with the roses . . ."

We did practice with the roses, beginning with those trained to climb some olive trees, and though she explained in her strange chattering way about the wooden stems and the buds facing away from the plant, it all seemed thoroughly capricious to me as she cut away perfectly lovely branches and left rather hideous ones alone. She saw something I could not, as a sculptor might with a block of granite. She had somehow forgotten about this "Formica" with clothes for me, and I decided not to mention it. My employer was exhausted after these exertions, which took us all around through the olive trees and back to the courtyard. She led me to a door I had not noticed earlier, and we went inside so she could rest. The room was cool and made of stone; the paintings on all the walls were of seaside towns—shipyards, waves crashing against the walkway, the sun behind a great bell tower, a statue of a golden globe held up by two Atlases—and this, along with the underground feeling of the place, lent it a freshness that must have been of her design. I studied each painting, then cast my eyes across the various decorations—the coatrack made of deer antlers, the mirror framed with shells—and, in preparation for at last beginning my cataloging, I took off the hat she had lent me and dropped it on the sofa—

I heard a scream and turned. The Baronessa was standing with her hands on her face. "Ma che cavolo hai fatto!" she shrieked. "A hat on the bed!"

I looked down at the sofa, covered with a thin blue cloth. It seemed utterly unlike a bed. "But . . . but . . . this isn't a bed!"

"It's a daybed!" she exclaimed.

"It's a sofa. You can put a hat on a sofa." Why was I arguing over a sofa when the entire proposition was absurd? How quickly one enters into the madness of others.

Her hands went out grasping into the air. "Give me the green thing. We will call Luciano. He'll know the answer. He's from Napoli."

I handed her the phone from her basket. "I don't think it's really—"

But she was already speaking with the sewage man from Naples. It surprised me he played such a large role in her life; I assumed a baronessa would call only someone of equal rank. But apparently, though she seemed a terrible snob about books and art and culture, people's rank was of no importance to her. I looked around the room and discovered it was a kind of office. There seemed to be boxes of papers and a filing system of some sort. From one pillow on the "bed," an embroidered pug sneered at me in crewelwork.

"I have bad news," the Baronessa reported, holding the phone away from her ear. "It *is* a bed. And this means death." She held up a quivering finger. "But he knows a remedy."

"Thank God."

She put her ear back to the phone, nodding as she listened, then turned again to me.

"He says whoever put the hat on the bed has to touch the palle of a nearby man."

"What is a palle?" I asked.

"The testicles."

We stared at each other for a moment.

"That can't be what he said."

"He's quite sure," she said resolutely. "And I am not yet deaf."

I searched my limited experience of life to sense whether this was of great cultural importance or something entirely of her own invention and thus another test of my employment. I asked if perhaps I myself could be the nearby man.

She raised her eyebrows and applied more Italian to the phone. A pause as she pursed her lips.

"Apparently not," she reported. "Grazie, Luciano," she said into the phone before handing it to me. I pushed the little button to hang up, but she was busy walking to the door. "Now who is nearby? Quickly! Someone will die!" Her face lit up. "We have Gazelle!"

I put out my hands. "I'm not touching his testicles, I'm sorry."

"Or Vinsanto!" she said, a finger to her chin. "He's not bad-looking."

I explained he had left to drop off her friend.

She put one hand on my arm. "Well, we can't wait around. A hat on the bed means death. Unless you find another man, I'm afraid it has to be Gazelle. I'm sure he won't mind, and you may do it through the trousers. He's always up for anything. Go, now, quickly!"

"Are you serious?"

She turned like those Venetian statues that swivel in the wind, presenting the full aura of her righteousness to me. "Young man. You do not understand Italy. Touch Gazelle's palle or I will send you back to Washington."

It was the most absurd sentence I had ever heard in my life. Somehow I could not find it funny. I walked out slightly stunned and got halfway to the chicken coop, but we will never know if I would have gone through with it, for I heard the Baronessa's distinctive call:

"Koo-koo! Koo-koo!"

I shouted "Yes?" and saw her pop out into the courtyard with a man in a jacket and a fedora.

"Giovedì! You may return! The matter is solved!" she

announced with her mischievous grin, gesturing to the man, who tipped his hat. "My friend Oscar has arrived!"

All my ideas about life in a villa, especially life with a baronessa, seemed now like the foolish thoughts of a tourist who has not bothered to read his Baedeker's. Antique paneled walls and crystal chandeliers? My reality was hand-painted animals and lamps that looked plucked from a pirate ship. Servants to iron my bedding and draw a hot bath? My mattress was "grumeleux," the bath had hardly any hot water, and, in any case, I was a servant myself. As for elegance and style, they were all around, but with the opalescence of a soap bubble—glimmering, gorgeous, trichroic—bursting when one is compelled by duty. Such as the last thing I wanted to do: touch the nearest man's palle.

Luckily, the Baronessa's friend was an accommodating partner in removing the curse, as well as amused. Oscar and I adjourned to the little studio decorated with seaside scenes. He removed his fedora (delicately placed on a table), revealing a bald crown that had seen many days in the sun. The silver hair above his ears was carefully trimmed, as everything about him was careful and deliberate, from the chestnut ascot, cobalt polka-dotted, to the chardonnay jacket and claret trousers, to the mustard-yellow socks. I would later learn that he believed the secret to growing old was to "always have a nice smile and a nice smell," meaning to keep oneself pleasant to be around. He certainly was, and he was as generous with his smile as he was with advice to young Americans. He smelled of rose and old leather and carried a few packages wrapped in brown paper, the size of large books. Here, I hoped, might at last be a reasonable person to consult.

"Young man, a favor I must ask." His accent was distinctly

British, but not the posh upper class of the princess; he talked like the voice of the London Tube, and it instantly put me at ease. "You are here to make this catalog for our friend."

I said the rooms were apparently not ready.

"Don't worry too much about detail. Paintings like this, no need to do anything more than describe them."

"Am I making a record for her estate?"

"Her estate?" he asked, surprised.

I explained that since she was ninety-two—

"Yes! I had forgotten. I am certain Estelle has explained everything."

I said that she certainly had not.

"Do you know where I met Lisabetta?" he said, quickly switching topics. "At an auction!"

I asked what had been on auction and he pointed to himself. I apologized and said I had not realized he was an artist.

"I have a very special but very minor talent," he said. "But Lisabetta found a place for me."

"Is some of your work in the house?"

He raised his eyebrows and said it certainly was, then deflected the conversation back to the matter at hand: "Do you know why a hat on the bed is bad luck? Here is why. In the old days, when a person was dying, the priest would come and sit to give last rites. And every time, he would put his hat on the bed. You see? His hat on the bed. Then, later, that person would die. And what do you think killed them? Well, it was the hat." He laughed merrily. "Obviously."

"Obviously."

There came a shout from the courtyard—"Pronto!"—that I recognized as Nimali's, but Oscar didn't seem in a hurry to attend to lunch. Instead, he asked me a little about my background. I told him I was a typical American, born to two scientists in the suburbs of our nation's capital and educated in the suburbs of a Puritan city, and had been to Europe only once, when I was twelve, on a trip focused mainly on visiting my supposed ancestral home in Scotland, with London and Paris thrown in for good measure. He nodded gravely, as if I had told him I'd been raised by mountain gorillas.

"Lisabetta and I were good friends in our distant youth on Capri," he said. "We had some fine adventures! And got into not a little trouble."

"By the way, my name's not really—"

"Shall we see what is for lunch?"

I suggested we should first perform the countercurse.

He laughed, showing his straight white teeth. "A gesture is as good as a deed," he said, adding that I had merely to touch his trousers. "Listen, I know my old friend is not always easy. There may come a point when you want to leave."

I stared at him. After all, I just spent a day with a pozzo and a princess, trying so hard to be allowed to stay . . .

"There will be one, I promise," he said, then smiled. "But do not go. As a favor to me and to yourself. It will be worth whatever trouble you have to go through."

I agreed and very lightly touched his trousers with my fingers. He laughed. And so we snatched one day from death.

We found the Baronessa already seated at the luncheon table in the arcade, chattering in French with Estelle. The wisteria hung in the courtyard, following the arch, and framed them like a Fragonard. Our arrival did not stop the conversation, but Estelle did stand up and gesture for me to sit between her and my employer, who seemed to be telling a story at length. Estelle had her hair up in a white headscarf and wore a loose linen dress, almost a poncho, in its natural dusty hue. She sent me what looked like a conspiratorial glance, but I could not imagine what we could conspire about, unless it was the faina, and anyway, since we were at that moment sitting down to lunch, how I was meant to do anything about it. Oscar took his position opposite me, and I saw that before him, instead of a white plate like ours, sat a bowl shaped like a head of cabbage and, in it, an enormous multicolored salad. Nimali stood beside the table in a pink apron, holding a bowl of pasta. Her glare was one of extreme impatience.

"Lisabetta, it is done," Oscar announced, gesturing to me. Somehow overtaken by the theatricality of it all, I found myself giving a little bow.

The Baronessa smiled and said to me: "That is all very well, but you must come instantly when Nimali says 'pronto'! The pasta will now be overcooked."

I apologized to her and to Nimali, who held the bowl out for Estelle to serve herself.

"Giovedì," said the Baronessa, "you must learn the rules of the Italian table. First is the oldest female guest, our very young Estelle. Then to our eldest man, who would be Oscar, if he were eating pasta. You will be next and you may blame it on your youth. Then I, the host, am last."

Oscar leaned over with a merry smile: "Oh, but it's secretly the best! We call it the priest's portion. His humility forces him to eat after everyone else—but we all know the sauce is at the bottom! So the priest gets the best bite of all." The Baronessa seemed amused.

Certainly it was true of the second-to-last bite; spaghetti dotted with mussels, clams, shrimp, and parsley, fragrant with garlic, and my portion was delicious. The pugs pushed at my legs, hopeful for a morsel. I found myself looking around the table, and the Baronessa caught my eye. "He is looking for cheese!" I sat up straight in confusion; this was hardly my first Italian meal, but heretofore there had always been—

"No cheese with fish!" Estelle said, slapping my hand playfully. "Never never never!"

"And no using the spoon!" interjected the Baronessa.

I sat up haughtily. "I think you're just making up rules."

"It makes perfect sense," Oscar said cheerfully. "Have you ever seen cows in a fishing village?"

Having never seen a fishing village, I said no.

"Or clams in the mountains?"

The mere idea made me smile.

He tossed his salad with a fork and a spoon, talking all the while. "Think of two hundred years ago, before refrigeration. They ate their pasta in the mountains with cheese, and by the sea with fish, but nowhere with both. Not because they were stubborn. Because it was their reality. And we have kept the tradition."

"But now we have both, we could—"

"Never say this!" he stated firmly. "Never!" Then he laughed. I wondered how many Anglos he'd had to teach about cheese, about hats on beds, about so many perfectly obvious parts of life.

The Baronessa chirped brightly: "You know that Oscar was thrown in jail for his art?"

He sat up straight. "Lisabetta. I was never in jail."

Estelle seemed to have tensed beside me; I could see her exchanging glances with the old man. I wondered if this was a sensitive topic, but my employer ventured on: "It was in Paris. He had stolen tubes of paint from an art store. Sneaking around in a trench coat with big pockets. Had been doing it for years, but the trick to pinching is to keep a sense of balance. Something missing here, something missing there, nobody minds—"

"So you often say," Oscar mused.

"But Oscar got greedy, went too often, and the owner had him arrested."

He opened his hands to me and Estelle, pleading guilty: "I couldn't afford it. It was one thousand francs."

"And you know what his defense was? 'I am a great artist and I need this paint.' "

He said, "I did need it."

I asked if his defense worked, and he nodded serenely. I asked what the paint was.

"Tyrian purple," the old man said. "Made from the murex snail. A fugitive pigment. Though I was acquitted, I was advised by the court, in the future, to use"—he paused to shudder—"*magenta*."

I gasped, and it made him giggle.

"Of course, magenta was no good to me," he went on. "I was doing a particular"—he raised his eyes to the ceiling, searching for the proper word, then brought them down again—"style . . . that could only be Tyrian purple. The subject was Hercules, using a local fisherman as a model, done in the ancient way. I never sold it, never could find a buyer. It was not where my talent lay. Anyway, we all have stolen something!"

"But we have not all been caught!" the Baronessa said, and for some reason this made the table laugh.

Estelle and the Baronessa began speaking again in French, and Oscar forced them to change to English. The topic was one of the utmost importance in this heat wave: water. Apparently Villa Coco, for all its charms, had no well or independent source of water.

"When you buy a house, make sure it has a well," the Baronessa advised me, and I nodded as if I ever expected to buy a house, much less find one with a well. "I was young and impetuous and loved this house too much. But every house and lover has a fatal flaw—"

I repeated that in my mind: *Every house and lover has a fatal flaw.*

"—All you can do is learn what it is beforehand, and I felt at least I knew this one's was water. I hired a rabdomante, a very esteemed one—"

Estelle broke in: "A man who finds water with a stick."

"A diviner," I said.

The Baronessa seemed intrigued by this translation. "A diviner! He was in fact the butler of my friend! A defrosted priest." (*Defrocked*, Estelle corrected.) "I remember he said he didn't like to do it, but if God gives you a gift, you must use it. He walked all around the property with his stick, and at last he came beside the house, and down it went! 'Here is water,' he announced to us. 'We should dig here.' I was very sad to tell him that he had found, on the other side of the wall, our refrigerator."

I laughed, and she sparkled at me. Estelle smiled; she clearly had heard this story many times.

"But the rabdomante was also a soothsayer, thanks God! This he also did not like to do, but this he did. He said that I would not die in this house. Which upset me greatly, I have to tell you. I love this house. I do not want to die in some terrible hospital with boring people and someone screaming in the next room. I asked him when I would die, but apparently his talent lay only in venue. Like a booking agent."

Oscar pointed out that she had always wanted to die at sea.

"Yes," the Baronessa said. "If he had mentioned the sea, I would be content. I am only really happy at sea. I want to die lashed to the mast like Ulisse!"

Oscar was shown to a room downstairs—the "White Room," where apparently he always stayed—and I was told I would not be needed for the next few hours. I stood there in confusion until the Baronessa made a gesture as of whisking away a fly and I understood I was to leave. I managed to occupy myself by making my own assessment of the house's needs. It seemed I would have to both prove myself to my employer and find a use for my anxious energy. I examined the bookshelves and discovered them in anything but alphabetical order. I looked at the stone objects in the entrance hall and saw no organizing principle, nor was there one for the miniature African warriors marshaled in my room beside a drawing of a Russian church; and in the kitchen's cutlery drawer, where organization must rule, I found a fork had run off with the spoons. The work seemed impossible; it was a house built specifically to thwart me.

And yet, good boy that I was, I diligently avoided the Baronessa and her guest, though they were hard to dodge; they seemed to be everywhere I wanted to be. I went to use the lavatory assigned to me and found the two elderly people crammed inside its close quarters, pointing at the walls and whispering animatedly. Oscar appeared startled to see me; I saw he was carrying one of his brown paper packages, which he drew behind himself. He touched the Baronessa's shoulder. She turned around coyly and said, "One would like a little privacy sometime," a statement that seemed odd for her to make in my bathroom. Later in the day, I happened upon them in the "captain's cabin" (as she called the office), standing together in the middle of the room and each staring at a different painted sea view. It was altogether peculiar behavior. I tried following their maneuvers around the house, but the two seemed either to stand for an hour before the same drawing . . . or else to vanish from sight. In any case, they provided no clues.

As for any questions I had, the Baronessa referred me always to others. “Ask Estelle,” she said. “Or my cousin Giacomo. He comes any day now. He is a character from a Mitford novel.” This was of no help; I wasn’t aware of what a Mitford novel might be.

Oscar stayed two days, and I found him in the kitchen early on his final morning, just as I was making my coffee. “Have you mastered the Italian coffeemaker?” he asked. He was dressed again in his ascot, his chardonnay jacket, holding his fedora in his hands. I wondered how he managed in the heat; it seemed a singular talent of Italian men. He was waiting for Vinsanda to take him to the train station and had beside him the same packages in brown paper that he’d carried when he arrived. I wondered if he had brought something to show the Baronessa.

I said I was mastering it better than the language.

“We must find you an Italian man,” he said. “That is the only way you will learn the language. A warm dictionary, as they say. Of course, finding a man is harder than it was in my day.” He said this very plainly, his gaze out the window to where two black kittens basked in the sun. “When I was young, you could hike across the hills and any man would be yours. A goatherd, a winemaker, a priest. It was wonderful! Simply wonderful. This was just after the war. I think everyone thought, ‘To hell with it! I’ll take whatever pleasure comes my way.’ Lucky me! I was there to give it. Think of lying on a hillside with a young shepherd . . .”

Do you know what? I was such a self-centered, parochial, cliché-addled fool that it had simply never occurred to me that Oscar was like myself. And still, looking at him in the kitchen, I could not separate what was a homosexual “tell” and what merely generational and Continental—the fedora, the ascot, the dentures, the scent of rose and old leather—when of course my surprise was the classic stupidity: the thought that someone has always been the age at which we meet them. Always a silver-haired man with a smile. Time works for no one but us. When of course of course of course one summer he lay on a hillside with a young shepherd . . .

"But my heart gave out at fifty," Oscar continued, turning to me. "An aortic aneurysm, inherited from my father. Who died at fifty. My doctor advised me to give it all up. Meat and dairy and bread, yes, and sex." He looked at the Mitsu-bitchy now arriving beside the door. "It was time, anyway. The era of shepherds was over, and I was too old for the new world. AIDS and parades. I did not want to be a fool in love. So I renounced it all. I don't eat pasta, I don't eat cheese. I don't fall in love. I am a very cheerful, very harmless old man."

I told him I saw so much more in him than that. Again, a bright, good-natured smile to cover whatever memory he concealed from me. I thought of my own vow, renouncing entanglements of any kind. I saw, in Oscar, a kindred spirit. Perhaps I was a harmless young man.

I asked him if he had accomplished what he had come to do. He raised his eyebrows in surprise. "You know, my American friend," he said, "I think our Lisabetta underestimates you."

My employer made ample use of each hour the day provided, but though we pruned roses, even in the continuing heat; hunted down books and magazines and drawings that seemed to her essential to have at hand; made numerous phone calls for hair salon appointments, doctors' appointments, and massage appointments as well as veterinary visits, we never approached anything like making the catalog I had been sent to prepare. This was a source of great frustration to me, and I fell into bed each night exhausted by both the physical labor and the circumlocutory conversation I partook in ten hours of each day. Mornings, however, were mine alone; since my employer did not appear at her balcony until eleven, and since the rooms were not "ready" for my cataloging, those hours were given over to my own pursuits. I took it upon myself to explore this bit of Tuscany.

I discovered that Villa Coco lay on a ridge between two deep river gullies and that the road Ghazel had brought me on formed a loop leading from a bright, sunny hill down to a dark, sunless valley and back up again into the light along another ridge that soon connected to our own. It took about an hour to make this Orphean loop on foot (Cesare always running merrily beside me), which began just below Villa Coco on the disused portion of road I had been warned so ardently against. Its overlayer of sand and dirt was so worn away by time and the elements that it was reduced to the bones of its former self: the flat stones of the Roman byway it used to be. I could make out, in the damp clumps of forest around me, here the remains of a grand stairway above a cliff, there of a door lintel leading to nowhere, and, at the bottom, a sign pointing to the nearby town.

Rising up from this dark valley, however, was a delight; I came across a lively stream whose course was directed, here and there, by concrete berms and dams and, in one location, an overgrown bridge leading to nothing but a dappled glade in which lay a contented cat. Higher up the ridge, the path became brambled, and one time I lost my way and emerged in a large field with myself at one end and a bull at the other. I watched as his awareness came gradually my way; his ears flicked to attention; I waited no more but threw myself back into the brambles from whence I'd come. There were other houses along the way, some utterly abandoned with entrance gates hanging rusty from the hinges but others neatly painted white, with vegetables growing in tidy gardens. I grew to know some of these neighbors enough to say "Salve": short, elderly Duccio, who owned the land beside us and was always working on a fence that seemed to fall apart at one end just as he was restoring the other; the middle-aged twin brothers, the thin one a painter, the fat one a composer, who had somehow made an artistic life in this bit of wilderness; the town baker, whom I often saw returning from work in his truck, singing loudly as he drove along (he had been trained for opera in his youth). At the end of my route, just before it joined our own ridge, I always passed the Cinghialaio: the Wild Boar Lodge, whose cardboard sign had been my first indication of my future home. As I passed only in the mornings, I found it always abandoned: a sort of log cabin with a slanted roof and a large area of fallen tree trunks placed around a fire. Later I learned it came to life on Saturdays, when men would arrive in Jeeps to hunt the area's famous wild boars. Sometimes, on my walks, I did not come across another human being, nor have anyone say a word to me—anyone, that is, except the elderly woman seated in her red chair at the crossroads . . .

"Ah, Signora Guicciardini!"

I asked the Baronessa about her at our next luncheon. "She's always there. What is she shouting all day?"

"All day and night! She will not let them bring her in until it is time for bed."

I asked again what the woman might be saying to passersby for all those hours.

"She is—" But then the Baronessa put a finger to her lips. "When *you* are able to tell *me*, then I will know you have kept your promise to learn Italian."

How I was to learn Italian was a mystery; we were in the middle of the countryside and I had no easy access to a car to attend a school. I searched the bookshelves and came across a lesson book, in English, from the 1960s, which contained full scenes of dialogue such as VISITING A TAILOR and TALKING TO CLERGY, with phrases such as "I want to look groovy" and "I don't believe in God," neither helpful in proving my worth to my employer. I wondered how I would ever translate the mysterious pronouncements of Signora Guicciardini or accomplish speaking Italian with my employer "in macchina." And yet I did, in my way, begin a series of Italian lessons through pure force of necessity. My teacher was none other than Nimali.

Early in the mornings, I took down the coffeemaker (what is called a "moka") and carefully unscrewed it into three parts, filled the lower region with water and the perforated middle section with coffee, screwed them back together, placed it on the flame, and waited so long for it to boil that it seemed a wonder of thermodynamics. Nimali would inevitably arrive in the kitchen during this procedure and launch into impassioned Italian as if we were lovers parted by circumstance. "Joe!" she would shout, without even a buon giorno, and begin a series of complaints about either her husband or "lei" (her), and of course there was no "lei" except the Baronessa. Nimali never seemed sad despite her complaints. Instead, complaining seemed merely a habit of morning; she often smiled while listing off the faults of each member of the household, most of which I did not understand. She wore her hair unbraided and, dressed in one of the "maid's outfits" the Baronessa bought her (which Nimali hated), her hands clasped before her, she resembled a Tuscan soprano singing her morning song, and the chorus seemed to be "La vita è dura!" Life is hard. To which

I learned the proper response was "Ma andiamo avanti!"—but we must go on! On she would go, appealing to me with those eyes, clasping her hands, shaking her head, then reaching the chorus: "La vita è dura!" I said we must go on, and on she then would go with more complaints. There seemed to be innumerable verses. All while I waited for the moka to sputter out my morning coffee. Eventually I learned enough Italian for another phrase: "Caffè prima, dopo italiano." That is to say: Coffee first and then Italian. She admired my resolve and usually took a turn through the downstairs while I prepared the moka, reappearing just as the coffee had finished brewing. "Joe!" she would shout. "Piano, piano," I would say, and she would nod as sagely as any professor.

In return, I taught Nimali some English that she might find useful, including the simple word "Enough!" We practiced; I would begin by saying *La vita è dura*, *La vita è dura*, over and over until she slammed her palms on the counter and, in her lilting accent, shouted, "Enough!" Then we both had a great long laugh.

Eventually, I reported these morning lessons to the Baronessa, who seemed delighted. "But you must be careful," she told me. "Nimali has decided not to learn gender. It is not for political notions young people have. I think it simplifies the language. So all the world is feminine to her! It makes for a very rose-colored conversation. You will become as fanciful as Gazelle! And the last thing I desire is someone else in the house I do not understand."

Estelle was not often at Villa Coco, and I had not yet received an invitation to her house, but our paths did cross on one of my morning walks. I had just passed the signora in her chair and was making my way down the shadowless stretch of road before it dipped into the forest. Dry and beautiful, with a view of hills covered by centuries of cultivation—vineyards and olive groves in their regular lines—that contrasted so much with the thorny wilderness below; I was already sweating from my efforts and glad I wore a broad straw hat borrowed from the villa (in a closet with a dozen others) when I was surprised by a high honking sound behind me. It was an Ape—a miniature breed of truck on three wheels, its name meaning not a simian but a bee—and behind the wheel was Estelle. She pulled up beside me and asked if I needed a ride. I said I enjoyed the walk every morning before the Baronessa arose.

Estelle leaned out the window. "You took the lower road? We never use it, it's certain death to drive on. How is it on foot?"

I told her it was fine.

She asked if I was finding my days too empty, and I responded that I hoped they would soon be filled with something more than pozzos and pruning gardens and pugs.

"Are you unhappy?"

I paused a moment. "It's just not what I expected."

"You have to get used to one another."

"I wonder if she'll get used to me. She didn't want an American."

She laughed. "No, *I* wanted an American. She wanted a blond British boy, that's the kind she likes. An 'Anglosaxophone,' is how she put it." We shared a laugh. "But Americans are . . . honest. You're honest. We don't need some twit who knows every object and can cite the provenance of every painting. We just need an honest list."

"That's what Oscar told me, too." It seemed strange they would both say this.

"Oscar!" she said. "Well, he'll make everything speed along. They have an important trip to Ferrara coming."

"And who is this cousin who will be visiting?"

"Giacomo-Giacomo!" She laughed. "He's very shy. Coco saved him from a terrible mother. I do not know how they are related. It's possible they aren't at all! Does it really matter? He ran away from home and lived with her for I think a year before his family clawed him back. He became . . . what they wanted him to be. Afraid of them, I think. He is an editor at a publishing house. But he always comes back to see his cousin. I think being here with her was the best time of his life."

She started up the truck's engine.

I put my hand on the door. "Maybe this is too personal, but the Baronessa. Is she in good health?"

She asked, "What do you mean?"

"I mean . . . a woman of her age . . . and you've called me in to . . ."

She cut the engine. Behind her was the valley, blue smoke rising in the air from somewhere and, from another corner of the landscape, a chain saw droning sharp and high. "Yes, I insisted on it. She will never be free of her vertigo and it will get worse over time. Though of course," she added, "she'll never die! She wouldn't allow it!"

I laughed, and so did she, though there was something serious in her tone.

Before she took off, she pointed at my head and smiled: "You do look good in Coco's hat."

Oscar returned after a week, and I was glad it was not yet another of my extraneous tasks to retrieve him from the San Drogo station, mostly because I was terrified of the Mitsu-bitchy, which felt more like an early experiment in flying machines than a truly functioning road vehicle. It was also clear to me, after the warnings I had received about the treacherous lower road and my own experiences on the upper one, that only an expert such as Ghazel could navigate the ruts and stones and fallen branches. I was, in a sense, trapped at Villa Coco. So, I understood, was the Baronessa, which was perhaps why she invited her friend to visit her rather than the reverse.

I heard the clatter of Oscar's arrival while I was upstairs making my lumpy bed, but, as he was immediately whisked away to my employer's chambers, I saw nothing of him until he appeared at lunch, neatly dressed in pale linen pants and a pressed shirt in deep green. "I look like a bottle of Chianti!" he announced before kissing me on one cheek and then the other. His familiar scent was comforting. From behind him the Baronessa emerged all in white, raising her horse-headed cane. "After lunch, we will visit the Formica!" she announced.

"What is this Formica?" I asked.

"The Formica!" she insisted, spreading the fingers on her free hand. "Oh, what is the English? Tell me, what is the name for the creature at a picnic? The creature that bothers everybody so you are forced to leave?"

"A baby?"

A smile. "The ant! The ant. But this ant is not at a picnic, she is at Rignano. And she has clothes for you."

Oscar said this was a place of great treasures.

"HO HO HO!" the Baronessa chortled. "The great treasure is Oscar and what he has brought me."

"Shall I bring another toe?" he asked, and they had a great laugh. I assumed this was some untranslatable example of Italian wit.

Lunch began with a baffling dish of what seemed to be giant flower buds, deep-fried. "Zucchini blossoms," Oscar explained to me. "Filled with ricotta, with one acciuga in the center. An anchovy."

"But you told me fish could not go with cheese!" I said. He shrugged.

The Baronessa chimed in: "The anchovy is not a fish!"

And that was the final word on anchovies. It seemed the universe could be just as one decided.

They were delicious.

We did not go to this mysterious Formica after lunch. I suspected my employer had forgotten again, and I had no desire to remind her, so we went about our normal activities (work on the roses, her correspondence, a search for a dog's toy), and I could see she was growing weary, possibly simply of me, and she suggested I take Oscar out on a walk. I found him in the loggia, playing solitaire, Pushkin and Gorky at his feet. I mentioned a walk and he smiled. "Lisabetta still thinks of me as a great hiker," he said. "Why don't we just sit here?" And so we did.

"We must broaden your knowledge of Italy," he told me. "For instance, Ferrara. Where Lisabetta and I are going next month. Not far away at all."

I told him I had never heard of it.

"Ah, a marvelous city! It is the birthplace of Antonioni and Vancini and is where they filmed *The Garden of the Finzi-Continis*. I wish you could come, but unfortunately it is a very important matter for the two of us to deal with. And Napoli. You must go there as soon as possible."

"Maybe one weekend when I'm free—"

A shake of his head. "But you can't simply go there."

I sputtered in confusion; he had not a moment before told me to.

"You can only visit Napoli with a Neapolitan," he said. "Otherwise you will either have a merely touristic experience or be swallowed up whole. It is very hard to find the middle way. Only a Neapolitan knows the middle way."

"Are you a Neapolitan?"

An intake of breath. "What, *me*? Are you mad? I'm from Genova!"

I made a gesture of apology, still ignorant as to how far Genova might be from Naples or, in fact, how far Tuscany might be from Naples. Or from anything; I had not left our little corner of the countryside.

"When you go, of course you must have the pizza. That's famous."

I said that was obvious.

"But something more important," he warned me, turning over a card. "The sfogliatella. Try to say that. Sfogliatella."

I tried and it fell from my mouth in broken pieces.

"Something like that, yes. Sfogliatella. It's a pastry. Too heavy for breakfast. You have it midafternoon, let's say. But the important part is there are two kinds of sfogliatelle. Riccia and frolla."

"I see."

"Once you try riccia, you will never go back." Another card. "The same with frolla."

"What's the difference?"

A stern look. "One is riccia and one is frolla! Curly or short. That is the choice."

"And which should I choose? Curly or short?"

"Ah!" he said, sitting back. "Ah." A pause. "This I cannot tell you. But once you see them, you will know. The choice you make in this moment sets the course of your life."

"My life with pastry, you mean."

He looked to me, then to his cards, and said, "One never

knows." He turned another over and moved it to a row. "I'll bring you some slippers from Venice," he added as he leaned back to survey the game. "I know a place where they make beautiful ones in red velvet."

At this point the Baronessa appeared at the door with Estelle. I saw that my employer had not been resting at all but had been at one of her own mysterious tasks.

"What time is it now?" the old lady demanded. The pugs awakened instantly.

I answered this: "A quarter to three."

Her hand went dramatically to her heart, as her language went to French: "Sacré bleu! We must get to the Formica before they close! Everyone, into the Mitsu-bitchy!"

It was a race to get outside—a peculiar race, as two of the contestants were over seventy and one had a cane and vertigo. But we stumbled outside, and I was made to climb into the driver's seat, with the Baronessa beside me. The others gathered snugly in the back. The manual transmission was somewhat foreign to me, but I started up the poor vehicle and began to head jerkily uphill, on the route I had taken on my arrival. But I felt the Baronessa tapping me desperately with her cane.

"There's no time!" she shouted, and pointed toward the forbidden forest behind us. "Take the other way!"

I looked back at the dark and twisted road below. "But you said!" I sputtered.

"The other way, Giovedì!"

"You said never to—"

Another tap from the cane. "Italiano in macchina!"

The old abandoned road went along the fields without a bump but soon descended into the shadowy woodland, where it switchbacked on its way toward the valley. And I am afraid to say that, with the Baronessa hitting me with the cane to go faster and my other companions urging me on, I took the hairpin turns at a dangerous speed, plunging through foliage and making life-or-death decisions about which rut seemed deepest. There was no question of Italian in the car; there was nothing *but* Italian in the car, being shouted from all sides. A Vesuvius of Italian erupted at the sight of a log fallen halfway across the road that nearly meant the end of us. But it was not the end of us. And when we emerged from the forest between two stone columns, their finial lions gagged by ivy, the only sound remaining came from the Baronessa, laughing at yet another absurdity of her own invention.

We burst into the shop like bank robbers—it turned out La Formica was a church thrift shop. Our clamor startled two nuns out of the clothing racks like pheasants flushed from the bush. The nuns greeted us with reverence. It's possible that, as nuns, they greeted everything with reverence. Perhaps even cheap plastic wallets glowed with God. "Baronessa," one said, but the Baronessa paid her no mind, striding toward the men's suits and dragging me along. "We must find someone your size who has just died," she told me. Her thin hands felt the fabrics. Estelle suggested a dead man named Tonino. Down came one suit after another, and I was bid to try them on; there was no dressing room, so Oscar shielded me from the nuns until I found a pair of trousers long enough to reach my shoes. Soon I had Tonino's entire closet hanging on a hook: button-up shirts in plaids and stripes, suits of camel and tweed and linen, sweaters and shoes and ties. They seemed, to me, hopelessly out of style. The Baronessa scoffed; she said a high waist and pleats were always in style. "Take them all," she insisted.

"Maybe just one," I said doubtfully.

Estelle said they were each about a dollar. But I felt if I bought them, I would be required to wear them. I knew the chill of autumn would be here soon, but in this heat they seemed absurd. I caught Estelle's eye.

"I'll think about it," I said with a smile, making to return the clothes to the rack.

But the Baronessa did not smile. She lifted her chin and narrowed her eyes, placing her hand on the clothes to prevent me from returning them. She said, very firmly and clearly: "We won't be back."

I laughed. Speaking of a shop she told me she visited every week or so, it seemed the height of absurdity, another one of her dramatic moments. But she did not laugh, and neither did my companions.

Oscar leaned in and spoke to me gently: "Lisabetta is right. If you want them, take them now. Will we be back? Who knows?"

And so I came home with Tonino's wardrobe and began the slow transformation from an American into a man.

It was after Oscar's departure, during a trip by the Baronessa to the hair salon, when the house was empty at last, that I was finally able to make a complete tour.

The downstairs, for the most part, I already knew. The entrance hall had three doors: one leading to the kitchen, one to the library, and one to a white-tiled bedroom with a ceiling lamp hung so low that pieces had been broken by unexpectedly tall guests. This was where Oscar stayed. It was decorated with Turkish paintings that, on closer inspection, seemed all to be of mild foot torture in which the victim smiled with either atonement or delight. French doors looked out on the garden, and a closet held no surprises except that the serving platters seemed to be stored there. Through the library was the captain's cabin, with the views of the sea, in which Oscar had removed the curse, and another door leading to the main living room, which I had passed through many times but never had the occasion to enjoy. Objects were everywhere, but most striking were two great mirrors above the white corner lounge, painted with dancing ladies. Naked. Nearby, and leering slightly, was what the Baronessa had informed me was a painting of a Venetian courtesan, in folds of velvet, wearing the foot-high clogs necessary for her profession in high water. How did the Baronessa know it was a courtesan? "No pearls!" she told me. "Prostitutes could not wear pearls." As if this were something everybody knew.

Upstairs was the truly undiscovered country. I was reluctant to enter her private chambers, so at first I went along the flower-painted hallway, peeking into the room next to mine (yellow, prints of *A Rake's Progress* above the twin beds), the room beyond (linens and an imposing antique steam iron), and the Baronessa's parlor. Pushkin and Gorky looked up languidly from the sofa. Here I had been before; the lamps were chrome and from the 1960s, illuminating furniture from the 1980s and books, on shelves to the ceiling, from the 1880s. A door led onto the balcony, and I could see a storm boiling on the horizon. From this parlor, I passed through her office (lit overhead by an enormous lamp, which she told me was a streetlight from Milan, and darkened by black furniture and bookshelves) and delicately opened the door to her secret realm. Her sunken bath, her cluttered vanity, up two stairs to the Nimali-made bed and television and there it was. A woman with a jug. The Picasso.

This was the first item I put in my catalog. I had begun.

After the Picasso, and until two arrivals (one that would send the house into a panic, one that would ruin my best-laid plans), I focused entirely on my job as archivist. I want to make it clear that my discomfort at Villa Coco was organizational, never moral. Something was going on that I was not being told about, but it was a source merely of interest, not of judgment.

Or so I felt at first. But as I kept being excluded from certain rooms, inhibited from opening drawers and so on, this erratic behavior seemed to touch on my occupation—not only what I had been hired to do but my occupation of leaving behind the distractions of frivolity and thereby building a life of consequence. I did not seem to be achieving any of the above. I found myself trying to explain the systems I had been taught, but the Baronessa dismissed these as fads.

"One room that is ready is the library," she offered, and I felt a great relief. Here was a place I was comfortable setting rules.

"I will make sure it's alphabetical—"

"Are you mad? Some of these are in Russian! No, I have found another solution. By country of the author's birth."

"Okay," I said, swallowing. "That should be easy."

"Not so easy as you say! Where, for instance, is Yugoslavia? Or, for that matter, the Ottoman Empire? Prussia? Austria-Hungary? So many nations I knew as a girl. To simplify things, I refer to the map you see here on the wall."

It was dated 1912.

I did manage to ambush my employer one morning on her descent down the staircase with Pushkin and Gorky. I asked her to name every item in the entrance hall, the room with the bronze sculpture of the boat and the vitrines. To my surprise, she was delighted to do so; she sat in a cane chair and pointed at random at some object—say, a wooden statue with an enormous phallus—and began a story in her old wild way: "This not only came from an Italian archaeologist but resembles him . . ."

This did me no good for my catalog. Nor could I make use of the perfectly ordinary category of "value." At one point, I broke in on a tale about a rabbi in Beirut by saying, "We should move on to another of your treasures—"

"HO HO HO!"

"What is it?"

"Treasures!" she scoffed. "Not any longer!" Then seemed to stop herself from saying more. I wondered if all these beautiful objects had been found at a thrift shop, and was about to say so when she broke her silence:

"But do you know," she mused, "there is one truly valuable object remaining here." She put her hand to her chin and surveyed her crowded little room. "One thing that is worth all the rest."

I asked her what it might be, but she continued her musing:

"Priceless, in fact. It belongs in a museum, someone told me, only I said it belongs with me. Can you guess it?"

Frantically I looked around the little hall, every inch crammed with paintings with Cyrillic writing, engraved brass bowls, ivory and tortoiseshell inkstones, vases of peacock feathers, ceramic busts of young men and women, an ornate tasseled camel's saddle, Bakelite hairbrushes and combs and makeup boxes, carved wooden angels, and Native American fetish dolls arranged on a shelf. Of course I knew the value of artifacts—appraisal is one of the practices of archival science—but estimating the value of the objects around me was a puzzle. Was she sitting on a fortune? Or a trash heap? I pointed to a piece of stone, carved in what I took for Arabic, which was set into the plaster of the wall.

"Ah! That is from Cairo. I was invited to dinner at the house of an Egyptian publisher. There was Arabic writing on the wall of his dining room, and I asked him if he would give it to me. So he had that portion of the wall chipped away and sent to me, and there it is before you." She smiled, admiring it. "It's worthless."

My eyes fell in defeat. I had thought myself, if not an expert, then at least someone interested in beautiful things, and in college (before amorous entanglements consumed them) I spent my solitary hours eyeing objects in antiques shops and imagining that I might one day possess them. But there the objects were labeled, or the owner would provide a fanciful explanation, and nothing was "junk"—its value was its cost, and thus the same for all. Among my parents' things, worth was weighed in status. It was a foreign country, this one I had entered, a country in which the currency changed daily, in which an object's value was elastic and depended only on the individual.

"But yes, in this room," I heard her saying beside me, "there is something that is truly a treasure."

"Show me," I begged her.

Her eyes moved to me, and a smile flickered on her face, as if she were not fool enough to tell me. "You didn't ask what was written on the stone. It is 'Alayam dewl.' "

"Alayam dewl," I repeated.

"Days are like countries," she said, not moving a muscle as I digested this. She gave a little cough, then tenderly added: "Meaning they will change tomorrow. One day is for us, the next against us. So it goes."

I had not thought of countries as changing at all; the continent of Europe seemed as fixed as a sculpture group. But then I looked at her map of 1912 and saw that, for someone who had lived as long as she, alayam dewl, indeed.

"You ask about organizing principles. These," she said, gesturing to the vitrines, "are by affinità."

"What does that mean?"

"Their obvious attraction to one another!" she said. "I will show you, and this is something to learn. The Bangladeshi dolls and Afghan blanket together bring to mind the Mughal Empire, and isn't it amusing to see this Robensky, a terrible antisemite, below a Jewish Greek bridal shawl?" She gave a little giggle; it baffled me completely, for was not the drawing worth something and the shawl a yellowed rag? Not at all, not here, not to her. Because, as I was slowly learning, it depended not on training or learning or even experience but on having an "eye."

An "eye." It did not mean the ability to spot the difference between a topaz and a brown diamond, a real Tiffany and a fake, or even some "soul" in an object that all could attest to; it was to spot the echo in oneself. I scanned the room and could not sense it, but then again, this was a room filled by someone else's impulses and caprices. To find an echo in oneself, one had to know oneself. That seemed an impossibility. Would I ever become a person who bought a bridal shawl and draped it above a work by some well-known artist? Would I ever become a person who asked for a stone to be chipped off a wall?

"These tigers and lions, from Kenya and from Zanzibar," she went on with obvious delight, "go with the camel's saddle but not with the mating hippos. Those"—and here she paused, her gaze rising mischievously to catch mine—"go with the other erotic objects, like the prostitute and wooden penis, of course."

"Of course," I echoed.

So were my hours filled in those early days.

A child will draw the arm holding the tennis racket twice the size of the other arm, to convey its importance, and a director often puts a character in red so the audience can catch her in a crowd, but life does not provide these clues. So with all the people coming and going at Villa Coco, I could hardly know that the next visitor, a surprise one, was of any importance at all.

It was three weeks into my stay at Villa Coco, and we had reached the middle of October. Estelle, my employer, and I were sitting at lunch under the fading wisteria when all of a sudden Cesare began to bark. There was a sound of clattering metal from inside, like the imitation of offstage thunder in amateur theatrics (Nimali had dropped something); and then from around the corner staggered a curious character: all in cream, about as tall as a baronessa, a meringue fedora on his head, a gentle manner of walking like a windup toy, a friendly smile, and yet his circular sunglasses and way of jutting his chin out made me think, instantly, of a diamondback terrapin I kept as a boy. "Sacré bleu," said the Baronessa, and Estelle stood at once. "Buon giorno, tutti," the man said in a thoroughly American accent. His smile was also that of a diamondback terrapin. He switched to a Carolina-accented English: "Ah hope Ah'm not botherin' your lunch!"

"Not at all," the Baronessa said, recovering and looking over at me. "Giovedì, this is an old friend of mine, Pullman—"

"Furman," the man said, seemingly used to her way with nicknames. "Furman Childress. Ah've known . . . the Baronessa here . . . since Ah was very young. About your age!"

"You're still young, Pullman! You look just as you did on Capri, with Oscar," she told him flirtatiously, and I goggled at the notion. He seemed not as aged as she, but gone soft and pale instead of thin and crisp as paper.

He passed a linen handkerchief across his forehead. "Ah was her friend's paramour!"

The Baronessa said, "My friend Prince Mariano of Sicily."

"A prince!" I said. "Wow!"

She batted this away with her hand. "Sicily is nothing but princes."

"Lisabetta," he said, bowing in his courtly way to her. "Ah can only stay a moment. Ah was passin' by on my way to Florence and thought we could have a chat."

Of course, the Baronessa said. It was always nice to see an old friend, especially when so many now were lost. He removed his hat as one removes the lid from a pot, then smiled to all of us as if sure we were admiring the single blond lock that clung to his otherwise bald forehead like a price sticker to a melon. I rose to collect the plates and planned to let the old friends talk, but instead I found the Baronessa pulling at my sleeve. "Giovedì!" She then introduced me to this Furman character in the strangest way: "Here is the young expert come to help us!"

He took off his sunglasses, revealing startling blue eyes. "Ah! A pleasure, young man."

Estelle broke in: "Expert in archives and records."

He looked me up and down. "Ah've heard so little about you."

A strange thing to say. I felt instantly uncomfortable. It was like being in an actor's nightmare, where you are thrust into a scene in which you know none of the dialogue, none of the blocking, and yet everyone around you goes on as if you did.

Me: "Oh, my name's not—"

"And American!" the Baronessa exclaimed, this time as if it were the highest honor one could achieve.

Pullman (or Furman) gave me a pleasant smile and bent, rather than bowed, toward me. He said it seemed that I was a suitable addition, and hoped the rest of us would understand if he and his old friend had a little privacy . . .

"I remember him on Capri," the Baronessa told me once he had left and we were having coffee in the living room, below the portrait of the Venetian courtesan. She seemed somewhat shaken. "The most beautiful boy. How astounding he has not changed at all."

I stayed silent; it seemed incredible to compare the man I'd met to a beautiful boy. But I realized we were two people looking at the same object from different ends of a telescope.

"By the way," Estelle said to me, " 'Pullman' is Italian for a tour bus. She enjoys pretending not to remember his name." Then she turned back to the Baronessa. "Tricky how to handle him."

I asked what she meant. Glances were exchanged; I felt we were playing a parlor game to which I did not know the rules.

"Very tricky," the Baronessa said. "Before my friend the prince left him, Pullman managed to get a diamond out of him."

"Do you mean he stole it?"

"That I would admire!" she said. "No, he seduced it, I suppose. My friend had very particular tastes. I believe Pullman turned the diamond into buildings on the Amalfi Coast and so on, and look at him now. Rich as anything. But his taste is still . . . After all these years in Italy he has remained utterly American." Then she added, nodding to Estelle: "As we knew he would."

I still had no idea what this might mean; being American seemed to me, before my later travels, the natural state of being in the world. What could be wrong with that? And yet

I should have guessed from the fact that she used only his nickname after such a long acquaintance: she despised him.

"Our friend Pullman tells many stories about me," she said, leaning toward me. "But do not believe him. Only some of them are true."

I nodded sagely, but I supposed I would never meet this person again.

"I have called our friend Oscar," she said to Estelle with a grave lowering of her voice. "We must move things forward. And Oscar says he plans to procure slippers for you?" She turned her head, and I was startled to realize she was talking to me. A flame of a grin. "He says they will make you feel like the pope!"

What did not make me feel like the pope was working with Ghazel one morning, a week or so later. Moments after I had finished my coffee, the small man emerged from nowhere, stripped to the waist like an oil wrestler, holding out a gleaming machete. He shouted, "Giovedì!" It could mean only one thing: the faina.

The "wall of dogs" had failed to stop our enemy and it appeared he had a new plan; the machete seemed a sign we were meant to hunt the poor animal. Nimali looked at me with amusement as I was led away to the chicken coop. There, Ghazel laid out his plans in his own peculiar way: "YALLAH! TAGLIARE! FAINA! YALLAH!" Almost every other word was this "YALLAH!" pronouncement, which I took to be his personal form of punctuation. Only later did I realize it was an Arabic interjection along the lines of "Come on!" or "Let's do it!" I also gradually realized we were not to hunt the faina but to build a cage from bamboo that would somehow be triggered to fall and trap it. Details were vague.

The weather had been chilly when I awoke, but hacking away at bamboo with a machete under the command of a barking tyrant had me dripping with sweat and I was forced to remove my shirt. Ghazel, in the meantime, prepared the ropes. For the entire length of our labors, he talked to me about various topics, none of them comprehensible. It didn't matter; he did not require a response. "YALLAH!" He also had a habit of vanishing without explanation; I came back after a bathroom break to find the tools everywhere, bamboo half cut, and Ghazel nowhere to be seen. He did not return. It was as if he had been raptured.

In addition to providing a bamboo cage, I was to trim long leafy canes to decorate the entrance hall where I had first met the Baronessa. More macheteing, more dragging the things across the lawn. I was shimmering with perspiration, decorated with scrapes and cuts and sickle-shaped leaves, carrying the bamboo into the house, when I found a small conference taking place in the hall. Here were the Baronessa and Estelle. I was surprised to see my employer dressed in her finery earlier than her usual arrival at eleven.

"This is an exciting appearance," she said, "but not at all suitable for our trip."

Struggling with the bundle of bamboo, I looked to Estelle, then to the Baronessa and asked what trip—

But I was interrupted by a commotion from the other room—a crash—and saw the Baronessa's head turn in terror.

"It's just . . . eh, ahem . . . the brass crocodile!" came a man's voice.

She looked to Estelle and said something in Italian I did not catch. Estelle smiled at a private joke.

There entered now a striking young man so entirely unlike the Baronessa that, had I not known they were related, I would have expected her to send him back out onto the street. Little gold-wire glasses, the dark blond hair parted in the middle, the angular face all wavering smile above a sharp chin, the light blue oxford shirt tailored to his broad torso and narrow waist, the navy sweater tied around his shoulders. He was a few years older than me, and I recognized him both from the lizard-green car I'd seen on my arrival and from his ancestor's portrait in my room—for this was the "cousin," Giacomo. Giacomo-Giacomo. Afraid of his family, as Estelle had told me. But somewhere within was the young man who had run away to his cousin's house and lived with her for a year. He caught my eye. And I thought: Oh no.

"Is it my cousin from Vicenza?" the Baronessa asked. "And has he broken something?"

The young man laughed and approached her, kissing her on each cheek. I saw from how he held her hand the affection he had for her, and the fact that she did not let go said the same for her. He spoke in a tentative tone peppered with pauses: "I always knock over that crocodile. It's . . . eh . . . it's indestructible. Like you. Ahem. I brought Asiago."

She clapped her hands in pleasure. "Buono!"

"Hello, Estelle," he said, nodding to her.

"You will want to meet Giovedì," the Baronessa said, gesturing significantly to me. "He is my man Thursday."

I said hello and that I was in fact the archivist, here to make a catalog. I was well aware that I stood sweat-slicked and shirtless before the man. He looked me up and down, then smiled in greeting. Oh no. This was the last thing I needed.

"The poor boy is American," she added, as one might add that a guest was completely deaf. "And he has met the faina."

"Oh!"

"I have," I said, then gestured to myself and tried to explain: "Ghazel and I were building a trap to replace the wall for the chickens—"

"It is a wall of dogs!" the Baronessa announced.

I contradicted her. "It is not a wall of dogs."

But she was on to more important things. "We need your help, Giacomo, and quickly. The American has nothing to wear."

I was afraid she gave the impression that I *literally* had nothing to wear; that I had arrived in this savage state, naked and carrying bamboo. I said I had not expected a formal event. The cousin and I held a look for a moment.

"Vabon," he said. "Vabon." I later learned this was a term in his native Veneto dialect—va bene, okay—and his speech was peppered with it.

"Today we go to Ferrara!" the Baronessa said, yanking on her red wool coat.

"But," I said, trying to focus on this new information, "but that's a month from now! With Oscar!"

"Plans have changed!"

We were going on a trip, though no one had told her man Thursday.

It took a great deal of trouble to extract further details: Ferrara was about three hours north, in Emilia-Romagna; we were to travel there in the Mitsu-bitchy, and while we would not stay overnight, the Baronessa would take a hotel room in order to change before her appointment. There was a package to be delivered. I would be responsible for my elderly employer; Giacomo was merely the driver.

"She has to see a friend of Oscar's," Estelle told me once the Baronessa had left for the kitchen. "It will be you and Coco and Giacomo-Giacomo."

We seemed to be missing an important member of the party. "Not Oscar?"

She shook her head; Oscar was unable to attend.

"I thought it was her trip with Oscar—"

"It cannot wait."

I ran upstairs for a quick bath—this involved dumping cold water over my body from a jug—and returned to my room to find Giacomo-Giacomo there, studying the clothes in my dresser. He turned around and seemed surprised to see me in my little yellow robe. There was no privacy at Villa Coco. I noticed how much taller he was than myself. Giacomo coughed and said, "My cousin said you couldn't . . . eh, ahem, that I should help pick out something for you." He held out the pants from a brown corduroy Tonino suit and a corn-colored sweater.

"I'm sorry I'm intruding," he said. "I should have told her no."

I said they were fine, took them from him, and stepped behind a shoulder-height Chinese screen. I asked if he had come all the way from Milan.

"She said it was a crisis," he said unsteadily as I undid my robe and began to dress. "Of course it isn't. It never is. But I have to get back Monday to my . . . eh, ahem, wife."

What a relief it was to hear he had a wife! I had been certain I heard the bowstring twang of mutual attraction I knew so well from my reckless college days, the distraction I so wanted to avoid. Clearly I had dodged the arrow. I stepped into the trousers—high-waisted, of course—and I mentioned to him his resemblance to the photograph beside my bed.

"My grandfather," he said. Then, without looking me in the eye, he left the room. And I realized that on the vanity, just behind where I had been changing, was a mirror reflecting everything behind the screen.

I found Giacomo-Giacomo standing outside beside the Mitsu-bitchy. He was facing away from me, arms crossed, and seemed to be thinking of something far away, as one does when one imagines nobody is looking. He heard my footsteps, turned, and raised a hand in greeting. "I am wondering what you are wondering," he said, rubbing his hands together in the morning cold. "Why am I here?"

I said I often wondered why I was there.

"No," he said. "Why am *I* here? I am not a very good replacement for Oscar, as my cousin has often told me."

"Apparently the Baronessa doesn't trust my driving."

"Oh? Then why are *you* here?"

I pretended to be insulted and he laughed.

Then the Baronessa herself appeared, in her red coat, followed by Estelle and Ghazel, who carried two suitcases in brown saddle leather. This seemed curious, as it was meant to be a day trip. "I have brought you together to amuse one another while I am occupied. And to carry a cumbersome article." This was even more curious: a cardboard package, about half a meter square but shallow, which seemed to have been made out of other, smaller cardboard boxes; I assumed it was a Ghazel affair. It was not heavy but awkward; it took both myself and Giacomo-Giacomo to place it in the back seat, where Estelle instructed us to belt it in; I asked what was in it, but nobody would answer me. Giacomo-Giacomo took the driver's seat, his cousin beside him, and I belted myself in beside the package. Estelle waved farewell, and it gave me not a little pleasure to witness, as things were being put in gear, that a cane emerged from the passenger seat and rapped the cousin on the arm. "Avanti!" came the voice of the Baronessa. And off we went.

My relief at not having to drive was short-lived; this cousin was a terrible driver. Or, rather, a suggestible one. He was tempted by every exit, and only the helpful thwack of a cane kept him on the correct road. He seemed unaware that the sun rose in the east and set in the west and, though cypress shadows provided clear compasses, was forever wondering where north might be. Even a sign for the very city we sought (FERRARA) puzzled him, and I could feel the car tilting off course, as if his wanderlust compelled him to see sights unknown ("Have you ever been to Forlì?" he asked more than once, receiving another thwack and the comment "Not Forlì! Not Forlì!"). He drove, in short, like a child in that game where someone is telling you "Colder, colder" and "Warmer, warmer, WARMER!" I saw a family resemblance to his cousin's penchant for caprice; I wondered if this was what drew them to each other. I also wondered if we would ever get there.

Not that I supremely wished to; I found myself, bouncing in the back seat beside the mysterious package, to be in that blessed interphase which transit brings, a place between places and thus between states of being. That is: I was, briefly, free. Free of all expectation and worry and doubt. The only irritation was the package, intruding upon my person at every corner.

I am sure there is a simpler route to Ferrara, but I prefer to think of it the way we attained it: through the Baronessa's memory, from a time before the large highways were built, which brought us not speedily through the large cities of Florence and Bologna, but through dark forests and villages so small in scale, so medieval, that it seemed sometimes I was in the back of a carriage, wandering into someone's fairy tale. We dipped into town squares, tilted at an angle to the landscape for reasons lost to history, rose along cliffsides protected only by the thinnest of wooden railings, passed post offices and pharmacies with their blinking green crosses and stark concrete government buildings with bare places where the Fascist symbols had been removed and water mills and trout farms and creaking old bridges, and every part of it intrigued me. Perhaps I was like Cesare after all.

"You met the principessa?" Giacomo was asking me. Somehow the conversation had turned to English, and I was not about to send it back into Italian.

I explained that we'd met my first day at Villa Coco.

"Cousin, wasn't she living in . . . eh . . . Zanzibar?" Giacomo asked.

"Indeed," the Baronessa said. "Just a few years ago."

"She found a great love," I added helpfully. "And a great disappointment."

The Baronessa nodded sagely. "Pippa knows all there is to know about love."

Her cousin encouraged her to tell a little more.

"Oh, Pippa and her little house!" the Baronessa said. "Not so little, in the end. She and I went together once to Zanzibar, in my boat. Pippa had made friends with a schoolteacher there, a remarkable woman who lived in a kind of hut on the beach. Before I knew it Pippa had bought the property next door. She also met a man on the beach and fell for him. He said he was an architect! He would design the house for her. You know her brilliant schemes. And, before we left, she also fell in love with a monkey."

I cut in: "I don't understand."

She turned to meet my eye. "Then you have never known a monkey. Her name was Fatima. It was a Muslim monkey, you see. Pippa had the zoo in Stone Town take her into the monkey house and arranged to give her very special food. Then she came back to Italy while the house was being built.

I did ask, Are you sure they're giving Fatima special food? Oh yes, she told me. But I wondered, How can they tell one monkey from another? That upset Pippa. She said anyone could see the quality of her monkey. You see how hard she had fallen for this monkey. And for the architect. You know, Pippa was quite a femme fatale in her younger years."

Her cousin cut in: "Vabon . . . you said this was only a few years ago."

"Oh yes, she could kill a man with a glance! And now I've lost my place in the story."

I told her there was a monkey in a zoo and an architect.

"Oh yes! Anyway, eventually she went back. The house was complete. But of course it was all wrong. The man wasn't an architect at all, he just fancied himself an architect, and he mixed up feet and meters. Her little hut on the beach became an enormous treehouse. A bedroom like a ballroom. That sort of thing. Impossible to live in. She was very distressed about it all."

"And the monkey?" I asked.

"Ah, the monkey! Of course it turns out I was right. They weren't feeding Fatima special food at all, they were pocketing the money. Pippa went to visit her monkey and saw it all, clear as day. Well, she took that monkey out of there. And Pippa said goodbye to her schoolteacher friend and her beloved Fatima and left again for Italy. And she has never been back!"

I pursued again: "What happened to the monkey?"

"It lives in the house! With another monkey for company. The schoolteacher throws fruit over the wall. I can't say what it must be like by now, but I imagine it is a very good life for a monkey."

"Did the architect break her heart?" I asked.

"Of course not! It turned out all right in the end, didn't it?

The house was built wrong for a person. But just exactly right for monkeys. Pippa wanted to get a happy ending," she said, "AND SO SHE DID!"

The Baronessa seemed very satisfied with her story, but I didn't see what it had to do with love. It seemed to me nothing other than the tale of a foolish old woman and her delusional schemes.

My employer said: "Ah, eccoci."

Here we were indeed, at a high pass where a small roadside bar, frequented by motorcyclists, served beer and focaccia stuffed with mushrooms, a delight the Baronessa told us she had not tasted in twenty years.

Northward we went onto a flat green plain where water seemed to shimmer in the distance (surely an atmospheric sprinkle or Po mirage), and we proceeded along a route marked, as for a triumphal parade, with long pink ribbons and banners. It was only when we stopped for gas that we learned this was the next day's route for some kind of bicycle race called the Gara Nazionale. The Baronessa was as uninterested in this as she was in all sporting events except the Palio di Siena (a medieval, thoroughly corrupt horse race around that town's central square) and began a droll summary of the towns we were passing through, mostly a tour guide of their ancient arts ("This one is famous for orange wool coats"; "This one is famous for majolica") or cuisine ("And here one has cappellacci with a filling of zucca"). She seemed to be getting nervous; I saw her checking her watch and urging Giacomo to make better time. She had, after all, an appointment in Ferrara.

Along our route (just past another missed opportunity for Forlì), Giacomo asked me about my past, and I obliged him.

I described the suburban neighborhood of my childhood as "Spielbergian," thinking the bike-riding preteens and cul-de-sacs of those movies would be universal; the Baronessa kept saying "Eh?" until I moved on to my parents. I said there was really nothing out of the ordinary about them. Or, to be honest, my childhood in general.

She seemed to consider this. "Once, in Rajasthan, my hosts made a fuss about taking me to a very special zoo, with very special exhibits. It was a long drive and very hot. I remember we arrived and I was led to the pen, which was painted all in gold, to discover it was an ordinary donkey and a deer. Exotic to someone from India!"

Giacomo asked what this had to do with American parents.

"Perhaps your parents are this to us."

I wondered if she was comparing them slyly to a donkey and a deer. I sighed deeply before saying we did not speak often, they did not understand me, they were scientists who saw only observable phenomena and ignored the messy inner workings of the world. The silence in the Mitsu-bitchy allowed us to hear its own dubious mechanical clankings. Giacomo cleared his throat.

"This is not a very funny story," the Baronessa said at last, "you must tell it again another time," and something in her tone communicated more than her words and silenced me.

Thwack. "Not Forlì! Not Forlì!"

What Americans know of Italy is a confection of movies and food; for expedience's sake, restaurants and filmmakers have grafted Naples to Sicily, Rome to Florence, creating a Frankenstein's monster of pasta and accordions and Leonardo and cheese. In fact, the nation is much younger than America itself; unification was achieved only in the time of Dickens.

It is the opposite of America: not a colonizer's canvas cut into political states but ancient kingdoms brought together into one nation. And so the passage from Tuscany into Emilia-Romagna was not like that from South into North Carolina, which, no matter how Americans may squabble, is hardly to be noticed, but more like the passage from Spain to Morocco (one I made in my later travels). There was a change of landscape, of culture, of history, of language, and, of course, of cuisine.

So it is astounding to report that the first city I visited in Italy was not the famous Rome or Venice, or even nearby Florence, where I had changed trains, but Ferrara, which the Baronessa began to describe in her peculiar, vagrant way:

"Of course, Savonarola was born here. You cannot escape Savonarola. I wish Oscar were here to explain it all. It is famous I think for a kind of sausage and the Palazzo dei Diamanti and for the House of Este, the last member of which is who we are coming to see."

"A friend of yours?" I asked.

"We have never met. And you will not meet him; you will be in Ravenna. I know you have been longing to see it."

"What?" I had been longing to see Florence. I had no idea what Ravenna was.

"How can you come here and not see the Byzantine mosaics?"

"But you—"

"There is nothing like them in the world," she said. "An Ostrogothic wonder. And it is not often you get to see the penis of Jesus Christ!"

It was not clear to me whether this was a figure of speech or the literal penis. "I thought we were here to assist you—"

She said, "I think you have perhaps overdosed on your time with me. It will be good for us to be apart."

"I see. How far is Ravenna?"

"Not far. But first I have told Giacomo you must drive through Comacchio, which is a little Etruscan fishing village that knows it is secretly Venice. Like a scullery maid who is actually a princess." She seemed quite proud of this comparison, but I found her descriptions were becoming as dreamlike as Ghazel's.

"It's not far," added Giacomo. "We have enough time to be back to join my cousin for dinner. If the car holds out!"

"It shall," his cousin insisted. "I have made a reservation at a fine restaurant. You must not be late." Apparently the Mitsu-bitchy honored reservations made at fine restaurants. But it was not the first time I had known the Baronessa to hold things together by her will alone.

So this was the new plan: to leave my employer to do her business in Ferrara while Giacomo and I saw the secretly Venetian charms of Comacchio and the Byzantine wonders of Ravenna, joining her later for dinner. I had no doubt that this scheme suited some wider purpose of hers, but what it was I could not envisage. I carefully examined her: the stern, sharp nose beneath her sunglasses; the coils of fine white hair; the gleam of a diamond earring bezeled in gold; the red wool collar edged in tawny fur. I do not know if it is practice, powder, or paralysis, but an aged face gives little away.

And soon we had reached the castle city of Ferrara.

While entering an American city is a slow process of submerging oneself in the shallows of car parts stores until one has entered the depths of the metropolis, entering Ferrara, or really any small Italian city, was not like that at all; from a pastoral setting we were plunged into brick-brown darkness, where tiny medieval alleys took us around churches and fortresses decorated with flags, until we were spat out at last into a large piazza, in which sat, of all things, a castle. With a moat and drawbridge and everything. Right in the middle of town.

"Wow!" I shouted. "What's happening?!"

The Baronessa asked if it wasn't indeed striking.

"Is it real?"

She demurred: "This is a very Vedic question."

Giacomo broke in with too much information: "It was built by the Este family in the fourteenth century. To protect themselves from invasion. Or maybe the . . . eh . . . plague. I forget."

"Oh," I said. "It's amazing."

But the Baronessa had her doubts. "I wonder if it was very comfortable. I once was forced to live in a castle. You may let us out here, Giacomo; the hotel is avanti. Oh, look! That cretino Savonarola." And, indeed, a large statue of the monk stood directly before us. I did not know who he was, but, as she had said, it seemed there was no escaping him.

The Baronessa carried her own luggage while Giacomo and I contended with the cardboard package which, after she checked in, would not fit in the elevator (an antique variety made for only two people), but, saying the porter would carry it up, she bid us goodbye. "We are to meet at dinner at half past eight," she said, stepping into the elevator. "At Orlando Innamorato. Enjoy! You are to see one of the wonders of the world!"

"And the penis of Jesus Christ!"

I heard her laugh. "Who knows? You might see two!"

We left the Baronessa in the elevator; her final words were a comment on the porter ("He looks just like Savonarola! There is no escaping him!") before the accordion gate closed and she began to rise in her small capsule within the stairs. Giacomo-Giacomo and I got into the car and made our tumbling way across the cobblestones out of Ferrara.

"What do you think of my cousin?" he asked once we were back on country roads. I noticed his fine blond hair had lost its composure in the struggle with the package; a few strands pointed straight upward.

"Well." I was very cautious in speaking about her; I had learned any conversation might be as trapdoored as a Jacobean stage. "I've never met anyone like her."

"There is not anyone like her," he agreed, frowning slightly as he drove. "She is . . . eh . . . sui generis. Sometimes it is like speaking to someone from a hundred years ago. She knew Man Ray and Malaparte. Graham Greene. Pablo Neruda. And that was all on Capri! Ask her about Salvador Dalí and she will tell you they went on a dinner date, and that when he turned his head, his long mustache would tickle her ear! And so forth and so on."

"I don't think you want to take this exit." I was not about to be led to Forlì.

"Vabon. I thought it was the main road. But sometimes . . . eh . . . sometimes she is more modern than anyone else. More modern than I am, or you. She has no . . . how do you say? . . . no morals."

"Morals?"

"No morals at all. That's what my father always says. He kept me away from her until I was thirteen, and then she . . . showed up at a funeral for my great-aunt Ursula. I remember she didn't wear black. She wore a . . . eh, ahem, a red robe. She sat directly behind me at the service. I remember she leaned forward and whispered to me, *You know, Ursula took me to my first movie. It was* The Gold Rush. *Charlie Chaplin, the first man I ever found sexually attractive*."

I laughed and wondered if she had been dressing me as Chaplin all this time.

"I found her fascinating, and, at one point, I ran away to Tuscany. And stayed with her for almost a year. My father was furious, but it was a great education for me. She had parties then, musicians and singers and artists, and so forth and so on. The things that went on! No morals. And no hang-ups. About sex or race or marriage. She is very protective of her . . . eh . . . gay friends." He nodded to me. "And, of course, protective of me."

I thought I understood what this married man might mean, but I had my vow. So I chose not to take this exit. "Something I've never asked her about, I think I'd never dare, is her love life. I understand she's never been married. Has she always been alone?"

At this, Giacomo laughed. "I think you misunderstand. In America . . . ahem . . . you always marry. You marry for health insurance and to protect the children from shame. We do not have these problems here. Here we only marry for inheritance and if the landlady complains. Otherwise we don't bother. Nobody I know is married except the ones who married an American."

"But you're married."

He took this comment very seriously. "Yes, I am. That is a good example of having to marry. Ahem."

Comacchio was a small town on the edge of an enormous wetland. Fishing shacks dotted the landscape with great poles jutting out, from which giant nets hung on square frames, ready to be dipped into the shimmering waters. I saw the shacks on our drive in, small but solid looking, and I had an absurd longing to live in one and wake every morning to the slightly pink-colored salt pans, make my coffee, fish and eat and sleep without a "koo-koo!" to disturb me. Was this the life I longed for? It struck me also as intensely lonely; more and more I was missing contact beyond that of Pushkin and Gorky and Cesare in my life. Giacomo told me that only thirty years before, flamingos had moved into the wetland as if it were a chic new spot to vacation. Like wealthy tourists, they first came only in spring and summer but, smitten with the beauty and the price of real estate, eventually stayed on through winter and became true citizens of Comacchio, leaving Africa behind them. It suited them perfectly; the pink of the salt became the pink of their feathers. Alas, we never saw a single one.

We parked and went on a stroll around Comacchio. The sights of the town itself were quick to take in: no more than five or six blocks of brick and painted houses, churches, and a tower, unremarkable except that they were intercut everywhere by canals filled with the gold-green waters of the delta, which prolonged our walk and, I suppose, the daily life of the citizens so even in their modest square meterage they could circumambulate as one does in a cathedral, following the lines of a labyrinth painted on the floor. What would it be like, to know you were secretly Venice? I envied the town, though of course in the canals were not gondolas but the local specialty—eels—which made the waters wriggle slightly in their courses. Yes, eels. They were the basis of the town's famous cuisine and were its familiar spirits, beloved, much the way other towns cherish their swallows or poplars or stags; if it had been an American town, the local high school team would have been the Fighting Eels.

Along the way, Giacomo asked me about my time at Villa Coco. I began with the pozzo and went on to describe the faina and the hat on the bed—

"But this is very serious!" he said, stopping us on a bridge.

The canal glowed in stripes on either side of us, a satin ribbon on a table. "You know a hat on a bed means death."

I said that had been well explained to me.

He peered at me over his glasses and his eyes caught the gold of the water. "I hope you found a way to undo it."

With amusement I described the solution proposed by the Baronessa.

At last he smiled. "The nearest man's . . . eh . . . palle. Of course. What a Neapolitan solution."

"Oscar was obliging," I said.

"Any man would be," he added, pushing his glasses up his nose. "With so much at stake! Ahem."

The main sight in Comacchio is the Ponte dei Trepponti—the Bridge of Three Bridges—a remarkable meeting of two canals to become one leading into the lagoon and, from there, into the vast wetlands south of the town. I looked up at the two massive brick towers sitting grandly above the canals, as out of place as two princes forced to eat at a wayside inn. But we were not allowed to visit them; apparently a Miss Comacchio pageant was being held the next day, in honor of the Gara Nazionale, and the bridge was needed for rehearsal. And indeed three teenage girls, in red, green, and white sparkling gowns, stood impatiently on the bridge, awaiting instruction. The one in red was tallest, held herself most like a woman, and had the best dress; she would surely be the winner. I felt bad the others had to rehearse something so clearly preordained.

We found the Mitsu-bitchy where we had left it, beside an old columned fish market, where perhaps it felt at peace, because despite many tries and entreaties, Giacomo was unable to rouse it from slumber. We raised the hood and stared at that alien interior; neither of us knew anything about auto mechanics. But I could recognize, from the bits of twisted wire and colored hoses mismatched to their counterparts, the odd piece of chewing gum or twine, the handiwork of Ghazel.

Giacomo found a mechanic nearby. I understood nothing of their conversation, but I watched with interest as a waiter came along the street carrying two coffees in a lidded plastic carrier meant, I think, for transporting cakes. He took off the lid and presented the coffees to the mechanic, then made his way back into the village. Another mechanic emerged to take his cup. I understood this must be a daily arrangement with the local café. I looked around and took in the brickwork and plaster, the not unpleasant scent of mud and fried fish. I wondered what life might be if one were indeed trapped here forever, under a mystic curse, not a mechanical one, with bridges to cross and canals to walk along. From the café door, a portly man emerged with a sandwich board, which he struggled to set up in the wind. LA CHEF CONSIGLIA!, it announced, and of course what the chef suggested was eel. I felt a shiver go through me. Almost as if—and this was impossible—the Baronessa had arranged this all as a diabolical joke.

"I'm sorry, Baronessa," I said to her on a pay phone beside the mechanic's. I had managed to reach her at her hotel. Giacomo-Giacomo stood outside, watching me as he smoked a cigarette. I was terrified of her response—not only to our abandoning her in Ferrara, but also to our missing the restaurant reservation. "It won't be ready until tomorrow!"

She simply did not believe me. She insisted the car was in perfect working order. "Gazelle told me so."

"The mechanic says it needs a new belt or a fan."

"A belt! Or a fan!" she said. "This is a very well-dressed car."

"I'm so sorry."

"You will miss an excellent meal."

"Tomorrow we can—"

"I will take the train home," she said firmly. "My business here is concluded and there is a train direct to Firenze. Savonarola will deliver me to the station here and you will arrange for Vinsanto to pick me up."

That there was a direct train, all this time, and she knew of it, hardly surprised me. "What about the package? It's too big for you to—"

"That is no longer of concern," she said, then gave a sigh that surprised me. "You and my cousin must find a hotel until the car is ready."

"I don't know if there's a hotel—"

"You can always stay with an eelwife." Sometimes her solutions seemed to come from a novel and not life experience. "I have fond memories of Comacchio. It feels like Dal Lake of Kashmir, where a boat comes every morning to replace your houseboat's flowers. Fifty years ago in Comacchio a fisherman loaned me his scarf on a bridge at sunset, and now I realize that I never returned it . . ."

We did find a hotel in Comacchio, but it was filled with cyclists. As were the two others. "Gara Nazionale," intoned each desk clerk. But at the Principessa della Delta, an elderly red-haired cleaning woman took Giacomo aside for a whispered conversation. He turned to me with lifted eyebrows and explained that she rented a room in her house along the canal. We stood patiently as she put away her cleaning things

(Had we arrived precisely at the end of her shift? Could coincidence be so cheap?) and bid us follow her down the canal past the Ponte di San Pietro, a brick bridge of incredible antiquity, the rough underside of which was covered in canal-reflected sun, creating bright scrivenings and loops of light that dazzled me. The bridge was simple (I later learned it was from the seventh century) and I could so easily imagine the Baronessa viewing a sunset there and accepting a scarf from an admiring fisherman. Perhaps fifty years ago, perhaps five hundred. One can find the experience, in America, of standing where it seems no person has ever stood before—on a wilderness peak or a rocky, inaccessible shore—but seldom do we feel that thousands have stood there, for thousands of years, and empires have risen and fallen and will continue to do so long after we have gone.

The woman asked us to call her Nonna, and when I kept thanking her, she made a gesture of crumpling up a piece of paper and tossing it to the floor. We followed Nonna, and her rheumatism, up the stairs of her small pink house to a bedroom, which she presented with the resignation of someone who assumes you have previously been forced to live in castles. It was a mint-green room with built-in closets, painted with wreaths and roses. Photographs of ballet dancers were arranged on the walls, each with a border of red velvet. The night tables were white-painted wood, as was the matrimonial bed.

Giacomo looked at me and shrugged. "Vabon. Shall we get dinner?"

Because of the chill, I wore a newsboy's cap I had bought at Formica. Giacomo said it made me look even more American. I asked how this was possible, and he said he could not explain. Except that I looked like an American trying to dress like an Italian.

"Why did your cousin want us to come here? Why not just go to Ravenna?"

"I'm sure she has some memory of the place. A little story of hers, maybe." By this time, I understood that "story" meant a romantic adventure, and I thought of the fisherman's scarf. Was it possible her "stories" were not confined, as I had imagined, to viscounts and princes? It was sundown and I had said we should find the Baronessa's bridge, which, as there were only three bridges, was not hard to achieve. We found ourselves elbow to elbow in the cold, standing on a small bridge that looked onto an older bridge, curved like a carved-out melon, behind which lay a strip of canal leading to the lagoon. The sun was nearly down, the horizon the deep purple of Villa Coco's petunias, but, as often happens, the sky above had lightened as the land below grew dark, the canal waters as well, so there was just this dazzling pathway before us to some supernatural realm above. To where? To the Venice we all are in secret? Then the sunlight shifted, the radiance fell away, and the streetlights came on, one by one, bringing the ancient brick buildings back into view. But when I turned, I saw that the brightness still remained, for a moment, on the round lenses of my companion's spectacles. He moved and it was gone.

We found a restaurant called L'Anguilla C'e! ("There's Eel!"), decorated, on its roof, with a rusted metal sculpture of the aforementioned creature. Inside was an enormous photograph of Sophia Loren dancing in Comacchio before a group of applauding fishermen. When it was time to order, there was no doubt that we had to try the town's specialty—because it was all there was on offer. As at every restaurant meal in Italy, there was a long discussion of the food and wine with the owner (a thin, gray-haired woman), part of which Giacomo seemed to struggle with; he later explained she was teasing him in the local dialect, Comacchiese, so different from Italian that he understood not a word. "February, for instance," he said, giving me an example, "is not febbraio. It's ferver. Isn't that something? Ferver!" I nodded. I had only learned the Italian word for February the week before. The owner suggested the house wine, which Giacomo declined ("I never drink unlabeled wine," he whispered to me). Instead, we had a bottle of Lambrusco, the fizzy red wine of the region.

"There's Eel!" announced the sign outside, and indeed there was: eel marinated and grilled; as carpaccio and in a soup; in risotto and with pasta and polenta; smoky and tangy and tender and sweet. Here on the menu was a dish I had never tasted before—had never imagined tasting—served as if there were no other ingredient on earth. There are birds who have evolved to eat only one particular kind of fruit—and these were the Comacchese and their eel.

I repeated a fact I knew: "I heard the sex life of eels is a complete mystery."

"What's that?"

"Eels," I said. "Their sex life is a complete mystery." I took a swallow of wine. "All eels go to the Sargasso Sea to mate, but no one knows what happens there. They are the most discreet of all animals," I finished, and Giacomo nodded with a bashful expression.

"Oscar says you are a romantic person."

"He does?" I didn't see myself this way at all.

"He says you should always have a young person or an American around because they believe the future will be better."

"And Italians don't?"

"We know it is not so. But it is nice to be around someone

like this. I admit I am a little romantic. That . . . eh, ahem . . . I have an artistic side that I do not discuss with my cousin. It is that I am writing a novel."

"A novel!" I said. "But I think she'd love that!"

"I think so as well, but she has known so many famous writers, I'm afraid I would disappoint her. I am also an editor and it seems unwise. But, yes, I take time every day to write a little something."

"Can I ask what it's about?"

He was shy despite the wine. "Vabon . . . eh, ahem . . . I can only say it's a very romantic story. Set in my town, in Vicenza, but long ago."

"It's historical."

"I have said too much. But, yes, there is something even about this place, don't you think? The old bridge we passed. It is something I made note of, for my book."

I asked, "Is there a beauty pageant rehearsal in your book?"

"Now you are teasing me."

I apologized. The food arrived: Smoked eel with oranges. Delicate, smooth, flaking on the fork but soft and unctuous in the mouth. I looked to Giacomo and saw that his lips were coated in the oil, shining. I was about to say something when music started. A live band, out on the covered patio, with an accordion prominently playing. I would have called it a polka band, but it seemed so unlikely—

"Liscio!" Giacomo exclaimed, grabbing my hand. "You don't know liscio?" I smiled and shook my head. "It's the music on the River Po! Look!" And indeed, through the window, I could see people were standing up, old couples holding each other two-step style and swaying to the rhythm. A man with dyed black hair stepped out, took the microphone, and began to sing. I could have been anywhere from Texas to Munich to Oaxaca. Was it the influence of the Austrian

Empire that brought the accordion to be so beloved? Because those old couples clasped each other so tight. We clapped and Giacomo sang along; I had forgotten he was from a nearby region, and he surely knew every word. Watching his delight, I decided I had made a vow I could not keep.

He leaned forward and said something to me, and I could only say "Eh?"

Louder: "Estelle said all Americans are heartbreakers!"

I coughed; I could feel that I was a little drunk. "Why would she say that?"

Giacomo shrugged. "Americans!" he shouted over the music. Perhaps he was drunk as well. "You always hug and kiss and pretend to be great friends and say, 'Come visit me!' and so forth and so on, but you don't mean any of it. That is the heartbreaker."

"Well," I said, shouting in return, "I won't tell you to come visit me because I don't have a home."

"You can visit me!"

"In your vast estate?"

He laughed and applauded the band. The dancers were dispersing. "I have nothing. My father has such a house. And my wife has a house, her relative's house." He looked down and cleaned his glasses. The music had softened and the vocalist was taking a break. "Maybe you already know, but my wife was a college friend. She had to marry, for reasons of inheritance. I have the same reasons. The houses, you see, and more than that . . . it's hard to explain. You can't survive in Italy without family. We cannot live the way we wish to. One day she came to me and said, 'I have a very simple solution to our problems.' "

My suspicions were confirmed. "She is gay as well."

He wore a private smile, slightly sad. "She has a . . . eh,

ahem, girlfriend, and this is our arrangement, and so forth and so on. Of course we do not tell our families. They do not know about the girlfriend, but they also do not ask. It makes life simpler."

It did not seem simple at all, to me. "She has a girlfriend. And you?"

"When I was very young," he told me, "I made a proposal to God. That I would be a good boy, a good son, even though . . . eh, ahem. I would be perfect. And in return He would not strike me down dead." He laughed.

I sat stunned at such an arrangement. "What did God say?"

"I never heard back from Him."

I thought of Oscar, who had sworn off pleasures for reasons of health. With a shock, I realized I myself had done the same—for different reasons altogether.

"Still," he went on, "I kept my part of the bargain. So that part is, for me, somewhat unfulfilled."

"You've never . . . ?"

"Oh, I have. Now and then. But no one . . . serious. I do my work and that is enough." He replaced the glasses on his face and his ancestor was before me again, lean-faced and vulnerable and full of thought. Neither of us spoke for a moment, and we heard the laughter of the owner and her friends. "Are you not glad the car broke down? Are you not glad everything went wrong? It is . . . eh . . . a nice change. I sound stupid, I'm afraid."

"You don't sound stupid," I said. "I know what you mean."

"Is it nice to be American?" The music was starting again, the singer trying to rouse the crowd.

I had never considered this before. "I guess so."

He smiled at that: "Except you have ketchup on pizza."

"That's not true! You've never even been to America!"

"Vabon." He drew back slightly, seriously. "You don't like to be teased."

But I did.

When we emerged from beneath the metal eel, the town had changed; what before were bright canals between darkened buildings and churches became, at night, quivering pathways of reflected streetlight, as if candles floated, as during a festival, on the water's surface. No one was on the street, and there was nowhere to go but back to Nonna's. We had finished two bottles of Lambrusco, and it fizzed within us as we stumbled home; I remember he helped me over the bridge with an arm across my shoulder. I responded by tickling him under his coat and he laughed, pulling me closer. Who knows what foolish words we exchanged as we shuffled through the cold or made our way quietly up the staircase to the bedroom? I only know we removed our coats in silence, then our shoes. He unbuttoned his shirt and stood there awkwardly, then cleared his throat and looked my way, and I took it as the sign I needed. My vow was long forgotten. I removed my hat, and the young man began to warn me of the danger I was courting. Then he caught my eye, and no further discussion was needed.

With a smile, I threw my hat upon the bed . . .

That morning in Comacchio, no boatman brought flowers; it was no Dal Lake. And yet we lay as contented as flamingos in pink salt. I remember Giacomo opened the windows and, standing by the bedside, I had a view of the ancient bridge, the gleaming canals, and his broad body with its tangle of dark hair at the center of his chest, his princely arms spread out against the frame of the window. He wore his glasses, and without his modern clothes, the resemblance to his ancestor seemed complete; he could have stood here two hundred years before, leaning naked against a window where his breath on the cold glass was like white smoke. He smiled; I wondered if it was for the view or the quiet peace of the morning or for me. He fell on the bed and we fumbled around again. Like any abstainer, I told myself it was only one lapse. What harm could it do? Where could it lead, anyway? I wondered what his God would think of us.

After we dressed and went downstairs to the dining room, Nonna provided cappuccino along with homemade doughnuts; she crumpled up our thanks and threw them to the ground. We made our way along the canal to the auto shop, where the mechanic sat outside, smoking, receiving another cake carrier of coffee as he informed us the Mitsu-bitchy was ready at last. Giacomo paid him, and we drove the short distance to Ravenna. I found it to be a baffling place: bland, ordinary streets of shops and ice cream, at the end of which might be a worn brick church, and inside that church: wonders! The saints in gold and lapis lazuli! A march through more uninspiring thoroughfares to a park and a low brick mausoleum, and inside: glittering stars and quatrefoils! We did indeed see the penis of Christ two times, as he was twice portrayed nude in baptisteries, but it was hardly the highlight; the highlight was this shock of inner poetry after such prosaic exteriors. The analogy to the human condition was too much. At the Arian Baptistery, I brushed against Giacomo by accident, and he seemed to tremble with embarrassment or confusion. At least, that is what I saw in his eyes, as wide and full of emotion as those of Empress Theodora, in her pearl headdress, staring down at us from the apse of San Vitale. I thought she was the spitting image of Nimali. Perhaps the effulgent beauty around us, as well as the raw day-after feelings, was as heavy, as delicate, as a pearl headdress.

The evening before, we had learned more about each other than just what we might look like beneath our clothes. He had spent his youth with a variety of girlfriends, and it became clear that his experience with men was, if not minimal, rudimentary. I was certainly no magicien du boudoir, but maneuvers that felt obvious to me simply had never occurred to him. But this was in that particular era—long after the easily had shepherds of Oscar's day and long before the marital affections of our present one—when everything between men of our sort was tense, hidden, whispered, confused. And exciting.

"I have a . . . eh, ahem . . . request to make of you," he had said as we lay in darkness, ready for sleep. There was no noise outside at all; the cyclists must have been getting their rest. "Two requests."

"Of course."

"One is that we cannot make of this a habit," he said. "My life is already confused with . . . eh, ahem . . ."

"Your wife."

"And my work. I hope you understand."

I said I understood completely.

"Vabon. It's not that I did not—"

"Listen," I said, propping myself up on one elbow. I could barely make out his face in the blue light. "I don't need a complication either. This was nice. But I'm leaving at Christmas." I did not add that I knew all too well what could happen. Handcuffs, for one thing. To be honest, I was relieved.

"Vabon. And a second request is not to mention this to my cousin."

I said I would never dream of it, but why?

He closed his eyes. "Maybe she would approve. Maybe not. But I worry it would all get back to my family and so forth and so on. That would be a disaster."

"I thought you were the only relative she spoke to."

"Still, you will promise?"

I saw this had nothing to do with my employer at all, merely with his own fears. I said I would be as discreet as an eel.

"And then?" the Baronessa asked.

"That's all, I'm afraid," I said. "We took two rooms in Comacchio, then came back here."

It was late afternoon by the time we arrived and found the Baronessa in the western olive grove, directing Vinsanda for the coming harvest with prolonged instructions. He stood staring at us as if he might lose his mind. I understood the feeling.

The Baronessa wore a tan belted jacket similar to ones I had seen on the wild boar hunters. Her eyes were surprisingly alert. "And Ravenna?"

"Amazing," I said.

Giacomo stepped forward. "We saw the Arian Baptistery and San Vitale."

She paused. "That is all you two have to tell?"

I nodded. "Amazing," I repeated.

She said, "I see." Her searching gaze scanned us both very sternly.

"Oh, I do remember one thing!" I said. "That the Empress Theodora looked precisely like Nimali."

"Nimali!"

"Yes," I said. "The eyes, you know."

She put her hands to her mouth and burst into her version of hysterical laughter. Tears formed in the corners of her eyes and she had to lean against her cane. "This is what you gained in Ravenna? That the Imperatrice looks like Nimali! I am very glad the two of you have seen this vision!" I smiled at Giacomo, who did not catch my eye or speak.

I asked the Baronessa about her appointment in Ferrara, and she sighed. "It did not go as I had hoped," she said. "And I admit I am a bit sad. I have said goodbye to an old, dear friend."

"Oh no! In Ferrara?"

She blinked, and her expression seemed to tighten. "Oscar should have been there. But it is done, thanks God. Now!" she said, her face flashing with resolve. "You will at last be put to work!"

I wondered what "work" would entail after days of sweating in bamboo and taking a mysterious package to Ferrara, but I said nothing.

"The rooms are ready!" she exclaimed. "So you can begin this project you are so eager to finish. You will have other duties on top of this, and will not be as free for such pleasure trips as this one."

I took a deep breath, about to say it was hardly a pleasure trip—then considered that perhaps . . .

She glanced at my clothing, somehow not remembering it was what Giacomo had picked out the day before. "I am glad to see that you are learning how to dress. Next you must focus on learning Italian."

Giacomo caught my eye, and I saw a look of amusement.

But my employer was on her own course of conversation: "Now come! The veterinario is waiting in the courtyard. It is a very special day." With these words, she began to make her way back to the main house.

I asked what this might be.

"Oh yes! Today!" she said, turning around again to face us. With an expression of delight, she threw her hands into the air. "TODAY WE SHAVE THE DOGS!"

part
II

Days are like countries, somebody once told me. Meaning: they will change tomorrow.

And indeed they had. When I first came, I worried if I would make it one more day, and here I had lasted more than a month and we were deep into autumn. Villa Coco embraced it as thoroughly as a teenager embracing some new fad; you would not know, from the giddy excitement over fallen leaves and the sudden profusion of apples, that this had happened, in just this way, each year since before Dante. The pool was closed (we had hardly used it). Nimali was seen rushing to Formica to buy a cardigan, as if somehow she had burned last winter's sweaters. Even the Baronessa, veteran of ninety-two spins through the seasons, had me searching her closets for a beloved shawl; it turned out to be the one in my bedroom. For my efforts, I was loaned a gray Afghan blanket trimmed in red and instructed to wear it "in the goatherd style." Every time I wore it, I was informed "that is all wrong." But no further instructions were forthcoming. Vinsanda was told to gather the cotogne, or quinces, and Nimali was told to boil them, strain the result, and form it into a paste to have with cheese. I later saw the whole lot in the compost bin. Ghazel, having failed to capture the faina yet again, reported he was trying a new method: POLLO BEN NATO, as he put it. "I believe he means venenato," the Baronessa said after some consideration. "A poisoned chicken. What he has said means an aristocratic one. Do we have aristocratic chickens?" It seemed entirely possible we did. And on cold nights, to my delight, we began to have full fires in the dining room.

There also arrived, with the cold, a new mystery.

"I have lost my pearls!" the Baronessa exclaimed one morning, sending the household into a frenzied search as we upturned wastebaskets, rooted through pockets, and sieved the contents of sock drawers as if panning for gold. No dice. She was shocked and aggrieved—but I was not. Things had been going missing for some time now.

A week had passed since the mysterious trip to Ferrara. The Baronessa's cousin had left and not made a return visit, and I was at last allowed entry to all the rooms, so I was finally able to focus on my archival tasks. I worked room by room, beginning with the art on the walls and moving inward toward smaller objects, like the Fibonacci spiral of a nautilus. Paintings, furniture, jewelry, the boat in the entrance hall, all described (as Estelle and Oscar both suggested) as simply as possible, without provenance or value. As to these household disappearances, they seemed, like sleight-of-hand tricks, to happen in the corner of my eye while I was otherwise distracted: Was I mistaken, or had there been a painting of guitars and newspapers? Where was it now? Then again, I could hardly have memorized the million objects in the villa, and I also had to take into account the Baronessa's decorating whims, on which pieces might be swapped or put in storage or sent for repairs without my ever knowing. One day, a drawing from my bedroom was missing. I went immediately to my employer. “I have a right to move things in my own house” was her reply. I suppose she did; I suppose she also had a right to move her pearls and forget where she’d put them. And yet, as the resident recorder in the house, I felt it: a thinning of the atmosphere.

Surely I was imagining things! Surely it was the effect of too many exaggerated stories, too many novels in translation, too much imagination all around. I put my wild thoughts aside and continued my work. I requested that all rearrangements and redecorating cease for the length of my time there “counting the spoons,” as she had put it. The Baronessa sighed and muttered something in Italian.

And yet I succeeded: within a week, the little drawing was back above my bed.

Despite my workload, I still made time for my walks, which became chillier and more barren as we reached November; farmers lit fires by the roadside and the boar hunters seemed to be out in force on weekends, parking their Jeeps along the path and vanishing with their dogs into the wilderness; the only sign of them was distant gunfire. Cesare followed me on these walks, glad to be with me and glad to run after birds and sniff the piles of leaves. The sky seemed lower, the hills farther away. It was as if the landscape had taken a potion. Every morning, I noticed the countryside changing. One day a tree would be as it had been since my arrival, and then the next, it would be completely scarlet. First, just one here or there would shift, but soon—as it goes with any fashion—half the forest wore the colors suddenly in vogue, only to have those original trendsetters turn to earthy browns, then lose their leaves completely. Eventually just the oaks kept theirs, fawn-colored and glossy, on the lowest branches, while the rest of the forest was bare above a landscape of boulders and fallen logs covered by the leaves. There were hardly any pines in our valley, but one could see that the mountains above us—holding in their folds the gloomy Vallombrosa Abbey—still wore cloaks of deepest green. The days grew shorter. And I grew lonely.

It was simple to keep my vow now that the Baronessa had run out of relatives, but I wondered what this vow revealed about me. Was it the same resolution as Oscar's? As Giacomo's? To combat whatever terror bedeviled us. The same awful arrangement with Heaven: basically a protection racket, in which the Almighty takes our lunch money in return for not throwing us against the lockers? Oscar had not freed himself of it, even in old age. Even eating salad from a cabbage bowl. Giacomo had fled into marriage. Had I chosen a similar path?

One morning, a call came in the kitchen, and, after hearing it ring and ring and fearing an Italian conversation, I took a deep breath and picked up the white wall-phone. I was relieved; it was Oscar on the line. I told him we missed him in Ferrara.

"Ah, Ferrara!" he said. "I'm so sorry I could not join you. Lisabetta sometimes moves too quickly for my old heart."

"I mostly saw Comacchio."

He laughed roughly. "She told me the car broke down! What did you think of Comacchio?"

I told him it had an astounding commitment to the eel. I said nothing, of course, of my brief interlude with Giacomo-Giacomo.

"Did you know it was eels they ate at the Last Supper? Or so Leonardo thought. Eels and oranges. Promise me you will try them." I nearly told him that was precisely what Giacomo and I had eaten on our trip, but I had promised to stay mum, and I was liable to give myself away.

"Oscar, tell me what that trip was about."

"Oh," he said, pausing. "Has she let you in a bit?"

"I've been cataloging things. But there's something she isn't telling me."

He sighed. "You must allow an old woman some mysteries!"

I said the mysteries at Villa Coco were thoroughly unnecessary. "Where the light bulbs are hidden, for instance. Which only Nimali knows. Or how to work the Baronessa's television set. Which only Ghazel can do."

I heard him giggling. "Maybe it simply amuses her. Have you found a warm dictionary, my friend?"

I found myself coughing in surprise. I said merely that the possibilities were very limited. I asked if he needed visitors.

"It sounds like *you* do! No no no no! I will come after the harvest."

"The harvest?"

"Olives! You are in Italy, my friend!"

"When is that?"

"In a week." He promised he would bring pesto from Genova.

Nimali continued teaching me Italian, but in addition I had to take a kind of remedial course in art and culture: part of becoming less American. I was seen as a typical product of the American system of liberal arts, by which was meant I knew everything about Lincoln and Franklin and nothing at all about Dante or Flaubert. I had about a thousand years of catching up to do. I began with *I Promessi Sposi*, by Manzoni, said to be the most popular Italian novel of all time, though I had never heard of it. On the Baronessa's shelves I came across a very antique translation, which I found hard going, and I asked her about it. "Oh, Manzoni!" she cried. "This is the one where the lovers, after many years apart and many trials, including a wicked nun, are at last reunited. And they turn to each other, grown much older, and say, 'What? All this? For *you*?' A classic." I made it through *I Promessi Sposi* with the difficulty of one forced to walk on foot along a route schoolchildren take by bus, only to discover that this was not the plot at all.

I found myself entranced by my next assignment; I don't know whether the translation from French was simpler or it simply suited me better. It was *La Princesse de Clèves* by Madame de La Fayette. I told the Baronessa and she said: "In it are inscribed the wonderful lines: 'There is a heavy price we have to pay for seeing things as they are. The price is of our youth.'" I finished the medieval romance, and enjoyed it thoroughly, but found those lines nowhere within.

The Baronessa also pressed on me an enormous, seemingly academic tome entitled *The Lives of the Artists* by Vasari, in which the author describes artists past and contemporary (contemporary to him being Michelangelo), which was in fact a fascinating portrait of Vasari's own pettiness. At least in the first hundred pages; I abandoned it after that. As, I think, did the Baronessa; I think she abandoned every book, which was why she got Manzoni so wrong. She had read everything but finished nothing; she imagined the endings and that was enough. That is, I learned, one way to go at it. It went on in this manner, with her throwing antique books at me and quizzing me about them at dinner, quizzes for which the examiner had all the wrong answers. Because her inventions and interpolations of novels were a literature unto itself.

Though she pressed me to learn great culture, I found

the Baronessa was herself more taken by television mysteries. Her favorite was one with a sexily bald Sicilian policeman as intrigued by food as he was by clues, and this program appeared on a rather haphazard schedule, or at least the Baronessa announced it haphazardly, mostly at dinner, when she would mention there was to be a murder that evening. I learned that what she wanted was for me to watch along with her. Not that I would join her in her bedroom; instead, I was meant to watch on the downstairs televisore while she watched above. It was said to be a lesson for my Italian. And I dutifully watched. There on the white sofa, with Cesare beside me. At each commercial, the house phone rang (Cesare would lift his reverent eyes at my departure), and it was her—"Chi pensi sia l'assassino?" she would ask in an excited voice—and in my own halting Italian I would offer ignorant guesses as to the murderer's identity. Ignorant because the show was not in Italian; it was mostly in siciliano, charming in a street scene but indecipherable to an American looking for clues. I understood nothing; this did not matter. She rattled off her own theories until the end of the commercial break and then rang off quickly, so we could both reenter the mystery (Cesare would lift his reverent eyes at my return). Of all my language struggles in those days, this was the least frustrating. I never guessed the murderer, but then again, neither did she. We were incompetent detectives, whispering together over the phone, and for once I felt in some way her equal when I would hear her voice on the line crying: "Giovedì! Someone has been murdered!"

I grew to know more of the local wildlife than just the faina. Now and then, on my daily walks, I would startle a black-eared hare out of the grass, and, with the sneering expression and long, ungainly limbs of an adolescent, he would lope into the field to see if I was worth running from, eventually deciding I was not. Two kinds of deer could be found—the capriolo and the daino—flitting in the shadows of the forest at twilight or running pell-mell away from me as I approached an olive grove, but no one could identify which species it was that screamed all night in the rutting season, sounding like a horror movie. Pheasants would sometimes cross my path, mostly the dully camouflaged females, like feathered toads in a panicked dash to the other side of the road, but sometimes also the males in their red spectacles, white starched collars, and coppery mantles, spotted in black and white, strutting along grandly like Oxford dons; I found it strange, when I asked our neighbor Duccio if he ever shot and ate them, that he shook his head determinedly: "That is for the English!" I understood they simply were not eaten in these parts, or at least not by him. The pheasants thus walked about in total peace, without a worry in the world, like cows in Rajasthan. Or Oxford dons.

Not so the most famous resident of our woods: the cinghiale, the wild boar. As for the boar hunters, we did not mix with them, and they did not speak to us. They were meant, however, to respect us; the Baronessa told me they were never to aim their guns toward a habitation, but they seemed to be lazy on this point, and she brought out a sunhat with a bullet hole through it as proof. I took to buying bright colors at Formica and wearing them the rest of hunting season, to my employer's despair; I had no plan for this to be how I met my end. Of course, to local Tuscans, the boars themselves were the danger; more than once Ghazel warned me about "I FILI!" at night—meaning wild boars with their children, as they were known to be vicious in defense of their young. I did not, however, come across them. All I ever saw were the distinctive marks they left as they rooted about in muddy embankments and, once, at night, a line of them in silhouette against the moon, racing across the top of a hill.

The greatest danger I encountered was on a morning walk when I came face to face with a spiny pig, a porcospino: a porcupine. I recall I turned the corner and found the little gentleman waddling along, late in the morning for a creature of his sort, though perhaps he'd come from a rollicking party; he certainly staggered as if he had. I stood shocked, and it took him a moment before he caught my scent, stopped, startled, and halfheartedly lifted the white tips of his spines off his back; I heard them rattling. It was like a drunk old soldier lifting a saber. Seemingly satisfied by this display, he ambled off into the forest in search of the safe bed of his home.

I became acquainted, also, with more miniature Italian creatures: the various harmless garden snakes, including one that kept appearing underneath rocks, terrifying me, which Ghazel somehow managed to inform me was not a snake at all but a legless reptile (an "orbettino"), confusing all my notions of animal life and taking away none of the terror; the spiders that inhabited every corner of Villa Coco's rooms like the silent but vigilant guards of a museum, including a particular favorite of mine, who lived in the ivy outside my window and picked her way among the leaves by lifting her long pink legs in a series of grand battements; the ants, which on dry or cold days made their way through a hole cut for the telephone line into my room, in a schoolchildren's procession across the floor, up my side table, and into my nighttime glass of water, ruining it; the stinkbugs that ambulated everywhere like pieces of a board game come alive, and that were bright green when I first came across them and by early November, as I kept removing them from my toiletry bag and hairbrush and suit jacket, had been reupholstered in bronze, after which they vanished and troubled me no further; not to mention the tiny fleas or mites or worse of which I only ever saw the evidence of bites along my backside. Of all of these, I mentioned one once ("There are spiders in my bedroom!") but never spoke of any of them again after hearing the Baronessa answer airily:

"Country living!"

I was beginning to find my stride in my cataloging, having now finished the entrance hall, library, and, of course, my own room. I had begun rotating my Tonino wardrobe with other Formica items, and deciding Giacomo was merely one last pint before the long, dry road of chastity, when one day the Baronessa made her usual entrance down the stairs, Pushkin and Gorky rolling before her, and I noticed she was dressed in a singular fashion—khaki trousers and a coat and a wide orange hat—as if she might be off to shoot a rhino. She looked over my own outfit of pleated trousers and a fresh white shirt, both Tonino purchases of which I had become very proud. "Why are you wearing these things?"

I was startled. I wondered if I was "comme il faut."

"I thought you wanted me to dress more . . . Italian."

"This is charming," she said, "but not appropriate for the raccolta."

The olive harvest. I had forgotten my conversation with Oscar. I said that might be exciting to watch, but I had too much work to do. I bowed slightly and turned back to one of the vitrines—

"HO HO HO!" I heard behind me. She stood there, arms crossed, with an expression of delight. "Today you will be working for the raccolta!"

"But I—"

"We all work for the raccolta," she told me sternly. "Even myself. We must harvest them all within a week or so. Where do you think it comes from, the oil you use so liberally at dinner?" I had assumed it had been purchased; it had never occurred to me that the groves that studded our landscape were, in fact, our provender. "You must put aside this affection for my treasures, as you call them. And you must change."

And so, just as I was getting under way, I was thwarted once again.

The olive harvest: it was not at all as I had imagined it. To begin with, I had not imagined that I would be doing it. I thought it might be a jolly time for Vinsanda and his friends, drinking wine among the trees and singing old Italian or perhaps Sri Lankan songs, gathering the olives from the branches and throwing them into great vats. But we were all under conscription. The Baronessa claimed the government would not let private citizens hire workers for the raccolta and that only family members could do the work; if a government inspector came along, she told us, we were all to say we were her cousins. "Giovedì, you are now cugino Giorgio," she informed me. "You are from Todi." Vinsanda cast me an expression that I took to mean this was all utter horseshit.

The raccolta was an interruption not only of my intellectual pursuits but also of my sartorial ones—after weeks of being trained in pleated wide-legged pants and fitted shirts and jackets, I was now expected to produce a "country living" look in which to pick olives, an activity I imagined akin to picking berries, one by one, but on an enormous scale. My arms ached in anticipation. I dressed in a sweatshirt from my college and jeans—precisely the kind of outfit previously found "too American"—and was told I had done well. My second surprise was that there would be no "picking" in the olive picking. Instead, I found Vinsanda had set up fine nets beneath the trees. Ghazel was present to give us long-handled rakes and describe, in his usual gibberish Italian, how one went about using them. Even the Baronessa took a rake. There was no wine; there were no songs. Just the pleasing patter of the fruit dropping to the ground when one had found a particularly rich cluster. The absurd rakes and nets turned out to be simple and ingenious methods for collecting olives, and once one of us had finished a tree, Vinsanda would gather up the nets and transfer the contents to a small plastic bin. With so little to show, it seemed hardly worth the effort, as with so much of life. But the Baronessa assured us we would make enough oil for the year if we did not miss a corner. She was very good at pointing out where we had missed a corner, particularly with me, and when I tried to respond, she would loudly shush me. "Cugino Giorgio! You are from Todi! You cannot be heard speaking English!"

The work itself was surprisingly satisfying: once I found a hearty clump of olives, I could rake a dozen together and hear them softly thudding to the grass. A wild gust shook the trees and, all at once, it was like those globes of tiny landscapes where it is not snow but glitter or colored confetti, because the last leaves of autumn all flew into the air, shining, gray-brown, innumerable, swirling around us. And when someone turned on the radio to Italian pop music, and the sunlight through the leaves tatted the shadows into lace over us, and smoke from the leaf fire blew our way, there was a soothing romance to it all. I am not the first to comment on the poignant beauty of autumn, or the gold-edged pages of its days.

The next morning, a visitor did arrive, but not our friend Oscar. I was still in the kitchen with Nimali, discussing the hardship of life; a knock at the outside door made me jump. I opened it and was met by a sturdy middle-aged woman with a bent nose and wild black hair held back by a clip. She had the sporting demeanor of a physical education teacher, and she carried a long canvas case. Nimali chatted with her for a while and eventually gestured for the woman to come in. The stranger went directly into the entrance hall and then upstairs. I asked Nimali (in my improving Italian) if she had come for the Baronessa.

"No," Nimali said matter-of-factly. From what I understood, she had come for my bed. But I was certain I had it wrong. Had the Baronessa really remembered our conversation from over a month ago? And where was the replacement mattress?

I headed out for another day of work in the olive groves. The Baronessa insisted that the "work cannot cease!" I remember her tapping her cane against the dirt road, and it might just as well have been the crack of a whip.

I wondered at the urgency, but my only companion was Ghazel, whose explanation was "PUTTA! MENTO!" Since this meant the chin of a whore, I waited until the Baronessa passed near our grove again for an inspection, and she made it clear it was an appuntamento: an appointment at the olive press in a week. "It was the best we could get. You have to book in advance," she said, raising a finger gravely. "Like the Ritz." Later I was also informed that storms were approaching from the west and it was no great treat working in a downpour. But that day was fine—sun so bright I had to squint as I raked the upper branches, the sound of birds arguing like tourists whether to stay a few days more or move on, as planned, to a southern spot. Soon the baker joined us, along with elderly

Duccio, with the promise that they could share in the harvest. The one character not joining us for the raccolta was our neighbor Estelle. Since everyone else, including neighbors, had been mustered (presumably pretending to be family), her absence seemed yet another of her innumerable mysteries, none of which revealed anything about another, like a crossword in which the answers you've filled in don't connect.

An hour later, I saw the mattress woman's car sputtering up the road before me. She passed with a wave, her mysterious case strapped in the back. I went immediately to my room, where Nimali was quietly remaking my bed. She raised her eyebrows and shook her head.

"It is a very old horsehair mattress" came a voice from behind me. I turned and the Baronessa was there in a white wool sweater and pants. Her hair had three olive leaves resting in it. "Only a few people know how to redo them. It has to be done," she said ominously, "*from within*."

"What was in her bag?"

"A pitchfork. She attacked that bed like it was a wolf!" She strode into my room and imitated attacking a mattress with a pitchfork, though she was a poor mime and it came across as someone fishing. "You have to have it in your soul, to fix a horsehair mattress! Of course, we won't need to fix it again for another hundred years." She paused for a moment in the hallway, then added with a smile: "I suppose we leave that for the next owner?" It was the first time she implied she might not live forever.

After two days of labor, the olive groves were barely a quarter done. I thought this was great progress, but my employer did not. "Ghazel is worried about the storm," she told me at dinner. Her expression was grave. "And your spirits seem to have suffered. I would like a pleasant dinner companion. So I have called in reinforcements for you both."

The weekend arrived.

And so did her cousin.

Giacomo's return to Villa Coco was after lunch, and this time he came in his own car, the lizard-green Fiat, which he parked in the olive grove where we were working; he stepped out of the car, rolled up his sleeves, and, after he had delivered his Asiago to the kitchen, was put straight to work. He was in baggy tweed trousers, a blue-striped shirt, a sweater vest patterned like an argyle sock, and a kerchief tied around his neck. Again the good husband from Milan. His blond hair, straight and fine, was staticky and floating above his ears. "Buon giorno," I said. Giacomo nodded at me, then turned away to ask Ghazel for a cigarette. We had of course not spoken since Comacchio, and this turning away seemed to signal how things would be. We worked separate quadrants of the grove for the rest of the day, as clouds blocked out the sun and distant rumblings joined with the constant patter of olives on the nets. I tried to put our past out of my mind—but then my eye would be caught by something bright, and I would turn to find it was always his blond head, toiling beneath a tree.

He was set up in the room beside mine—"la Camera Gialla," as I heard the Baronessa describe it to Nimali—and, before retiring to her television shows, the Baronessa kindly asked if I would mind sharing a bathroom. I did mind; within an hour, I discovered on my white oval bar of soap a blond hair bisecting it. I extracted it and tried to deposit it in the sink or trash, but it clung to me like a living thing. I began to wish I had never thrown my hat upon that bed.

Life with this bathmate was more awkward than our eel-town fling; the first morning of his stay, I heard shouts from the bathroom and he ran out in his towel, complaining that I had used all the hot water. But his childish, infuriated expression faded when he saw me. "Sorry, sorry," he said, shivering among the painted vines. "This isn't how I want things . . . eh, ahem, between us." I noticed he had wrapped himself in a hand towel that barely encircled his waist, and we both began to laugh. We arranged a bathing schedule: I was to take the mornings and he the evenings, and when I went to bed, I could hear him in there, splashing away and singing. Later, I heard a knock on my door and he entered, now wrapped in a larger towel, and quietly said he had been thinking about it, and we should keep our friendship as it was: "I am here for my cousin and the harvest." He said this with a stiff formality I did not recognize; he went so far as to offer me his dampened hand to shake. I understood we had had what his cousin called a "story."

He was polite with me, but I was shocked to find him speaking briskly with his cousin. "What am I doing here?" he would shout to her as he passed her in the field. "What am *I* doing here?" This despite the fact that it seemed he came every year for the raccolta. The first night, the Baronessa turned to me at dinner, leaning over her porcini and grilled polenta, beginning a tale about her time in Manaus—but he broke in, saying, "I've heard this story before. She ends up seeing a pink dolphin." I was surprised when my employer chuckled with delight. "You never know!" she said to him. "I change my stories every telling!"

Hiding a smile, he went on about the supposedly glorious life he was missing in Milan in order to harvest her olives. "Opera tickets," he said. "Wasted!"

His cousin inquired politely what opera.

"*Tosca*!" he responded.

"Will it suffice for me to throw myself from the roof?"

His expression revealed that perhaps it might. Then they

both burst into laughter. I understood this teasing was a habit of theirs, a sign of their old affection.

We of course made no trouble for his cousin; it turned out it was his cousin who made it for us. We were working in her groves, entertaining her at meals, keeping a vow of silence in the shared hallway, and otherwise leading the polite and chaste existence of young monks in an order. Naturally, at Villa Coco, nothing could remain polite and calm and orderly. I was only just learning how the Baronessa preferred an imbroglio.

"Tonight you dine with Estelle," she announced after our day of work. "She is in need of hands for her own raccolta and I have promised the two of you will assist." This was the explanation for Estelle's absence, though it turned out her harvest was not of olives but of uva—grapes—and that she not only picked the grapes herself but made her own wine. I saw Giacomo taking a deep breath and looking up into the sky. And so he and I found ourselves with a double nationality, recruited now into an evening of mashing grapes at Estelle's. "It is not foot work but hand work," the Baronessa told us, making it sound like Balinese dance, adding: "We may all enjoy a moment apart." I understood the invitation was entirely of her own devising; was she tired of us?

Though we could drive there, Estelle encouraged us to walk ("There will be wine, after all"), and from my frequent passeggiatas in the hills I knew of a shortcut. It was twilight when we left; the route turned out to be swampier and more deeply rutted than I remembered, and Giacomo seemed irritated by every step. We were mostly silent on the way over, talking only when he asked me to give him a flashlight once the light grew too dim. It was perhaps half an hour before we arrived at her little cottage, spattered with mud. Estelle appeared in the doorway with the fluttering light of a fire brightening one side of her jumpsuit, so that she looked less like a fighter pilot than a Pulcinella. She gestured for us to come inside.

It was an artist's space; every wall was covered in canvases or drawings, and an easel stood beside the window with a naked human form already sketched upon it. I had not known she was an artist; of course she was. Instantly, parts of the crossword began to fill in: why she joined the strange world of Villa Coco, why she was so far out in the country, why she lived alone, why she came and went at her own whims. She was an old-time bohemian in the form of a modern Algerian Italian woman. She was, in some way, the Baronessa. Reincarnated by a slipshod Heaven so she overlapped with her previous form, but she could have posed for Man Ray on a rock in Capri, or captured lizards with George Norman Douglas, or matched wits with Moravia and Morante. What a shame that, in our impoverished century, she had only myself and Giacomo to entertain her.

I approached one of her smaller paintings, and it seemed, somehow, that I had seen it before—

"Oh, don't look at that," she said, taking it off the wall and holding it to her chest. "It was just something I was trying for Coco. But I don't have Oscar's gift."

"Oscar?"

"And now. Before you get any wine," she announced commandingly, "we must crush the grapes." I had seen her vineyard from the road; it looked modest. But the tubs of grapes showed otherwise. She said the grapes would make two dozen bottles of wine.

It was indeed "hand work": nothing more or less than squashing grapes, shirtless, in a white plastic tub. Estelle left this to Giacomo and myself; she put on a Nina Simone record and stirred the risotto. I felt awkward stripping down, with the new climate between me and the cousin, but Giacomo removed his sweater and unbuttoned his striped shirt and revealed that broad chest and the curls of dark hair at his sternum. Estelle asked Giacomo about Milan. About theater and art; I noticed she did not ask about his wife. Like everyone I had met in Italy, these two were completely at ease speaking of a Pirandello play or an exhibit of Caravaggio and La Tour, as comfortable as people in my world would be speaking of a television show. I was surprised to hear Giacomo, usually so awkward in his speech, talk so easily about a subject that kept me in terrified silence. I watched as the grape juice spattered his upper body and began to stain his hands a royal purple. The two of us looked like homosexual serial killers.

"And what about your novel, Giacomo?" Estelle asked. "Am I in it?"

I was shocked by this turn of conversation. I had never dared to broach the subject, but Estelle had picked up the Baronessa's casual way of making everything suitable for conversation. "Eh, ahem," Giacomo began. "It is set far in the past, you know."

"I think I would be a wonderful character. So would Giovedì!"

I held up my stained hands. "I don't want to be in a novel!"

Giacomo smiled. "Vabon. I will not force Americans where they do not want to go."

"I think it's time to open the wine," Estelle announced.

She brought out a bottle, nearly black, and I think only his distracted frame of mind got Giacomo to break his rule on unlabeled wine. "This is Number Four," she told us, and explained it was last year's, her fourth attempt. "Pretty good. Not like Number One." Giacomo downed the first glass without pause. I thought it tasted like a bottle of chilled blood but said nothing; it was good enough for me. I asked what Number One was like. "Oh," she said, looking into the fire, "something funny happened in the fermentation. It's a bit dangerous. But now is the time to ask us all your questions, you know. With Coco not around. Have a little more, Giacomo."

With the wine, I was bold enough at last to ask what she was doing there.

"Me? Painting, mostly."

"But how did you get here?"

"In the middle of nowhere, Tuscany? Because of Coco. We're related, you know."

This was something I certainly did not know.

"In our way," she said, pouring me more wine as well. "She had a lover, an important art dealer in Milan, who would come down here every weekend on the train. He was very charming, very handsome. And I had a lover myself when I lived in Milan. Also an art dealer."

"And they were friends."

"And they were the same man."

"Visconti," said Giacomo.

"Visconti, yes. We knew nothing about each other, Coco and I. We knew the kind of character Visconti was, but we knew nothing about any other women. I was up in the apartment in Milan and she was down here, tucked away in the woods. How would we ever find out? It was a perfect arrangement. We were all very happy. Of course I was too young and spoiled it." I wondered how old she could possibly be. I had taken her for someone perhaps a decade older than myself, but to have shared a lover with the Baronessa she would have to be at least in her forties. The firelight revealed nothing further. She continued, "I knew he went to Florence to visit dealers there. So I thought I would surprise him. I knew exactly the hotel where he always stayed. Helvetia and Bristol. He always liked an English hotel. I took the train down and bribed the concierge to let me into his room, and I was that cliché of the naked girl waiting in the bed. I must have waited for hours; I fell asleep. I heard the turn of a key and a woman's voice saying, 'I certainly like how they make the beds here!' I looked and there was Visconti and, with him, a woman in a blue suit with gray-striped hair, laughing. Of course it was Coco."

It was so easy to imagine the Baronessa laughing at the situation. But not so easy to imagine her twenty or more years ago, carrying on an affair. If Estelle had been twenty, how old would the Baronessa have been? In her sixties? Nearly seventy? She herself claimed that seventy was her prime of life. It seemed improbable, but, as I was learning at Villa Coco, the improbable was hardly impossible.

"Anyway," Estelle said, "there was no going back after that. He had to drop us both."

"Probably you wanted to drop him!"

"Why?" she asked, and she sounded very much like her beloved rival. "I'm the one who broke the rules. I'm the one who broke his pride. He did nothing wrong."

Giacomo nodded in agreement.

"And so Coco and I were left without our lover, only with each other. We were bound to be good friends. I was out of an apartment in Milan, so I came down here and helped her out. Eventually I found this place to rent. I sold some things Visconti had given me. And for some reason I've stayed. I still help Coco. I visit her and I take care of her and she protects me."

I questioned this and she raised her glass.

"A small town, there are all kinds of problems for a single

woman. But people think I am her daughter. And she lets them believe that. It is valuable protection."

"Vabon. Alla famiglia," said Giacomo, raising his glass as well. We toasted.

But, as this was apparently the moment for questions, I asked another: "The princess who came, Pippa, mentioned something. And Oscar too. Her 'great love.' Was it this Visconti?"

Estelle laughed and announced the risotto was done and we must wash up and eat immediately. In the fuss of preparing the table, I saw the two of them having a conversation in glances and expressions. But I would not let it go. When we were seated and eating, I asked again.

"In Panarea," she said, then turned to Giacomo. "Did she ever mention the house in Panarea?"

Giacomo said, still not looking me in the eye, "I don't really know the story. It is . . . eh, ahem . . . a mystery. I do know she earned all her own money—"

Estelle interrupted: "She lost everything when her father died before the war. I think the stepmother took everything. So she ran away to Capri. A family friend had a house there is what she says. Lived among the artists. And started selling their art."

"So she wasn't rich?"

"You will meet many Italians with titles and nothing else," said Giacomo.

"Why did she leave?"

Estelle shrugged. "When I met her she was already a rich woman in Milan. Something happened in Capri, something with Oscar, I think. And that Pullman character. Some good fortune or . . . escapade of hers. And she made the most of it on top of selling art. She wanted a house in Panarea, off Sicily. With a view of Stromboli erupting at night. And when she had enough, she bought one. Just a little house on the sea. It was what she thought she'd always wanted. But it wasn't. Eventually she sold it. But she had to buy a house in Panarea to find . . . the love of her life."

"And?"

"Coco saw her one day on the water."

The shock of this revelation astounded me. "A woman?"

Estelle laughed, and so did Giacomo.

"A boat," he said to me. "A wooden . . . eh . . . two-master cruising through the waters."

"A yacht!" I exclaimed.

"Not a yacht. A boat," he said, a little annoyed. "She had a horrible name, but Coco renamed her. But at last she had her. *Caprice*."

Instantly the image came to my mind of the sculpture in the entrance hall, a boat in bronze . . .

"Seven letters is good luck," he explained. "My cousin had her for twenty years. I was on her many times. But then she had to sell her."

"Why was that?"

"I don't know. She always says it's not a very funny story and changes the topic."

"Maybe it was for a man."

He frowned. "You keep searching for a man in all this. That isn't her story. Maybe it's yours?"

Estelle put another bottle on the table and dimmed the lights. "I think," she said with a mischievous smile, "we should try the Number One."

It was the kind of potion one finds in Shakespeare. After just one glass, the shadows took on a greenish tint and our eyes began to glow like those of deer in a field. The fire, an odalisque, dropped the silk from its shoulder, and the flame lay before us totally nude. We laughed until we could not stop; the music changed and we were dancing. At one point, Estelle vanished and it was just Giacomo and me by the fire, leaning against a landscape of pillows. The potion gave me the courage to say, "I know why you're here."

"What?"

"You keep asking why you're here. When you have business in Milan."

"And a personal matter as well."

"Think about it," I said, trying to connect my words while my head was woozy. "She put us in adjoining bedrooms, and when that didn't work she sent us here to Estelle. I'm sure she asked her to bring out the Number One."

"Did you tell her . . . ?"

"Giacomo, no one needs to tell your cousin anything."

"Vabon." He leaned back, and firelight covered him. He had not, in Comacchio, been more than handsome to me, as much as a dozen other men. Now, all at once, he was unique. Like a flavor, or a work of art, or a song that must be listened to a dozen times before it is more than noise and becomes our favorite. His soft and boyish face kept changing in the firelight. Beautiful; cryptic; furious; gold.

I said, "She made you come here for me."

"Oh . . . eh, ahem, really?"

"Or, rather, for you. And Ferrara. She arranged that as well."

"What? Why?"

"I think she wants you to be happy. And maybe," I said, chuckling, "she likes a little drama."

"I have not often been . . . eh, ahem, drama."

"And I think the sooner we indulge her, the sooner you can go home."

He said something quietly in Italian that I did not understand. He shook his head back and forth, then looked into the flames as if deciding something—to throw himself into them, perhaps—then he turned to kiss me.

Just as I had often talked to someone in my growing vocabulary of Italian only to realize I had misunderstood a statement of theirs—that they meant precisely the opposite of my perceived meaning—in that way had I misunderstood this man. He took me with a desperation and passion he had not shown in Comacchio, where it had all been fun and exploration. Under the spell of Number One, Giacomo held me against the cushions and stroked my hair and put his lips all over my face and neck, staring at me with shining eyes, gasping as he unbuttoned my shirt and ran his hands over my skin. He was hungry, rapturous, relieved; he kissed me like a soldier home from war. I was confused and excited and let him have his way; it was so wonderful to be touched and adored, to be someone's treasure.

At one point Estelle floated through in a white cotton nightgown, saying, "I'm glad the Number One is working." Then she was gone again. We did not pay any attention to her.

We were of course useless the fifth day of the raccolta. I have no memory of walking home or of finding our way into the house and delivering ourselves to our proper rooms, but, with the same relief as finding nothing broken after a catastrophic fall, I discovered some part of me (some inner manservant) had brushed my teeth, folded and put away my clothes, and even dressed me in princess pajamas. No part of me, however, could save me from the headache that Number One had given me, like a mallet to my skull. "La vita è dura," Nimali said in the kitchen, in her daily report, and this time I agreed.

The thoroughly Italian remedy was a single chalky aspirina, given by Nimali with the reverence of a priest presenting the Host. It did nothing, however, to relieve my swirling thoughts about what had occurred.

Giacomo seemed to have fared better; he was already out, raking away in the remaining corner of the grove and chatting with the baker. He waved at me and kept chatting; only when I arrived for my duty did he confide "I have a face of wood," which I assumed meant a hangover. When it was time for a break, we both lay down in a leaf pile and fell promptly asleep. We were awakened by an elephant trying to bury us like game wardens; it turned out to be the Baronessa. She was throwing sticks in order to wake us. "To work!" she cried furiously. "We have only a few days!" She roused us to our feet and went to a tree and said she would show us how it was done. She herself worked very badly, raking the tree as feebly as a child brushing a doll's hair. And yet I could see, in her glance at the two of us, that she was very pleased her plan had worked. I wondered if she perhaps had become frustrated by her cousin's intransigence and my own sour mood, like a zookeeper who has brought together two pandas only to find them sitting on opposite sides of the pen. And so, with Estelle's assistance, she had forced our hand.

That night's dinner held an exquisite tension between me and Giacomo as we passed the salt (never hand to hand, as this was bad luck, but always in a chess move across the table) and briefly touched each other's fingers. The Baronessa was telling of her governess, called Madame, who wore old-fashioned ruffles and lace and had led the life, as she put it, of "an adventuress!" Her cousin and I, however, were not paying very close attention. She said something about the governess falling from a horse in the Indochine with no doctor around and asked, "Guess what?" looking expectantly from one of us to the other. Apparently we waited too long before saying "What?" because my employer frowned and said perhaps the story was too good to waste at a table such as this.

"No, no!" Giacomo said, leaning toward her. "Tell us what happened then."

The Baronessa paused and shook her head. But she had no self-control when it came to her stories; the absurdity overcame her pride. "She was left with no nose!" she burst out, eyes wide. "Just two holes, which I found very beautiful."

"She didn't have a *nose*?" I asked. I was beginning to detect a drop of invention.

"No nose at all," she said, avoiding my gaze, then leaned down to stroke the dog beside her. "This began my love of pugs."

The phone rang loudly, and Nimali scuttered across the kitchen to claim it. A moment later, she announced to the Baronessa that it was "Signor Pullman."

I struggled to think of who this could be until I recalled the strange man who had interrupted our luncheon before the sudden trip to Ferrara. I looked to Giacomo, who seemed unaware of this character, then to the Baronessa, who to my surprise stood up and accepted the call (something of which Madame would not have approved before dinner guests, even ill-mannered ones). The conversation was one-sided and in English and along these lines:

"He is proceeding."

"I have not decided."

"I said I have not decided."

"By Christmas. Goodbye."

She returned unsteadily to the table and seemed wrapped in her own thoughts. Her eyes caught mine, and she gave her signature flash of a grin. I wondered what worried her now. "If you are still listening to an old lady," she said, "Madame was once also in a harem in Suez. Before the nose, of course. Though that might have given her a special status!" Had this governess been her role model? Giacomo asked for olive oil, which we could pass hand to hand, and his touch was another turn of the knob, tightening the tension that would be released later when he crept into my room.

Oscar had said he would come after the olive harvest. My employer several times had me try to reach him by telephone, but he never answered; either I was forced to endure the cheerless Italian ringback tone droning into eternity, or else I was met with a different resistance: when his maid, Maria, answered. I was very proud of my developing Italian, but, as with a charm to which some are immune, somehow with Maria I was unable to communicate. At lunch with the Baronessa and Giacomo, I reported my frustrations. The Baronessa seemed subdued that afternoon. Her expressions, her responses, even a gesture she usually made for Nimali to start serving (a flourish of her hand) were lesser versions of her ordinary self, like the performance of a singer at a matinee, who, saving her voice for the evening show, omits all the difficult notes for which she is famous.

She did, however, offer a simpler explanation for my troubles with Maria: "You have been spending too much time with Estelle. She speaks a charming Italian but has decided not to pronounce the double consonants. One never knows if she is talking about her hair or her hats." That is: capelli or cappelli. I still could not hear the difference.

She said no more on the subject. We sat for a few moments in glum silence. Then, to my surprise, Giacomo brought up the story he had so precipitously impeded the other night. "You were talking about Manaus the other day," he said, looking over at me.

"You have heard the story before," his cousin said evenly.

"I'm sure Giovedì and I would love to hear about it." It was strange to hear him using my nickname; he had always called me by my proper name. And why mention this story from days earlier?

I said nothing, wondering how my touchy employer would react. "It is not suitable for a luncheon conversation," she said, though that had never stopped her before.

"Weren't there pink dolphins?" He knew this story well. "And a couple? I know you think we are terrible prudes—"

"HO HO HO!" she said, shaking her head and turning to her wine.

"And you were in need of a bathroom . . . ?"

"This is a story for a different audience, and you will both be needed in the groves," she said, then added: "Siamo alla frutta," just as Nimali delivered pears to the table, meaning both that we had literally come to the fruit and that our conversation had come to an end.

I did not think too carefully, in that time, about what we were starting, Giacomo and I; those days were like photos taken in an impetuous instant but left until much later to develop. It was a relief to have someone with whom to share a conversation about his cousin, about the oddities of life at Villa Coco, and about the house itself. One morning, I drew his attention again to the portrait next to my bed.

Giacomo explained his grandfather was attired for a costume ball. "He is dressed as the sculptor Bernini."

I mentioned how similar they looked, and he said it was

not true; he looked, in fact, similar to Bernini. He reached to his bedside and, from his wallet, brought out a fifty-thousand-lira note, on which was printed an image of the sculptor that indeed resembled Giacomo enough to be a perfect portrait (if he grew a mustache). I told him so and he seemed affronted—Bernini parted his hair to the side! I did not mention it again, though in my mind his own image now became confused with both his grandfather and Bernini on the lira note, so sometimes I forgot who had the little mole above his lip, Giacomo, Bernini, or his grandfather; or, in the early mornings, when he rose to slip back to his room, I was surprised to find him clean-shaven.

Giacomo-Giacomo. He was guarded and shy but also desperate for touch, desperate to laugh with someone. It took time—but those days were enough. Like getting to know a horse or a fox, with which you cannot communicate except in broad gestures, and only guess the creature's meaning. Desire is always inside the person: mute, invisible, but guiding everything. But what did he desire? Understanding this was as difficult as understanding Nimali in the morning before coffee.

He tried to teach me Italian; for instance, the word "riccio," which could mean a hedgehog, a chestnut, a sea urchin, or a curly-haired boy. He said I was all of them. And he did a startling imitation of me one night in bed, bugging out his eyes and shouting: "Oh! Wow! Hey! No! What's happening?!"

I said I did not talk like that, but of course this statement was itself proceeded by a contradicting "Hey!"

"You see? You can't help yourself." He jumped upon me.

"No!" I shouted, pushing him off, but his meek appearance hid an unexpected strength, and he managed to pin me to the bed. A moment later, he howled like a dog and pretended to sink his teeth into my side.

"What's happening?!"

Oscar had promised to come after the harvest but instead arrived a day before its end. The Baronessa informed me that because Giacomo, Vinsanda, and Ghazel were busy with the olives, it would be necessary for me to pick him up at the station. I understood she considered me the least efficient member of the harvest crew.

"What an honor to have you drive me!" Oscar said as he greeted me, raising his fedora with his usual charm but a slightly weakened smile. He again carried his brown paper packages and insisted on loading them in the trunk himself. Still a novice at a stick shift, I found myself bursting too fast out of the parking lot, then jerking to a stop, stalling, starting again, and bursting out again until I fell in behind a very slow-moving orange Ape.

Oscar seemed to notice none of this. He asked, "How are you getting along with our baronessa?"

"Oscar, I'm trained in archives and records. Organization. But Villa Coco is nothing but chaos."

He said, "You find Lisabetta difficult."

I did not know how to answer such a direct statement, but luckily he answered it himself:

"Of course she's difficult," he said. "But you have to think of her as a magic door. Every time you open it, it leads somewhere new. To the Ottoman Empire, for instance. To a princess or a dockworker or a dog."

I said I had not thought of her that way.

"There was a Greek theater in ancient times," he said, "so beautiful some listed it among the wonders of the world. And now? There is nothing left. Nothing but a single ticket, made of bone, for a seat in the fourteenth row."

"And she is that bone ticket," I said.

"No," he responded. "She is the holder of that ticket. She

has seen the show." I understood he was speaking of history and time. "Now. I hear you have found a warm dictionary?"

I coughed in surprise at this leap of conversation. We had entered a sun-dappled series of turns, around each of which might lurk some oncoming car, and I took every corner with trepidation. "I don't . . . I don't know if—"

"No need to say more. But it's why I have arrived early."

I said I did not understand.

"Lisabetta loves a little . . . shenanigans, is that the word? What a lovely word. Shenanigans around the house. Youth must have its fling. But it seems the two of you have been neglecting your host."

"What? We . . . I mean, I always—"

"She called me in to keep her entertained."

"I didn't know. She should have said something."

"Nobody likes to feel irrelevant. To be the old lady nobody listens to. Especially when she has such extraordinary stories."

"I'm so sorry—"

"Even ones we have heard many, many times before."

"Oh, Oscar."

He patted my knee. "Let us say no more about it. It is my turn to apologize, for I have neglected to buy your slippers. But!" From his bag, he produced a basil plant, wrapped in plastic, and he raised his eyebrows. "I have kept one promise!" he said in delight. "I have brought pesto!"

Once we were in the kitchen of Villa Coco, he placed on the counter a box of pasta, the basil plant, and two large potatoes; he looked like San Drogo with his attributes. He and Nimali had a very serious conversation, during which she held out an open palm and he a potato and only at the end of the discorso did he bestow it, gently, like a blessing. I whispered with Estelle, her hair wild and golden again, her collarbone adorned with a jade pendant, and she explained he had brought ingredients for pasta. "Trofie al pesto," she called it, adding that I was in for a treat. Foolishly, I informed her that I had tasted pesto many times before. "No, you haven't," she said, calling over Oscar and telling him what I'd said. "Ah," he said. "No no no, it is not pesto if it is not from Genova."

Perhaps it was Nimali's special magic with the mortar (she stood watching us, hands on her hips like one of our employer's amphorae) or indeed the provenance of the basil, but the dish was utterly unlike what I had tried before and certainly more than the sum of its humble ingredients (plant, pasta, potato). Layered with the last of the old olive oil, it was spicy as a North African market, somehow tasting both of roots in deep earth and leaves in the sun, the sauce sliding down the coils of pasta. I was beginning to understand. Everything I had tasted in America, everything Italian, was a distant memory of the old country. Like a spell written down but never heard. Of course some enchantment was lost.

"Not only can you not have pesto outside of Liguria," Oscar informed me at lunch, "but it used to be you could not have it out of season. You will notice this of everything. Artichokes are upon us! So we will eat artichokes as often as we can."

I said that while I loved artichokes, I did not relish the idea of having them at *every* meal.

"Ah!" he said, raising a finger. "In Venice, there is a tiny crab in the lagoon called the moeca, and it molts only twice a year. And only for a few days. When it is time, nobody eats anything but moeche. And then it is over."

"But it will come again."

"But maybe not you and I. We won't be back, as our friend likes to say."

I tried, though I was unused to this particular monogamy with food. And yet—the constant variety I found all through the autumn! Chestnuts, which Nimali boiled and pureed for use in lasagnas with various squashes; the carrots she roasted alongside rabbits or boar and which raised an eyebrow from the Baronessa; the pale green, slightly prickly cardoons, gratinati with bread crumbs and Parmigiano; the alien germinating chicory, with its spiky puntarelle, which Nimali somehow knew how to slice into ice water, where they curled into rococo shapes, later to be dressed in anchovy and garlic. ("More anchovy next time," the Baronessa would state. "I have never in my life had enough anchovy.") And then the artichokes now in season: stuffed with bread and olives and mint and baked; narrow and spiked from Sardegna, laboriously cleaned and eaten raw; globular romanesco, sliced with Parmigiano in a salad.

While the idea of days of eating artichokes, no matter how varied or ingeniously prepared, would previously have struck my American palate as a forestate of the afterlife's grim tedium, I understood these autumn days would end. And so I stuffed myself with artichokes. And puntarelle and cardi and chestnuts and boar. During that time, I believe some part of me was lost, like the broad pelvis of ancient humanoids that kept us tree-bound or the third eyelid we now no longer need, so that I might achieve one simple aim: become less American.

Throughout lunch, the Baronessa was brimming with delight with her Oscar. Much of the conversation was in Italian (I began to suspect this was purposefully to thwart me), and it seemed he had come with great news that was not shared with me. Then my employer began a long discourse that Oscar had to stop, saying, "Let the boy hear this! She is talking about her trip to Brazil." My employer said I had promised to learn Italian, that the ultimate test was to translate the Signora Guicciardini. That made the table laugh, but Oscar said the signora had great wisdom to impart. Then he persuaded the Baronessa to let me hear the story in English. To my surprise, it was the very story we had tried to pry from her the other day. I assumed it would be full of the great wisdom Oscar had told me about:

"I was very much in need of a bathroom!" the Baronessa began. Giacomo sat back and smiled at me. "It was along the Rio Negro. I was in Bogotá and I decided to see the Amazon. I wanted to see the pink dolphins. I heard they could become people and walk around town with a cane, always wearing white clothes."

"Excuse me? Could become people?" I asked. She pretended not to hear me, but I could tell she was pleased, at last, to have an audience.

"I rented a boat with a small crew," she went on. "I was the only passenger, and a woman, and they took excellent care of me. They liked to pull giant alligator-like things out of the water to show me, and piranhas. I kept saying I wanted to see the pink dolphins, but no, my sailors wouldn't find me one. I slept aboard very well, and every morning tiny little monkeys would sit on my shoulder, tiny like a mouse. But I was not talking about monkeys . . ."

Giacomo leaned in: "No no no, go on."

"The bathroom! Well, it was on our return, when I had left the boat and was staying in a little village. Airão! That was the name. Airão. I was in what they called a hotel and decided to go out for a walk and suddenly . . . I suppose it was something I ate . . . suddenly I had need of a toilet. Desperate need. I have never felt such a desire in my life, I wanted it more than a diamond or a man—"

"More than a diamond?" Oscar asked with amusement.

My employer ignored him: "I began to yell to people on the street, who pointed toward the water, but that was not possible for me. And yet I did find it, beside the water, a shabby little hotel where the man behind the desk pointed to a back room. The kitchen, it turned out. So there I was, rushing through the kitchen in Airão, and on the kitchen table . . . were a man and a woman making love."

"Cousin!" Giacomo said in mock outrage.

She ignored him. "I apologized in Portuguese, but they did not cease. The woman raised her arm and pointed to a door as if this happened all the time. My desire had to be satisfied. And, Giovedì, since you like a happy ending, SO IT WAS!"

"I am so relieved," I said.

"Not more than I! But even better, after I left the bathroom, the couple, still in flagrante, waved me goodbye. I saw they had left their clothing in a pile on the floor. All white. And a cane in the corner. Do you see? I had wanted to see pink dolphins! AND SO I DID!"

She made the gesture for Nimali to serve us the next course—and this time, it was the full flourish. I caught Oscar's eye; he seemed to be beaming. And my employer: I saw a delight now in her face, and something more to her story, this woman seated in the fourteenth row of history. A bawdy travel tale, of course. But also: a resolution that the world not lose its magic.

What began as one of the charms of "country living" ended, of course, in monotony, especially for the Italians who had suffered the olive harvest annually. And yet Giacomo refused to complain, as much as his arms grew tired. "We must have the olive oil," he said to me when we were at lunch and I brought up my sore arms. "And so what else is there to do?" I mentioned that some, in the wide world, *purchase* their olive oil, and have fine autumn days free to do as they choose. The withering glance he gave me implied he regretted sharing a bed with a barbarian who *bought* his oil.

We finished the harvest—but the storm never arrived. Instead, a fog appeared, and it seemed the countryside wore a blanket "in the goatherd style." I had my coffee and morning lesson in Italian ("Andiamo avanti"—we must go on) and stood outside the great wall of ivy, staring at the cloak of fog; so dense from afar, of course up close it resolved into tiny floating droplets, like old newspaper photographs made from a thousand dots. Eventually, from this fog appeared a little dark green vehicle—Estelle, come to visit the household now that her own harvest was done and fermenting. Vinsanda told us to carry the crates of olives to the garage in case the storm should still arrive, while he gathered up the nets and rakes to be put in storage until the following year. We moved in the wet fog like ghosts.

That evening, the crates of olives were piled into Vinsanda's vehicle and all of us made our way, at midnight, to the frantoio. Only Oscar and the Baronessa stayed behind; it was far too late in the evening for them both, she said, and I understood that what she wanted to do was watch her television shows. Oscar whispered he was going to sneak a nip of gin, and not to tell his friend. I wondered if this was wise. I brought Pushkin and Gorky to her bed and bid her good night, and Giacomo and I crammed ourselves, with Estelle, into her little three-wheeled truck.

The frantoio was called, inexplicably, I Bonsai (The Bonsai), and getting there was a rough ride (bumping constantly against Giacomo, who took every opportunity to bump me back), bringing us down a back road past a gloomy castle I had never seen before; in the thick fog, it all seemed imbued with a mystery that in sunlight, surely, would have vanished, revealing only factory buildings. We found ourselves at an old stone structure whose parking lot was packed even at this late hour; Estelle (narrating the whole business with the hushed gravity of someone explaining a religious ceremony) told me they were pressing olives all day and all night. Two workers in blue uniforms loaded our crates—one dozen of them!—onto a conveyor belt, then slid a plastic sheet between our olives and those ahead of us, belonging to a party named Vaggia. Estelle explained this was to be certain we would not mix olives. "Who knows what our neighbor uses on their trees? Who knows if they have the olive fly? This way we are sure the oil is ours, and not," she added with disdain, "*Vaggia*." The wait was long, but the workings of the mill fascinated me—a shining steel structure inside, with transparent tubes in which one could see the olives being rushed overhead to the presses, great crushing wheels, and more tubes transporting both the olive remains (for a second crush, a donation to the frantoio) and the first-crush oil itself. That was incredible to see: pouring from the metal spout into our large containers, a bright green liquid, almost unnaturally chartreuse, swirling like sea-foam and carrying into the air a scent of pine forests and grass. But an even greater surprise awaited me.

"Vinsanda booked the back room," Estelle told me as Giacomo and I wheeled the containers along. I looked over at Vinsanda, who grinned sheepishly. "It is his birthday."

The "back room" was at the far end of the mill, a dim stone chamber, where a simple wooden table was set with plates and silver—and there sat Nimali, smiling as if la vita were not dura after all. Estelle produced a ceramic pot, a loaf of bread, and a bottle of her wine. Vinsanda took a seat at the head of the table, smiling as I worked my way through bad Italian in trying to thank him for all his help over the past months. Nimali had the expression of a piano teacher at a recital, powerless to correct her student. Then it was time for the oil. The pot contained white beans Estelle had made, the bread was broken, and with the wine we tasted the very freshest oil I may ever have. It stung like nettles. The unexpected sensation brought me out of myself, and I could see the room with clarity, as if I had wiped my glasses and returned them to my face, now with the ancient stones making of it a painting of workers celebrating a harvest, myself merely one of them, or even (perhaps under the influence of Vasari) a Caravaggio in which we were about to recognize in our companion Vinsanda the divine. The formal placement of the bread and oil, the shadowed wall and bright faces, the shine of oil on Giacomo's lips. I sat very still, trying to keep this remoteness as long as I could, to hold in my mind this moment, plain and ordinary to the others, which my foreignness alone found beautiful.

"It's a bit harsh on the first press," Estelle said, and I was brought back to the table. She had noticed my expression at the first taste of the oil. "It will be mellower in spring." I smiled sadly and took a piece of bread. I would not be here in spring.

High above our little villa brooded the mountains of Vallombrosa, and I had long heard of the abbey sequestered there, where monks sold honey and medicinal liqueurs and it was said that wolves still hunted among the silver firs and beeches. A hike in the mountains seemed, to me, a fine escape for Giacomo and myself, and, it being Sunday (a day when my employer often liked to dine alone), I proposed to the Baronessa that we remove ourselves and find our own dinner in a nearby village.

"High spirits!" she said with a tight little grin. "I approve."

"You'll be all right?"

"You know I do not require attention," she said, turning to her half of the newspaper. She sat in her parlor with the windows open to the autumn air. "But have you perhaps neglected a guest in need of an outing? Our friend Oscar does not want more of my old stories."

She was as wrong about herself as she was right about Oscar; once again, my "high spirits" had led me to abandon an old person, and one who had so recently come to my aid.

Oscar, however, declined the invitation when Giacomo and I proposed it, saying his days in the mountains were behind him and that an attack by wolves no longer held the charms it had in his youth. He sat in the loggia below the Baronessa's window, beside the fading orange tree, dressed in a camel cardigan and reading the other half of the newspaper. "You should consider visiting Cascia di Reggello," he pointed out. "It is an unassuming village with a masterpiece in its church, one that is seldom visited." I thanked him for his advice and was about to leave when I felt Giacomo's hand on my arm. His glance told me I had missed something. As always, the American, taking people's words too literally.

"Would you come and show it to us?" Giacomo asked.

Oscar's eyes rose above his reading glasses. "I would not put you out of a mountain adventure. I think fondly of my own."

Giacomo said, in Italian, that it was we who would not want to miss a guided tour of a masterpiece. Oscar looked to me and back to Giacomo and surely understood, for he smiled as one does when one is offered a special wine. I tried to curb my disappointment at the loss of a mountain hike and a meal with Giacomo. The house phone rang twice; it was the Baronessa, suggesting we make a reservation in Cascia at the restaurant Lala and ask for a view of the piazza. I thanked her and wondered how her deafness had been so magically cured.

The route to Cascia took us over the hill on which I had walked so many times and onto the main road from town. I drove (I could no longer trust Giacomo's whims) and, as Oscar and Giacomo chatted in Italian in the macchina, I found that after I had conquered one curve above a terrifying cliff, there would always come another, so that in the end I was wrestling a snake that took us back and forth across the hills until we reached the other side of the valley, and there, with a bit of straight path ahead of me, I was able to glance out the passenger window and see flashes of light reflecting the evening sun—the windows of the Baronessa's balcony. My life at Villa Coco, seen now from the world outside. We passed a row of cypresses and then it was gone.

The town itself appeared to be falling down the hill, the houses held back only by a low, plain Romanesque church before what I took to be a sloping parking lot. Parking seemed to be prohibited, however, with a sign that read merely NINA! And yet a truck and trailer had clearly found a home there. Rebuffed, I put the car under another set of cypresses, on which were tacked more signs of NINA! "Nina!" Giacomo said with a poignant cry. He explained this was a famous rock star from the 1960s. "Andiamo avanti!" he sang merrily. "Andiamo lo stesso!" Both Oscar and I were mystified.

The old man turned to me as we entered the church. "Did you read about Masaccio in your Vasari?"

I said that I had but could hardly be expected to remember. Giacomo paid the fee for the museum, which seemed to be no more than a narrow passageway leading to a distant, gloomily lit room tacked onto the church.

"Ah. Well, he is an important one. His name was not Masaccio, of course, no more than Parmigianino was Parmigianino." I was pleased that at least I knew Parmigianino. Oscar went on as we made our way down the hall: "His name was Tommaso. Thomas, and I think they called him Maso. Tom. But there were so many Masos in those days, they had to give him a nickname, and since apparently he never bathed and was a very filthy boy, they called him Masaccio. 'Dirty Tom.' And so he remains for eternity. Ah, here we are!"

The only object in the chamber was a triptych on wood, displayed on the wall. The left and right panels each held two saints, one of them looking at his book like a student caught unprepared for a test, and in the middle sat the Virgin Mary and her child, attended by two kneeling angels. Everything appeared just as I had seen it many times before.

"Do you see?" Oscar asked, glancing to me and to Giacomo. We must have seemed like students caught unprepared for a test. "The angels. They look away from us."

It was true; each was at an angle facing Mary so we could make out only part of their faces.

"And the chair," he said, pausing to allow for dawning comprehension. I did now notice that Mary was seated in a chair with rather grandly jutting armrests. "It recedes into the distance. So does the platform on which she sits. You see? You could draw a line from every corner to the point where they meet in the distance. The vanishing point. The famous Renaissance perspective. You have probably studied that in school." Giacomo nodded. "Well," Oscar said, "this is the first time it had ever been done. This painting here. By Dirty Tom."

"Lala" turned out to be a restaurant directly beside the church, and it was Lala herself who served us: a papaya-shaped woman with short blond hair and dark eyes, who accepted Oscar's flirtations with an abashed expression as she led us to our table. He winked at me; moments later, a bottle of white wine arrived. "I still have some charm left," he confided.

Oscar ordered a cacciucco, a Tuscan seafood stew, for us to share. When I asked about the rules of the mountains and the sea, he replied: "In some places, the rules don't apply. Lala has a nephew in Livorno, and he brings her seafood every morning. So at Lala, and only at Lala, that is what you eat." The stew was easy to love. Deep red, autumnally red, from broth and tomatoes; aromatic with garlic; and in it a pirate's trove of clams, mussels, varieties of shrimp, and sweetly cooked fish whose names meant nothing to me, as they are found nowhere outside the Mediterranean. The trick, Oscar told me, was to cook the broth with bones for many hours, then add the seafood at the last moment. A combination of intensity and freshness, patience and immediacy, all soaked up with the Tuscan bread that suddenly needed no salt.

"We were a great pair on Capri," Oscar was saying. I had lost the conversation in the stew, along with my mussel shells. Perhaps the white wine helped as well. "I came after the war, and the island was a bohemian outpost, and I found it wonderful. But I did nothing but bad sketches! Lisabetta was quite a bit older, and she found my particular talent. The timing was perfect—rich people were coming to the island. They always follow where artists went first."

"You sold your paintings to them?" I asked.

He didn't answer directly. "You can't imagine life after a war. Genova was bombed, and the Fascists were no treat."

Giacomo asked if he left Genova during the war.

"I was eighteen when Italy entered the war," Oscar said, smiling as if this were a merry tale. "We were anti-Fascists, of course, so my father had to hide from time to time and I was left all alone in a house of women. They were afraid the Fascists were going to take me into the military. So you know what they did? I was never tall, as you can see, but I was already a man. So they shaved my legs and dressed me in short pants and gave me a hoop! There I was, eighteen years old, and I had to pretend to be a little boy, with a hoop and stick running down the street. The most humiliating time of my life!"

"Did they catch you?" I asked.

"No, but I was furious! So furious that I refused to speak to my mother and my aunts. I took a piece of chalk and I wrote on the soles of my shoes." He lifted one foot off the floor, and then the other, pointing to them: "*Sì* on one shoe and *no* on the other. For two weeks I would only answer in this fashion." He lifted each foot. "*Sì. No. Sì. No.* In that time, my father came back. And he said, 'Oscar, I've heard you've been a real brat! That you refused to speak for two weeks and only answered with the soles of your shoes, is it true?"

He paused in his storytelling. With a sly smile, Oscar lifted one shoe off the ground, showing us its bottom and murmuring, in the voice of an abashed teen: "*Sì* . . ."

I felt protected by the wine and laughter and the fog of twilight descending around us. I let Giacomo's finger curl around mine under the table and I leaned close to him as he whispered something foolish in my ear. Oscar watched us, patiently looking on us with a smile. I was careful not to act as we had with my employer, and when Giacomo went inside to find the bathroom, I asked Oscar to tell me more about Capri. Instead of answering, he leaned forward and said:

"Do not be lazy in love, my friend."

I was startled. "What? I'm not!"

"You are," he said quietly, looking at the trailer in the parking lot in front of us. "You take what comes."

"What . . . I . . ."

"I recognize in you myself." He readjusted his hat. "I spent years in a life I did not want, and not for love. It was because I did not think another life was possible. But it is always possible." He turned to me with his charming smile.

I wondered how he had seen any of this in me. For certainly laziness had taken me through all my past "stories." Laziness or lack of will. Did I give it off as a kind of pheromone, the sign of a rudderless man? Or was this simply what he assumed of all young people?

Giacomo returned, wiping his hands on a linen handkerchief. He was the kind of young man who carried a linen handkerchief. He smiled at me and took his seat.

"Hey!" I said, pointing across from us, for just then, I noticed the trailer doing something trailers are not known for doing: it began to transform. The entire side near us lifted into the air and folded back onto the roof, which folded back again to reveal a gleaming contraption within. It was a kind of flattened pyramid, all in silver, and it seemed at first as if it were a device delivered by an alien species, or perhaps planted millennia ago by the Etruscans, and the time had come for it to awaken. Awaken it did: it began by rising high into the air, and then, sliding out first from the bottom, a series of steps extended onto the parking lot, one by one, until at last an enormous staircase stood before us, leading up to emptiness. By now it was growing dark and people had begun to gather in the lot, which I realized was the town piazza. Then the whole thing burst into a blaze of lights: the frame of the trailer glowed in reds and whites, spotlights turned on to illuminate the structure, and the edge of each stair began to glow eerily. From behind the stairs rose a curved sign with one name splashed across it: NINA.

"Wow!" I said.

"Nina!" Giacomo shouted beside me. He was joined by other shouts from the crowd, which rose into a chant. "Nina! Nina! Nina! Nina!"

The device heard the invocation, and obeyed, for a moment later it delivered up, on a pneumatically powered platform, a tiny, somewhat elderly person in a silver wig and deep blue gown, seated in a chair like a saint's image carried in a town procession or, it occurred to me, like the Madonna herself as Masaccio saw her; she even cradled a microphone in her arms. She sat very still until she arrived at the top of the glowing stairs, then stood unsteadily and, raising the microphone to her lips, and now utterly unlike the Madonna, began to sing . . .

I could only shout: "What's happening?!"

The next day, Oscar and Giacomo took off before the coming storm. I stood in the kitchen doorway with my employer, saying goodbye. She turned to talk to Nimali, and as she did, Oscar raised his finger to his lips; I was certain this was because, the night before, I had secretly brought him some gin before bed, which we knew the Baronessa would not approve of. Somehow I could not say no to such a charming man. Before he got into the car with Giacomo, he turned and said, “Come visit me in Genova. Then you can have those slippers I promised you!” I waved and told myself the gin would surely do no harm.

I had said goodbye to Giacomo in our shared hallway, after hearing him singing the songs of Nina in the bath (he requested a morning one). I was leaving my bedroom when I saw him in his red bathrobe, a vanity kit nestled in his arms like a lapdog. His toothbrush was still in his mouth. He was the very image of helplessness, and he turned and saw me staring at him. I said I hoped he would have a safe journey. He nodded, mute because of the toothbrush, and shuffled down the hall to embrace me. The vanity bag was uncomfortable between us. I pulled him into the bathroom with me and closed the door. He pressed me against the wallpaper of medieval creatures; I felt them galloping through my system as he kissed me. How sweet the first flush of romance is: the overture, as it were, providing all the thrilling chords of an opera whose plot we cannot yet know. Then he nodded and left and closed the door and I was alone. I tasted his fennel toothpaste and it made me smile as I ran the bath. So this was what it was like, to feel like you are secretly Venice. A moment later I was cursing his name: he had used all the hot water.

And the Baronessa and I stood in the little kitchen doorway and waved goodbye to the lizard-green Fiat taking them both away. One could feel the coming storm prickling on one’s skin, and I looked above the bare trees to see a sky of scattered bones, but what those oracles said about the coming winter I did not know.

“Do you know what I was thinking about?” the Baronessa said to me. She was leaning once again on her bastone, with gloves in its mouth. Her vertigo must have been troubling her. “The time Oscar and I visited Istanbul. Long, long ago, when we were quite young and did foolish things. I did something very foolish, in fact. You have asked me about my greatest treasure."

"Yes?"

"I stole something on that visit to Istanbul."

I turned and looked at her. A little old lady with her hair recently done in a white dome. "What was it?"

She did not answer me but followed some private thought: "Those were wonderful days," she said. "With Oscar working for me. You know the entrance used to come from there?" She pointed into the woods, where among the trees I could see faint traces of a road leading off into the wilderness. "See the cypresses? That was where the road came through before a storm brought it all down." And indeed, just as she said the word, I could make out, in that expanse of oak, the tall, dark sentinels of cypresses still lining a vanished road, as they used to when she came here forty years before.

She said quietly, "Maybe it really is time to go."

I assumed, of one so elderly, that she was thinking of her own mortality.

It was just Estelle and myself at dinner with the Baronessa. The fire was crackling below the mantelpiece cupids, and lights flickered in the chandelier. The meal was wild boar and polenta. The Baronessa said she had great news for me but became distracted by curiosity about Masaccio and the Madonna and, after a brief detour onto Nina (of whom neither of them had ever heard), arrived, of course, at the subject of food. I had begun exclaiming over the fish stew at Lala ("Buono!" cried the Baronessa) when suddenly Estelle dropped her fork on the table.

"Coco!" she exclaimed, looking at me with surprise. "What potion have you given him? He now speaks Italian!"

I did not even realize I had been doing so. Estelle was staring at me, but the Baronessa did not seem much impressed. "Then let us test him," she said. "Have you listened to Signora Guicciardini? Who shouts from the crossroads?"

I said indeed I had.

"Oscar sees her as a sibyl," Estelle said, "shouting prophecies from her cage in Rome. I think she is Old Italy yelling at the New!"

But the Baronessa was fixated on me: "And what, Giovedì, do you think she is saying?"

The room was so quiet I could hear the far-off sound of Cesare barking in the forest. For I knew exactly what the signora had been saying, the great wisdom Oscar told me she was imparting.

I cleared my throat to imitate her: "Hedgehog-fuckers!"

The Baronessa exploded with laughter and grabbed Estelle's arm.

"She's mad because people pause at the crossroads," I explained. "She's saying, '*Choose* something, you little hedgehog-fuckers!'" I thought of what Giacomo had taught me and added: "Though it could be chestnut-fuckers."

At this, she laughed and laughed and laughed and could be calmed only when one of her pugs began to bark in alarm. She pulled the dog into her lap and sat there, firelight gleaming in the tears now in her eyes. More laughter convulsed her, and she held her hand before her face as if she could hardly look in my direction.

For the rest of dinner, I bathed in the warmth of an acceptance I hoped would endure.

part III

Nimali announced the arrival of the bora: the winter wind. The sky seemed to harden into a gray mass like porridge left on the counter, and we hardly ever saw the sun. One day, I found Vinsanda and Ghazel dragging enormous iron frames of plate glass across the courtyard and was informed they would be fitted to the Baronessa's balcony and to the eating porch, which would become an "ARA NERA!" as Ghazel put it. That is to say, a black parrot. I understood immediately he meant an aranciera—an orangery for the single orange tree. What it in fact became was a sleeping porch for Cesare. The kittens I had seen on my first day were growing into cats, and took over the garage. The Baronessa's balcony placed one more pane of glass between her and the world. The air was full of the scent of burning leaves, and every night at dinner, Vinsanda prepared a fire that took only a single match to set ablaze. I was often made to sit near this inferno, and a Tonino jacket received a scorch mark, which the Baronessa found very fashionable.

And yet her energy did not cease. How she was not exhausted I do not know; from the first "Koo-koo!" midmorning to the final evening brush-off ("Perhaps we've seen enough of each other today"), there was not a moment when one could rest. There was the garden to visit, which we did even in deepest chill, supervising the rows of dormant plants like teachers walking between test-taking students; there were various fantasies to entertain, such as restoring the captain's cabin's fireplace, which, when lit, leaked smoke into my bedroom; there was the hair salon to visit; there were seasonal clothes to be brought out, brushed of mothballs or unwrapped from tissue, all the while brushing mothballs from her old stories and unwrapping her peculiar thoughts from the tattered tissue of her discretion ("Estelle will grow even more beautiful as time passes, don't you think?" then with a donkey's laugh: "NOT ME!"); and of course her letters, which she dictated to me not from across the room but sitting close beside me on her salon sofa, peering at my calligraphy and spelling—for the letters were often in Italian, and as our alphabetical pronunciations were noncorresponding ("Chee ahkkah eepsilon eeloongah, you have written something very amusing, but we will have to start over"), the process was so slow it seemed as if I were not inking the words onto the page but embroidering them. And there was, of course, my catalog. I was making progress, having conquered now the kitchen, the white bedchamber, and the living room. My employer insisted on what she called a "longhand ledger," which I am sure was an invention of her imagination. I used her computer in the mornings for the sake of speed and efficiency, and after lunch, I transcribed everything on a yellow legal pad, to her apparent approval. Thus I spent the final month of my time at Villa Coco.

After the first snow, I accepted an invitation to dinner from Estelle. It was on a Sunday, when the Baronessa often preferred to eat alone and was happy for me to find my own amusement. Estelle had walked to Villa Coco that day (though I had not seen her; again she was involved in some mysterious closed-door conversation with my employer), so she accompanied me back to her place. I remember the frozen ruts of mud on the road that led to her cottage and the extraordinary sighting of a bird—all-over celeste, underwings a deeper blue—hopping from branch to branch above us, surely a migratory vagabond. Estelle nodded to it as we walked. She wore a green jacket and, on her wrists, a set of amber bangles that clattered with her gestures. She asked me about Giacomo.

I shrugged. "You know? When I came here I promised myself, no affairs!"

She laughed. "Hard when Coco is around! She always loves somebody having an affair."

"I suspect," I said, "that she pushed the two of us together."

"She wants her cousin to be happy."

"And the Number One?"

She put her hands up. "What wine does I am not to blame!"

Calling Giacomo in for the trip to Ferrara and for the olive harvest—had the Baronessa done it to entertain her cousin or myself or both? Or was it to distract us? "But, Estelle, it's just a story, as you all call it. After all, I'm leaving in a month."

"Now that you have had a story, she may want you to herself. And what happens after a month? What do you want to happen?"

The bird reappeared above us, turning its beak back and forth. I did not know.

"Do you have a story . . . ?" I asked.

I let the ellipsis float there like a pontoon bridge she might take to complete the crossing. She paused, as one might before a pontoon bridge, then gave a wry smile and a shrug.

"Who would I have? Duccio? No, they're all as rough as wild boars and talk like they're coughing something up." She imitated the peculiar Tuscan country accent, where *c*'s are replaced by hacking coughs. "Either that or aristocrats who have handmade shirts and shoes but not a lira for anything else. No, I'm fine by myself out here, thank you. I make a little money arranging things for people, Coco included. And soon I may be leaving too—" She stopped herself with a smile and rubbed her hands together in the cold.

I was startled. Estelle seemed as much a part of Villa Coco as the signora at the crossroads. "You're leaving?"

She strode ahead of me, stumbling slightly on the icy path. "I may have an opportunity."

"But you'd be leaving . . ." I wanted to say the Baronessa, but in truth I could not say what duty they had to each other.

"I haven't said yes. It's maybe a terrible mistake, but we will see."

It made me somehow sad, the thought of Estelle gone from the place. Everything seemed to be sliding away like the hillside after a storm. Giacomo and Estelle gone. The odd sensation that the house was dwindling. As if some enchantment had reached its limit. I stopped at the spot where the path rose up to her cottage, now visible among the trees. The bird stretched its wings before it. "Estelle, I wanted to ask about Oscar."

I thought I saw her head jerk slightly in surprise. I went on: "His visits. His packages."

"Oh, that?" She smiled as if I'd asked a foolish question. "Don't worry about that."

"And the Baronessa seems . . . She has an urgency that wasn't there before. I don't understand."

"Old people, there is a certain impatience, no? Not hard to understand."

And off the bird flew into the gray sky; I hope it was headed somewhere warm, one who had lost its way home.

We had rabbit in white wine and rosemary and talked of foolish things around Villa Coco: Ghazel's son, who it seemed was a math genius, and Vinsanda's heretofore unknown mastery at cake decorating. I could not, however, learn anything more about Oscar or my employer. It was only later, when stumbling (a little tipsy) through the darkness from our villa's kitchen to my bedroom, that I nearly ran into something in the entrance hall and, steadying myself against it, pricked a finger on a sharp edge. A bit of moonlight was in the room, and I could see the object shining a dull gold—the sculpture in bronze of the boat. I had passed it daily in my cataloging but had paid it little mind. Now I touched its nameplate, and though I could not see it (how had I not noticed before?), I could feel each letter as it passed beneath my fingertip: *C-A-P-R-I-C . . .*

Giacomo began to call me at the house, so much so that even Nimali, answering the kitchen phone, became a mother handing the receiver to her teenager, one eyebrow dramatically lifted in semaphore for "Again?" Our calls would periodically be interrupted by a clicking sound, a sigh, then another click, which I finally realized was the Baronessa because, eventually, she cut in on our conversation and called for "an intermission so the audience can take refreshment." She proclaimed to her cousin he could call only once a week. "On giovedì." Of course, since I had only a handful of weeks left, we ignored this directive.

"Let's meet in Florence," Giacomo said on our next call. "Sunday!"

"Oh! I'd love that!" I said.

"Vabon. We can have a hotel bed instead of that horsehair mattress."

I heard the telltale click.

"Um," I said, "I will have to check with your cousin, but as Sunday is my day off—"

Of course my employer could not resist breaking in: "Eh? What is happening Sunday?"

Giacomo ahemed and said, "We were thinking of Firenze."

"Oh no," she said. "Impossible. There is so much to do before our friend leaves."

"But, cousin, it's *Sunday*."

There was a silence on her end of the phone.

"Baronessa?" I said.

"Impossible," she repeated, but this time her voice was somehow quieter, weaker. "Let us think of another time." She reiterated that it was impossible, quite impossible. What was impossible, I began to think, was my stubborn employer. I did not then understand that her motive was never to separate us; she was not thinking of us. There were other worries that had nothing to do with a cousin and a callow American.

Soon after, we had a winter visitor. He made a sudden appearance by knocking on the kitchen door and terrifying Nimali. The Baronessa and I were having gelato and making plans to watch a murder mystery on TV; we peered from the dinner table, but I noticed she did not rise, merely nodded her head; the visitor was not for her. He was a slight, bearded sepia-toned man in a blazer and kerchief who, when he removed his fedora, revealed himself to be bald as a hazelnut and as brown. Although he was as slender as Ghazel, and perhaps the same age, his movements were slow and gentle compared to the other's nervous energy—a loris compared to a gazelle—and he was talking to Nimali in a tone so quiet I could not make out what he was saying. Both of them were focused on a small dark object in the palm of his hand. The scent was unmistakably that of a truffle, and the Baronessa confirmed he was the tartufiere who had brought us Cesare.

She said, "I asked him to come to train him, but he says it is impossible." Because of the chill, we were both dressed in blankets "in the goatherd style."

"Maybe we should let Cesare just be a dog," I suggested.

"You're right," she said, resigned. "It is not everybody's duty to fulfill their destiny. But it is a disappointment. Think of the truffles!"

I pointed out that the visitor seemed to have one.

The Baronessa went on: "It is a gift to us. A very precious one, as you can imagine. He is explaining to Nimali that there are only three ways to prepare a truffle. The first, which I well know, is scrambled with eggs. It's my preferred. The second is with fresh tagliatelle. The third, he says, is exquisite. You layer the slices of truffle . . . with anchovy!"

"You're kidding."

"He says it is how the ancient Romans ate them!"

"What does it taste like?"

She paused for a moment, listening to the man's quiet words. "He says he doesn't know. He has never dared to risk it. Too bad, I would be curious to find out."

"Well, we can try!"

"Where angels fear to tread?" she asked, eyes wide. "I admit I am intrigued but also afraid. Is this to be my last truffle? Then I will have it with eggs, thank you."

"Don't be silly," I said. "It's not your last truffle."

She folded her hands thoughtfully. "These notions come to one at a certain age. My last trip to Paris may have already passed. My last hamburger surely has. The last of everything is approaching now."

"You make it sound so sad."

She flashed her smile. "You are not considering that not all of life is a pleasure. The last trip to the dentist! The last taxes to be paid! It is not all bad, growing old! By the way, you are wearing this blanket in the wrong way."

She took another bite of her gelato as if she had indeed had her last trip to the dentist.

And then there was the Baronessa's vertigo, which seemed to be worsening. One snowy day, Estelle and I took her to the doctor in town, Dr. Ibrahim. I never met him, but I certainly knew his office, as it was next to the hair salon among whose metal drying bonnets I spent precious hours of my life, reading *Oggi* magazine and inhaling that particular scent of sanitizer, coffee, rosewater, and burnt hair. On this particular occasion, I was the chauffeur and walked past the salon (a decidedly ancient lady was being led out by a middle-aged man) to linger in the piazza of our little town, a tiny tessellated trapezoid with an ancient arch, a post office, and two bars: one proto-Fascist and one proto-Communist. There was no outward difference between them except the newspapers displayed in the windows. Elderly men sat outside each in folding chairs, arguing among themselves and judging passersby, unless there was a construction project, in which case they could all be found loitering there together, judging the progress and, political differences set aside, agreeing it was all being done wrong.

I went through the arch and found the third café: an anarchist one. I sat in the window, with a braid of garlic as my companion, sipped my coffee, and tried to read *Rivista Anarchica*. The Italian was knitting together nicely in my mind when, out of nowhere, it became tangled by an American voice:

"How long have you been with yours?"

"What's that?"

Though twice my age, he was about my height and build, dressed in a much older man's style of wool coat. It was the man from the hair salon. Baldish, pinkish, aquiline nose, in a purple scarf with a green scarab pin. It struck me that his elegance blurred his looks as much as it enhanced them. He held a dollhouse espresso on a dollhouse saucer, and the spoon seemed about to topple.

He gestured with his chin toward the doctor's office. "Your signora. How long have you been with her?"

I waved my hand. "Oh, I think you don't— We're not—"

"I know, I know, you're her right-hand man," he said, laughing a little. "Her maggiordomo. So am I."

"Oh."

He sat on a stool to my left and rested one foot on the rung of another stool beside it. Placing his saucer on the narrow bar that ran along the wall, he lifted the coffee and took a sip. "I've been with mine for fifteen years. She's ninety-eight."

I said that was a long time. I had been working for the Baronessa for only a few months.

"A few months." He began to rock slightly, propelled by his foot on the stool. "How's it going?"

It was going fine. And my position was to end at Christmas.

He chuckled. "How many pugs?"

"What's that?"

He merely raised an eyebrow.

"Two. She has two pugs."

More rocking, looking into the piazza. "Mine has four. Four pugs. Ninety-eight and four pugs." He faced me again. "You won't be leaving at Christmas."

"No?"

A warm American smile. "Mark my words. She'll come to you and say, *I have an important trip. Stay long enough to help with that.* It will be something like that, a trip or a family crisis. It will seem like an easy thing to do. After all, she's going to die any day now, right?"

"Well—"

"And then fifteen years will pass."

"Ah."

"I'd planned to travel Europe, maybe try living in Paris. And here we are, at the hair salon. I haven't had a weekend off in five years. You know the last woman I was with? Her cousin. Isn't that sad?"

I was startled at the whole situation. I wondered if he had gotten his coffee "corretto"—that is, with a shot of grappa. "Well, it's—"

He clattered the cup in the saucer and put up both hands in mock surrender. "I'm sorry. You don't know me. Forgive me. It's none of my business, I'm sure you'll do great." His hands went down, his eyes out again to the piazza. "But I never leave her side. I'm always with the ninety-eight-year-old contessa and four pugs."

"I should—"

"Look, do you want some advice?" he said, edging a bit closer and whispering. Yes, I could smell the grappa. And he was interested not in what I wanted at all but rather in what he wanted. It was to tell me to steal things.

"What?"

"Steal things. She'll never put you in her will, never; you're not family. She'll promise to, but she'll never do it. *Steal things.*

You're the one taking care of her, not her family, and they'll drop you and the pugs off a cliff when she's dead. Steal things, but be careful. I took her grandmother's jewels. She thinks the Ukrainian maid took them, but it was me. I took her first-edition books. Sold them all and invested it so I'll be okay." I felt sorry for him as he grinned and whispered, with his scent of coffee and alcohol and lavender cologne made by the monks high on the mountain. He seemed so glad to tell me, a stranger; he was the servant in the myth of Midas, burying his secret in a hole in the ground. I managed, afterward, to extract myself by pretending to see my employer across the arch from us, and he paid for my coffee and his cornetto and I thanked him and felt grateful to have escaped what I thought of, then, as some old man trying to seduce me. Rather than trying to warn me.

"Things are not well," Estelle said, supporting my employer, who wore a green suede jacket and slightly dented hairdo after her visit to the doctor. The Baronessa seemed to struggle along the snowy walk. Estelle wore a deep green swing coat with her gold-tinged hair floating wide. I could see, on the other side of the arch, my new friend tipping an invisible hat to me from the café window.

"Merely dizzy," my employer insisted. "I am fine for my age, thanks God."

"There is no fine for your age," Estelle said.

"Doctor Ibrahim says to me, 'You are ninety-two, what do you expect? You're not going to repair yourself! This is what you've got!'" Her demeanor changed as she broke into laughter.

Estelle shook her head while I opened the door of the Mitsu-bitchy. "She should stay in bed and watch her soap operas and basta!"

A dismissive sigh from my employer as she climbed into the passenger seat. "That is not my plan, as you well know!"

Later, after we guided the Baronessa up to her parlor to rest, Estelle confided in me that the doctor said her vertigo had not improved and that, though she had survived wars and heartbreak and pug after pug after pug, a woman her age who insisted on living in a labyrinth of statues and staircases must prepare for a fall. With that, Estelle kissed my cheek (scent of rosemary), buttoned her green coat, and went outside to where her Ape waited. Nimali caught my eye in the kitchen and shook her head. I went upstairs and found the Baronessa outstretched on the white-linen-covered sofa. Her eyelids, onionskin, were closed, and her expression was so free from the usual frenzied ideas, antic grimaces and grins, and watchful stares of daily life that it seemed I had never seen her so at peace. A pug on her breast, sleeping, was the attribute of a saint (Catherine's wheel or Peter's keys), which they are never without, and with her hands folded below the creature, a thin coverlet draped over her and falling to the floor, she resembled a figure on a sculpted tomb. She had seen the show from the fourteenth row. It seemed a beautiful way to go.

I sat there for a long time in a bentwood chair, reading the newspaper and regarding her. Outside, the fog made the world as white as a Japanese room formed by paper screens. I thought of how I had been racing against time, and if the end for her were not now, it would be soon, and so I had failed; I had not managed to finish the catalogue raisonné of her life. But did it matter? Wasn't my employment just another ruse to keep Death waiting, as one invents an important project so as to preclude dismissal, or as the rifle heiress who built one room after another onto her mansion, having been told Heaven waited on home renovation? I smiled to think this was the way that she would choose. And I thought of what I would do now—if the inevitable had been set in motion—and I began to miss my home. America, with its water towers set like playing pieces across the cornfields and its vast emptinesses of space and history and memory and style and curiosity. My reverie was ended by a sneeze from the dog—and instantly the Baronessa's eyes fluttered open. Herself, again. Embattled with life.

Her glance came to me. "Giovedì. I must tell you about Oscar."

"What's that?"

"What I popped in my purse!"

I struggled to grasp what she might be saying; was she still in a dream?

"Do you not remember? I told you Oscar and I stole something of great value."

I did remember; I urged her to say more. She gave a little laugh and uttered something I'd surely misheard. "What's that again?"

She repeated it loudly.

"A toe?"

"A big toe," she said, as if this explained everything. She pulled a newspaper that had been tucked, hidden, beside her and covered the pug with it; the creature did not respond. "Of one of the four Tetrarchs of Rome. I plucked it off the ground in Istanbul."

"I don't understand."

She sighed and closed her eyes again as if my ignorance alone might do her in. "Then I will explain another time. I'm feeling tired today. Can you ask Nimali to make some tea?"

I did not ask Nimali; I made it for her myself. But I learned nothing more that day and assumed she was somniloquizing about Oscar and Tetrarchs and a toe, in that strange improvisation the dream-mind makes.

Giacomo called again on a Thursday; I found it awkward to have our conversation in the kitchen, since I knew Nimali understood more English than she let on ("Enough!"), and I felt each tarnished plate and goblet and ewer displayed in the cabinet was bending its ears to me. Thus, my responses were necessarily curt.

"Hey!" I said, taking the phone from Nimali's hand as she went back to clearing the table, one Byzantine eye on me.

"Sorry I haven't visited," he said. "Things have been difficult here with my parents. Let's try again for a weekend in Florence. This weekend. I have a room at the Porta Rossa. We'll be right in the center of town; I can take you to the Uffizi and you can see the Caravaggios and Botticellis and everything my cousin prevents you from seeing. And so forth and so on."

"You know I have to ask your cousin." I listened for the click of my employer's intrusion.

"I will *manage* her somehow," he said. "You must be nearly finished with your work by now! You leave in a month."

"I'll see, I'll see."

"And this is more than just a way to see you without my cousin. And treat you to a bistecca. I retained two rooms at the Porta Rossa. One is for us and . . . eh, ahem . . . the other is for Laurine."

Laurine, you see, was his wife.

He was bringing me to Florence to meet his wife? So soon before my departure? Wasn't it instead time to bring our "story" to a conclusion?

"As for my cousin," he added, "I will manage *her* somehow."

I brought him back to the subject of his wife.

"She is coming with her girlfriend, Carlotta. So you see it

will be . . . eh, ahem . . . a family outing! You and I will have the day together, and they'll come for dinner."

"C-C-Carlotta is c-c-coming too?" I stammered. The odd arrangements of his life came suddenly into view, but it occurred to me the attendance of Laurine and Carlotta might add dignity to our farewell. Again, Nimali's comprehending eye was on me. "The Baronessa—"

"I will manage her *somehow*," he said.

I submitted to the overwhelming enthusiasm of his voice.

"I'll bring Asiago," he said, as one final promise.

I found myself answering: "Buono!"

With that, I ended the call. Nimali smiled and asked how was the cugino? Before I could answer, the phone rang again, twice. It was the Baronessa.

"Giovedì!" she shouted. "To the television, quick! Someone has been murdered!"

The nephew did it, in the end. The clues were a necklace and a chicken.

I was searching for clues myself, in the phone call I'd had with Giacomo. Why this mysterious invitation? Why, now, the introduction to his wife? But at least I would see, at last, the splendor of the city I had glimpsed only in passing on my arrival.

I was also searching for clues about the house and what had changed. I remember standing in the captain's cabin and feeling something was off. Was it the antler coatrack that was missing? Or the little metallic bust of Homer? The broken pot? The ass? I looked around and studied the paintings that had so engrossed Oscar and the Baronessa months before. Of course, I saw them almost daily on my trips through the cabin for stamps or paper or hidden light bulbs, but this time I paid attention. Four paintings, each a sea view from a different harbor town: medieval merchants hauling crates onto wide-sailed ships, the water all a-swan, the ladies veiled and nunlike; later, rowdier Renaissance crowds gathered in reds and blues to watch a waterlogged angel rise from the waves; men in eighteenth-century frock coats bustling before gilded barges on some exotic waterfront; and, last, nineteenth-century soot-stained sky and sailors laboring behind nursemaids with parasols and prams. I tried to identify each location, but they blurred from English to Moorish to Indian fantasies, and I began to wonder if they were real places at all.

As for Giacomo's cousin . . . he did not manage her somehow.

The Baronessa and I were in her parlor, cataloging decades of photographs for inclusion in a series of albums; she wanted them organized not chronologically but thematically: all the times she'd been to India, and so on. I was trying to convince her this would not be helpful, archivally. I was building up the nerve to ask to borrow the Mitsu-bitchy on Sunday when, to my surprise, she brought up the subject herself.

"I have heard my relative is coming to Florence. But not to here."

"Yes." I wondered if she had listened after all; I also wondered, from her tone, why she was so against it.

"And that he desires your company."

I thought I would appeal to her artistic side: "It is a chance for me to see the Caravaggios. And the Botticellis."

"My cousin is unlikely to be a helpful guide to either of them."

"The Vasari you gave me is an excellent guide."

But she would not accept this. "Even better would be my friend Lisa, who works at the Uffizi. It is pointless to go with all the crowds! You will spend time before minor works and miss the important ones. Do you know who was the Duke of Urbino?"

"You know I don't—"

"See? You would miss him, and he is fantastic," she said, picking up another photograph of Jaipur. "He chopped off his nose so it would not block his side view! For assassins! Isn't that wonderful?"

"Wonderful would be loaning me the Mitsu-bitchy."

She looked up at me at last, and I saw shrewdness in her eyes. "But that is out of the question. Ghazel has taken it for repairs."

"What repairs?" I said, more loudly than I would have liked. I was exasperated. "And why not take it Monday? It's just sitting in the shop through the weekend."

"I am going to have a rest."

What was her angle? Merely to have me by her side? To prevent whatever romance Giacomo and I might rekindle? She herself seemed to have had many "stories." It was hard to believe she would begrudge us our own.

"Baronessa!" I said firmly.

"I am feeling poorly. Ah! My vertigo!"

"Baronessa, I am going to Florence."

"I had not known you cared so much," she said, rising with the help of her cane. "Another time. You have much to do here before Christmas, as you so often point out to me. And Nimali and Vinsanto are gone all Sunday." She seemed to be using everything at hand to prevent my departure. She was also letting me know not to count on a ride from Vinsanda, as he would be gone along with his truck. And why? Mere spite, at having lost some of my attention to her cousin? Territorial behavior like her pugs, barking from her side? All to lay claim to a mere American? It seemed absurd.

"He asked me to meet his wife!"

"Nimali?"

"No," I said, growing infuriated by her little jokes. "Giacomo has asked me to meet his wife!"

"Eh?"

Now I lost it by shouting: "HIS WIFE! I have to meet his wife!"

"We all have our problems," she said tartly, then added: "You don't need to wear the horrible colors to dinner. Cinghiale hunting season is over."

I was furious. *There may come a point when you want to leave,* Oscar had said to me on our first meeting. But I had missed something; I was so caught up in my own concerns that I had not seen those of the Baronessa, nor was she adept at communicating them. I had not thought of old age and its particular cares. It was only much later that I understood.

To tell the truth, what struck me about the whole exchange was not merely her unfeeling attitude toward my affairs, or her stubborn show of how thoroughly she had me under her control, or even the white lies and jabs and slights. It was that I had not known, either, that I cared so much. And—furious, freezing, startled, sweating—I stumbled to my room, fell upon my bed, and wondered why I did.

And then it snowed.

I had walked to Estelle's many times before, though I got very damp this time tramping through the snow, so I was relieved to see her near the window, staring at a canvas. She was happy to see me, and when I told her about the car she said: "I don't think it's about Giacomo. She's been worried recently." I said that didn't excuse her keeping me trapped at Villa Coco, and it was a weekend and my day off and by God I was going to take it . . . and the train station was too far to walk and could I borrow Estelle's car? She laughed, because of course we both knew her "car" was not a car at all but the Ape I had seen shuddering along the road since my first days.

And it was in this Ape—motor hiccuping, exhaust sputtering, suspension shaking me to pieces—that I arrived, in a triumph of fluttering ticker tape snow, into Florence.

The domes and towers of Florence were like the silvered bottles and brushes of a watercolor painter, set before the paper of the sky, and something about the stately outline of the city in the dove-gray snowscape, as I approached in my putt-putting vehicle, made me into a peasant arriving by mule before the gates of some vast kingdom. I had to park outside the city's old wall and walk, from there, along the Arno to the hotel. Americans are so proud of our old things—"This inn has been here a hundred years!"—but we are absurd youngsters showing off their apartment, with its brand-new furniture, to an old couple who live in paneled rooms with cobwebbed chandeliers, and who have not bought a chair for generations. An inheritance of beauty, but also of stagnancy and neglect. Nothing more beautiful would ever happen here than what had happened long ago. And yet—how could one resist the pang in one's heart at such magnificence? And there he was in the lobby of the Porta Rossa. So tall! Looking at his watch, at the grandfather clock, until he heard my voice.

As it turned out, there was no time for the crowded Uffizi. Instead, Giacomo offered a more subdued experience: Fra Angelico's frescoes decorating the cells of his own convent at San Marco. I understood why the Baronessa had made me read Vasari; I saw there the "rare and perfect talent" he described. I stood for a long time before the annunciating angel, winged like a tropical bird, and an unusually austere and bookless Mary hearing the news with seeming terror. I saw, also, the cell of Savonarola and imagined the Baronessa whispering: *There is no escaping Savonarola*. I had come all the way to Italy to escape my own Savonarola, and indeed had failed.

All the time, I was noting Giacomo's hand on my arm as he led me down an alley. On my elbow as he pointed to a cherub in the corner of a fresco. On my shoulder as he brushed away the sugar dust of snow. His nervous smile as he cast his eyes downward. He was like a man with a delightful secret. Was it me?

Near San Marco we sat on a bench and ate the Asiago he had brought; nearby, a radio played a song by the famous Nina we had seen perform, and Giacomo sang along. We bought gelato and found, to my delight, that a little rolling cabin had been set up in the square and was beginning a puppet show. A crackling sound system sang "Pulcinella Pulcinella Pulcinella!" to gather children around, and when it had stopped, up popped two puppets—surely the solo puppeteer's two hands. Understanding nothing, I watched as our white-clothed, black-masked hero foolishly quarreled with his master, slapping his hands together loudly, and finally they descended into an all-out assault on each other. This was followed by the appearance of Pulcinella's wife. Rather than the feuding Punch and Judy of my youth, these two seemed to be accomplices in some wild scheme, and before she vanished below, they shared a papier-mâché kiss. "Do you call it Pulcinella's secret?" asked Giacomo beside me, finishing his chocolate gelato. I said I had no idea what he was talking about.

"You don't have this? But it is famous! Pulcinella's secret is something everybody knows. It is no secret. But everyone *decides* to call it a secret. The only person you can't mention it to is Pulcinella." He turned back to his gelato.

"How is the novel?" I asked.

He immediately became bashful. "It's tricky to do romance in . . . eh, ahem, fiction. I got my characters as far as escaping by carriage," he said. "And then I realized . . . I do not know where they are going!"

I laughed and so did he.

And then it was time to head to the train station. We were a little tipsy on wine, walking arms-over-shoulders across the Piazza di Santa Maria Novella; shadows were long across the broad square, castellated to the east and west by hotel rooftops, making a kind of upper and lower jaw open to expose the great fangs of its twin obelisks before the vanilla swirl of its church. "You will love her," Giacomo said huskily. "And she will love you."

At the platform, at precisely the correct time, the train arrived. Giacomo called her name, for there she was:

A beauty—almost unnaturally white-blond hair in soft curls around her shoulders, widely set eyes of an antelope or other wild, quiet creature contrasting with her sharp smile as she saw me, the grin of a wife who knows more than she should—and as she stepped from the train beside a tall woman in a beret and belted safari jacket (presumably Carlotta), Laurine's shining raincoat billowed out, revealing tailored trousers and dark leather boots, a silver chain around her neck bouncing on her white satin blouse, her little jump onto the platform with a checkered weekend bag in one hand and the other waving merrily beside her girlfriend, but all this is utter nonsense to write because it ignores the only important fact about her, the only point worth mentioning, the obvious thing that brought understanding of everything about this Laurine and her husband and myself. You see, it was this simple: she was pregnant.

Every house and lover has a fatal flaw, as an eccentric friend once told me.

It was only the next morning that I was able to speak properly with Giacomo. The rest of the evening had gone from dinner with the two women, during which I found it impossible to focus on the promised bistecca alla fiorentina and, once the conversation slid into Italian, found myself compensating with too much red wine, after which things unraveled rapidly. We had returned to the hotel, and, loaded with wine and doubt, I was eager to get Giacomo alone, but just as we two couples were saying buona notte at the doors to our respective rooms, a surprise: "Laurine!" came a shout from down the hall. It was her elderly aunts, staying in a room down at the other end. Why had Giacomo not picked a less famous hotel? The chiacchierata of chatting went on endlessly, and I realized the pair would not leave us until we had gone off with our "wives." This meant Giacomo and Laurine heading off as he cast me a pleading look and Carlotta and I finding ourselves as roommates. We shared a bottle of prosecco and a meal of complaints in Italian before a weak knock came at the door: Laurine. I switched rooms with her and found Giacomo apologetic in his pajamas. I was furious; I would not speak to him. I slept very little. I got up early for breakfast and that was where he found me, on my third cup of coffee.

He led me to an alcove near the breakfast room, bright red wallpaper all around us and a display of truffles behind glass. He was pressed against the wall, a pained expression on his face. He looked like a wadded-up fifty-thousand-lira note.

He apologized again, and tried to explain and explain about Laurine and her family and—

"Giacomo," I said. "I'm sorry I was so mad last night. But I already came out of the closet. I don't want a new closet. Even in the oldest hotel in—"

He said it would never happen again, that it was a fluke, and with Laurine being pregnant her family was—

"That wasn't a surprise I enjoyed," I said. "You and your wife—"

He explained that it was his child, of course, but that they hadn't—that is, eh, ahem—there was a doctor and a clinic and so forth and so on . . .

"I like you, Giacomo," I said firmly.

He exhaled with relief. "This is . . . eh, ahem, good to hear."

"I like you, but what am I doing here? What am *I* doing here?"

"I thought . . . I thought . . ."

"I'm confused," I said. "Before, I was your American until Christmas. But this is—"

"You could be my American . . . also after Christmas."

I stated the obvious: "You're going to be a father."

"Yes."

"And you are asking me to stay in Italy after your child is born?"

"Yes, I suppose," he said, then seemed full of intensity as he said, again, "Yes!"

It was clear to me now that Giacomo knew himself, and what he wanted, so little that, like a magician's apprentice, he had simply put everything potent in the pot—his wife, his American, his future child—and waited to see what might be conjured. It had conjured, as they say in Italy, a pasticcio. A kind of baked dish but also: a mess. And yet, as my anger began to transmute into pity, I thought of what he was saying.

To stay in Italy with him after his child was born. Forget the pasticcio of the night before, the Pulcinella show I had been forced to participate in. Was he offering a solution to my time at Villa Coco ending? A way to prolong this strange dream or, rather, enter a yet stranger one? My rage was abating; I told myself I must consider it. I thought of Oscar's words. Perhaps this was exactly what he meant; a lifetime of experience had taught him not to let an offer like this pass by. Not to be lazy in love. Perhaps: the secret to a lavish life, a satiated heart.

Giacomo took a deep breath and began: "I have wanted to tell you our idea—"

"Signore?"

We had not noticed a slim mustached man from the hotel holding a sleek black rotary phone. He said my name, and I nodded. Giacomo turned away. The mustached man extended the phone and said there was a call for me.

"For me?" I asked.

"It is a gentleman named Hassle."

"Hassle?" I asked.

"Hassle."

I glanced over at Giacomo, then at the man, then, absurdly, at the phone. I saw my face reflected there, stretched like chewing gum. Then suddenly I looked up and said: "Gazelle!"

Apparently Ghazel knew I would be staying at the Porta Rossa, but how he had managed to report my proper name to the hotel clerk is beyond me; perhaps he understood his employer's nicknames as well as any of us.

"BARONESSA!" he shouted on the other end of the line.

I asked him what he was talking about. Surely he had not called thinking I was the Baronessa. My mind was clearly still on Giacomo.

More shouting: "BARONESSA! TORNARE!"

I said the Baronessa had no need to return. She was in the house.

"TU TORNARE!"

I was to return. Well, of course she would demand this.

"CAGARE!" he said firmly. "CAGARE!"

This was a surprisingly obscene verb, and I was certain either he or I had it wrong. I pressed for more information and learned it was "cadere." To fall. Understanding came over me; the worst had happened. Here was a woman of ninety-two who insisted on living in a house of stairs and rooms like a rummage sale, with pugs always underfoot, and the rest of us had been too timid to protest—or too focused on ourselves. For had I not abandoned her, left her alone for the night with no one but Ghazel? She had been right; I should have stayed. All this time I had been hectoring her about my day off, worrying about completing my catalog, when I should have offered my arm. I should have noticed she was afraid.

I asked him about her condition, but he merely answered with one word:

"OSPEDALE!"

Hospital. I thought of her words from months before: *I do not want to die in some terrible hospital with boring people and someone screaming in the next room.* Of course this was how things were always going to end. I had been too young to think of it.

"YALLAH!"

Estelle's Ape seemed even clumsier on my return. I left Giacomo quickly, saying I needed time to think about all this. I packed my few belongings and walked to where I'd parked the truck. It was late morning by then, and I was juddering so violently along the streets, I thought the vehicle would fall to pieces over the hour's journey from Florence. But the Ape endured, and I took it down the long dirt road to Villa Coco, parked it quivering out front, and entered through the kitchen to find Ghazel at the dining room table, before a roaring fire, eating what looked like a turkey leg. The scene was an engraving by Hogarth. I interrogated him about the Baronessa and the hospital and he seemed unwilling to understand. I asked about Estelle and he perked up. He used the turkey leg to point above his head. "SU!" he shouted, and so I headed upstairs.

I took the steps two at a time and, hearing a man's voice behind the Baronessa's door, I thought: Dr. Ibrahim is here with Estelle. They are preparing for her return from the hospital. I should be ready for hard news. I paused a moment, smoothing down my shirt, then turned the knob and entered.

No doctor was there. But Estelle was, seated at the foot of the bed—and, to my surprise, so was the Baronessa.

She was fine.

She lay there in a pink silk dress embroidered with golden dragons; she looked as if she'd come from a party. Pushkin and Gorky sat on a pillow beside her. The room was full of greenish, underwater light from an impending storm. All four of them turned to me as I entered, but as I was about to speak—to say something like "I thought something terrible had . . ."—the Baronessa shushed me loudly. For there was someone else already speaking: the man's voice I had heard, coming over the phone in vivavoce, or speakerphone, in husky Italian. I recognized it.

"The best in Genova . . ."

The Baronessa's eyes were bright as she listened. I saw Estelle reach out to take her hand.

"They are giving me oxygen . . . I feel much better . . ."

My heart tumbled; it was Oscar, not the Baronessa, who had fallen.

I looked from one woman to the other.

From their expressions alone, I could tell that something quite dire had happened, but Oscar's voice conveyed his determination to remain the pleasant old man who caused nobody any trouble.

"When I am back home . . . the first night, what will I do? I will have a little gin! You will be so mad at me, Lisabetta!"

When the call was over, I took the phone from the Baronessa, and her expression was reproachful. "A word before you vanished in Estelle's car might have been kind. We were unsure if you had returned to America."

"What happened? Is he okay?"

Estelle: "His maid found him in the entry hall this morning. Apparently he had been lying there all night."

The Baronessa asked: "Did you see this Caravaggio that meant so much to you?"

I accepted the sarcasm: "I did not."

A raised eyebrow. "Well, I hope you enjoyed your adventure."

"In fact, I didn't. I'm sorry I—"

The phone rang again, this time Maria, Oscar's maid. Again on vivavoce, she asked to speak to the Baronessa privately. My employer gave me a long look before Estelle took me out to the hall so she could be alone.

Estelle led me by the hand to the Baronessa's parlor. We took seats on the white-linen-covered sofa. Estelle rested her head in her hands for a moment.

She said, "We were certain he would be fine through New Year's. Christmas. It was all planned."

"You were *expecting* this?" I asked. "Has this happened before?"

Estelle lifted her head, and I could see she was quite tired. "We have known he has been getting weak. Ferrara, you know, he couldn't go because he was quite ill. And Ferrara was important."

Suddenly I understood how dramatic his absence had been. "But he said he's okay? Did I hear that correctly?"

She said something in French, then lifted her head. "I do not know. He said they had him in a kind of helmet with oxygen. A diver's helmet, he told us." She smiled. "And Coco said, 'Ah, the Genovese, you are always thinking of the sea!'"

I gave an uncomfortable laugh. I asked when Oscar was getting out of the hospital.

There was a pause. "We will wait to hear from Maria. Now, tell me how things went with the cousin."

I told her as much as I had energy to tell, from arriving in the Ape to the Pulcinella show and Laurine at the train station, to afterward when Laurine's aunts appeared in the hotel out of nowhere, and the next morning, when I spoke with Giacomo. At a certain point, Estelle put her hand on my arm and said gently, "Years from now, Giovedì, you will realize this is a funny story."

I could not imagine what she was talking about.

"I am afraid I have not very good news." The Baronessa strode into her parlor from her bedroom and said this evenly as she approached, with her hands in the pockets of her emerald quilted housecoat. The collar of her dress stuck out above, like the frill of a carnation. She leaned against the sofa's arm as if she had lost some equilibrium. "I have talked with Maria.

She is an excellent soul. The doctors told her that he is very, very sick."

"His heart," I said sadly.

A sigh. "It is not his heart. He has la leucemia. I do not know the English." I let out a sharp cry, which caused her to blink in surprise. "We must prepare to go to Genova, although I do not know if they will let us visit him or if he wants to be seen." She paused and looked at me. "You seem shocked."

"How can he have leukemia?"

"He has had it for some time. But now it has struck."

"But his doctor said . . . He said when he gets home—"

"This is because we have not told him about la leucemia."

Her expression betrayed no emotion at all. It took a moment for me to understand, and when I did I was furious. "You knew?"

"The doctor took us into his confidence months ago. I had thought we had much longer."

"You have to tell him!"

She asked what good would it do him?

"He should know what he has. So he can make choices. That must be a right in Italy as well."

She was stern. "The doctor thinks it is kinder our friend believes he will get better."

"But it isn't!"

"You are so sure!" she said. "But our friend Oscar will not get better. He will not leave this hospital as he thinks."

"But still . . . his choice of . . ."

"There are terrible treatments for la leucemia. Terrible, painful. Oscar will not have them—thanks God—because it was too late when the doctor discovered it. It was too late and so we decided he did not need to know. We would allow him to keep his sense of humor, to have a final adventure. But now . . ." She broke off.

I was enraged nonetheless and told her this was monstrous, that we could not stand by and let our friend die of cancer even if he had only weeks or days left. I could not control myself, even as I saw her hand shaking as it held on to her cane. When I stopped, breathing heavily, she looked at me furiously and I thought she might strike me. She squeezed her eyes tight.

"He cannot go!" she said bitterly. "He cannot! We had such plans!"

She said this, I believe, not out of a sudden surge of empathy or understanding (her empathy had led only to keeping Oscar free of the terror of death) but instead from a surge of clarity—clarity of her own terror, which she kept locked in the strongbox of the mind. Now I had pried it free, and she called for a new plan of action:

"Give me the little green thing. I will make a call to my friend the marchesa. Nimali! The marchesa knows people in Genova, she knows the best doctors. I know how to do it. I will send one to Oscar this minute. And then . . . and then . . ." Her imagination seemed to falter as she leaned upon her cane, but she straightened. "And then we will go to Genova. You will drive me." Nimali appeared at the door. "Nimali, prepariamo le valigie . . ." And so, after ordering Nimali to prepare her things and holding her cordless phone, already ringing this marchesa friend of hers, she made her brisk way back to her quarters.

Like a guest who has written the wrong date in their calendar, a storm blew in just in time to pause the Baronessa's plans for Genova. Water lashed at the windows and battered the trees until a river ran down our dirt road, cutting even deeper the old ruts, and the promise of mudslides made travel an impossible thought. We spent the day going through the books in the Baronessa's bedroom, one of which turned out to be a first-edition Byron ("My great-aunt knew him on Capri" was all my employer would say). The pugs crawled on and off her lap and Cesare sat on the floor, looking up at us with adoration.

It was after a rather desolate Monday dinner (two of us with the lit candelabra, wind howling down the chimney, a roast with a knife plunged into it—basically a Gothic novel) that the Baronessa went to bed with Pushkin and Gorky. I had returned to the kitchen to do the dishes (it was Nimali's night off) when the phone rang. I answered.

"Please don't put down the phone," Giacomo said.

"This isn't a good time. We have to keep the line free . . ."

"I'm sorry. I had to . . . eh, ahem, hear your voice."

I put aside my confusion about our last talk and explained the awful truth about Oscar. Giacomo was shocked and aggrieved; he asked if his cousin was handling it well and I told him about the strange agreement she and Maria and the doctor had come to about Oscar's illness, hiding it from him all this time, sure they were doing the right thing. And then her sudden decision not to accept Oscar's prognosis; to find a new doctor, a new possibility; to travel there in person, as if—like some hero out of myth—she herself were the talisman to force Death to call back his hounds.

"I'll come down right away. We need to—"

"That's not a good idea. Giacomo—"

"I know I did everything wrong. You want—"

"I don't know what I want," I said, then thought of Estelle saying someday I would realize it was a funny story. "But that was too much."

He was frantic, I could hear. "I know, I know, I should have . . . eh, ahem, told you before. I should have never invited Laurine and Carlotta. Somehow I thought you would understand. I forget how different our worlds are. But I never got to explain my idea—"

"I understand."

"No no—"

"I don't think there's a place for me."

He had called to tell me there was:

His idea had to do with a building in Milan. A pink building. It had been in Laurine's family for generations, and the recent death of a relative meant it was hers; this was the kind of luck they had been hoping for, family luck, one of the reasons they hid behind a marriage. The building was on via Abramo Lincoln—

"There's a street named after Lincoln?"

"There is," he confirmed, "and it is at the corner of . . . eh, ahem, via Beniamino Franklin. You see, you must come. We have made Americans so welcome!"

The plan was this: They would reconfigure the three floors into three connected apartments. The lower level to present to parents and relatives as where the married couple lived with their child. The second level for Laurine and Carlotta. And the top floor—including a terrace garden with lemon trees and a laurel—for Giacomo and myself. An elevator to connect them all. But I could move in right away, before renovations. He raced on; I understood that this time he had tried to think of everything: "I'm sure you can find work in archives, now that you speak Italian. Milan has everything. We have connections. It's a wonderful city, we even have Chinese food! You could come at Christmas and we can . . . eh, ahem, have a look at the place. I will get a tree. It can be our first Christmas. As a . . . eh, ahem . . ."

He could not say the word "family." But that was, in effect, what he was offering. No one had ever offered something like this to me before: a life, complete and shared. With lemon and laurel trees on streets named after Founding Fathers.

"What about the baby?" I asked.

"You could be there with us," he said, and I understood he was not insisting I be some uncle or second father, something beyond my imagining at that age. Simply the man who lived with Giacomo on the top floor.

He asked, "Could it be something you want?"

I live in Milan, I imagined explaining to someone at a party, *on via Lincoln near via Franklin, in the pink three-story house.*

"I know this seems very . . . eh, ahem, new to you. Very strange. But arrangements like this have been around a long time, you know, in Europe. Royal families have always done it. We are no royal family, of course, but it is the same idea. I had an uncle who lived with another woman in a connected apartment and so forth and so on. It is the way things can be."

"I never met anybody who—"

"I will give you some time. But isn't it beautiful, in a way? Wouldn't it be a grand adventure?"

Who would not want it? To be so adored, to be brought into a family, to have one's life taken care of? Life was feeling very dear and precious to me that evening. A building in Milan; I imagined some pink structure decorated in gold tile, an elevator within resembling the trelliswork of Versailles or a birdcage, the parquetwork of the floor swollen with age and covered with old family carpets, the walls painted gray and lit with modern lamps. Who would even pause? Four weeks before Christmas, four weeks before my life at Villa Coco was ended. A solution had appeared. *Do not be lazy in love.* Was this what Oscar meant? To seize something beautiful when it appears?

"Giacomo, I have to think."

He took a deep breath. "I am saying come live with me and—"

At that moment the lights in the house went off. The telephone still worked, but I could not make out what Giacomo was saying because I was yelling that I had to go. I hung up the phone and stumbled around the kitchen until (a miracle) I came upon a flashlight. My first thought was to run upstairs to the Baronessa, whom I found bolt upright in bed with a candle burning beside her, saying this had of course happened just as she was about to learn who was the murderer in her show. "There is a little house across the road," she said, and at first I thought she was talking about the murderer, but instead it seemed in this little house was the "salvavita," which I took to be circuit breaker. I made my way downstairs again—I heard the phone ringing once more but ignored it—and out into the downpour, across the muddy road, and into the little house I had seen the very first day of my arrival. Here, my flashlight lit up cisterns of water, boxes of light bulbs, and, in a white plastic box set into the wall, a series of circuit breakers. I flipped them all down and then up again; something whirred into action, and when I went back into the rain I saw the house lit up. Wet and tired, I climbed the stairs to the Baronessa's room once more.

She lay in her bed, in the plain nightgown she had bought at Formica. Pushkin and Gorky lay asleep on either side of her. The phone was on her chest. Her gaze was on the painting on the wall beside her, the painting of a woman with a jug. The famous signature. I could see her hand moving across the bedsheet as if searching for a pen or a pad or a book, but it kept searching and searching and found nothing and returned to the phone in its cradle, holding it close to her. I looked on her jagged profile and understood she was not seeing the painting at all. She looked lost. Lost in all dimensions.

I knocked on the door, and she turned to me. "That was Maria," she said. "Our friend is with us no more."

The storm came to possess the entire countryside that night and the following day; it felt as if our part of Tuscany had caught a violent cold, wheezing and shivering in its bedclothes. Oscar. The Baronessa did not come down the next morning, and so I searched for some activity to lift me from the grief that weighed me down. I helped Vinsanda bring wood in from the shed, where it lay under a blue tarp, and watched as he built one of his amazing fires in the dining room, ready to be lit. Nimali and I put away the glasses from the dishwasher. I laid the table for lunch and adjusted the blue-speckled candelabra, also unlit. Oscar. I wished we could have been there for him, as the Baronessa had planned. And of course she had not only wanted to be there so he would not be alone; she had wanted to race to his side so that, in this awful final moment of her friend's life, *she* would not be alone.

You never know the last moments you will have with someone. My mind went back over the previous days and months, seeking to find some meaning in them, but of course there was no meaning. He and I had last talked of love—or no, that was wrong. That was what I wanted to be true. The last time I saw him was at the dinner table, showing us the bottoms of his shoes, and the last words I'd heard of his were how angry we all would be at him for having a little gin!

The story of Villa Coco; I understood I had it all wrong. I thought it was of a young man coming to Italy and having a fling that, during an olive harvest, turned into something more until suddenly he was offered a life in Milan. I thought *I* was the story. As we do when we are young.

But here was the actual story: A wonderful man was dying. Only his best friend knew about it, and she brought him constantly out of his home and made him laugh with the same "high spirits" they had in their youth, all to brighten his final days, which she had expected to last just a little bit longer. I was not the protagonist at all; I was merely a hired player. My job: to be utterly charmed by him. To love him. I had been charmed and I had loved him. A man with silver hair and a bald spot and a smile and bountiful stories and education and advice for a young American. I was persuaded to take him out to view a Masaccio and eat fish stew and warm himself by the fire of our young romance. And now that the story had come to an unexpected end, I had no lines written to express what I had lost.

All those years denying every pleasure for the sake of his heart. And it was la leucemia that got him. I thought of the special salad bowl the Baronessa had found at La Formica, in the shape of a great cabbage, kept in the cabinet just for his arrival; it was brought out with great ceremony and placed before him while we all enjoyed our pastas and cheeses and roasts; he was always a good sport about it. I thought of his renouncement of love and of pleasure in all its forms, how the excesses of his youth—sleeping with shepherds in the countryside!—had been locked away, like sharp objects, and how he had made himself into a "very cheerful, very harmless old man." When none of that would kill him. It is possible he could have slept with shepherds and dined on roast lamb until the day before, and it would all have come to the same thing.

But the Baronessa, to my surprise, was of a different opinion when she came, at last, down the staircase in a gray woolen cardigan over a pale blue dress and began discussing her friend. "It was the gin," she said firmly, taking a pug in her arms. "He should not have had all that gin at the end. I told him it was bad. But he insisted. He said after all these years he wanted to enjoy something."

I said, "You if anybody can understand that. Somebody at the end of his life—"

She stared ahead of her at the storm-darkened window. "He could have stayed longer. We had such plans!"

"Maybe he just wanted a little pleasure—"

"How dare he?!"

Her fist had slammed onto the prayer desk and caused a pen to tip onto the floor, where it rolled into the corner. I thought of a little girl, in a wintry castle, being told her playmate had gone back to London and would never return. The selfishness, the utter hopelessness of her grief broke through the mask of age as blotches of pink appeared on her cheeks, her neck and ears, as if that little girl had been there all along, trapped beneath the thin fresco of an elderly baronessa. I took her hand and she accepted it. She did not cry. It was rage, fury I saw there.

"There was no one else," she spat out, "who could talk about roses!"

I nodded, as if this were the only reasonable explanation for her grief. Death tears down the veils. Of custom, of decorum, of emotions; it lays everything bare for us to see at last. Hidden in that basement made for treasures never on display. It is released from a great broken urn. And those are the tears we shed. Sorrow, yes, but not just sorrow. She was trying to explain that she'd loved him.

Of course we made no trip, but the Baronessa told Nimali not to unpack the bags; there would be a memorial. The next day, the sky's fever broke; the rain calmed, the temperature evened out, and the road became passable again. Immediately Estelle was with us, knocking at the kitchen door in her olive-colored rain poncho and running up to see the woman who had once been her rival. I heard them talking for a long time behind the closed door of the Baronessa's bedroom, and I left them alone as I did other tasks. Finally I went to the door and heard Estelle speaking in Italian:

"We can't just do it two women alone."

The Baronessa: "It was for Oscar. He was the whole point. Now I just don't know."

"Giacomo?"

A sigh. "There is a child on the way."

"It may be time to . . . rethink everything."

Silence. I thought I could hear the pugs snoring. Then the Baronessa said, "What about the American?"

"Who?"

Before they could say the name, I knocked and entered.

Estelle was sitting on the bed, her poncho thrown to the floor, where Cesare lay upon it. Both women looked up at me with pain in their faces. It was clear they had gone through a terrible discussion and did not care to return there soon. But that expression was soon replaced by one of startled curiosity. Like astronauts on a moon who may have discovered signs of life.

The Baronessa said simply: "The memorial is Saturday in Genova."

I asked, as her assistant, if she wanted to make plans to stay the night.

"Eh?"

"Do you want to stay the night?"

She turned, and her face had transformed. "What a brilliant idea! No, no we must not stay the night. We will tell them we are headed to a hotel in Torino. But we will *not* head to Torino. Because here is what we are going to do," she said, gripping the bedsheets as she leaned toward me. "We are going to steal the urn."

I asked what urn. Did she mean to pinch some valuable artifact of his?

"I mean the ashes."

I gulped. "WHAT ashes?" Surely she could not mean—

"Oscar's!" she said. "Where else would he go but here? This was his favorite place in the world."

"But that can't be—"

"Yes, we'll tell them Torino. It will buy us some time. In case," she added with verve, "they give chase!" And I understood that the only way she could handle her rage and grief was to create one final caper.

The memorial was to be held at Oscar's apartment—which, the Baronessa told me, now belonged to Maria, along with all of his worldly possessions ("As it should be, except of course for Oscar himself"), and though it was only three days, my employer found the wait intolerable. This impatience was set off by either boredom or its sister: dread. For isn't boredom merely another kind of dread—being trapped in time instead of in a place or a weakening body? I was still learning her ways, but it should not have surprised me to see this impatience awakened, like a recurrence of malaria after years of dormancy, by the death of her dear friend.

At last the morning of our trip arrived; because it was, to my mind, a funeral, I wore one of Tonino's black suits, and so I was surprised, as I pulled the car to the entrance, to find the Baronessa in a scarlet wool suit. Over her shoulders was draped a camel-colored coat. Estelle helped her into the car, and the Baronessa greeted me with the brief grin that was her signature, quickly replaced by a look of determination.

She bid goodbye to Estelle and to her dogs. She tapped her cane against the steering wheel as one might tap a horse into motion. I started us up the dusty path between the raked olive trees.

"I would have liked to wear my grandmother's pearls," said the Baronessa beside me. "They are said to once have belonged to Marie-Thérèse, and perhaps Marie Antoinette. People say many things about pearls. But as you know, they are missing."

"You look lovely," I said.

"You look very comme il faut" was her reply.

"Not in a good way," I said. "Vabon."

"You look like you're going to a funeral."

"Signora," I said, and of course all of this was in Italian, as we were in the car, "we *go* to a funeral."

She corrected me: "We are going to a luncheon. Oscar organized it long, long ago. The guest list, the music, the food. You recall he was always particular about what he ate." It seemed to me a person would not be so particular when that person was in an urn. I thought of the sfogliatelle he had warned me of in Naples, how I had yet to try them and how, if I did, he would never know the path my life would take. She was still talking: "I think it is very generous of Oscar to plan things. After all, who else is going to do it? Turn right at the signora." We had reached the old woman, shouting from her chair, like a witch in a fairy tale.

Then the Baronessa asked me if I had ever stolen anything before.

"What? No. Nothing."

"You do not know if you have the talent until you try. This may be your opportunity." I struggled with how to express my concerns in Italian, but she took my pause as me digesting her words. "We may have to rely upon my expertise. But this is a gamble. I am no longer seventy!"

"Vabon," I said. "Your expertise in Istanbul?"

She turned to me and said, "Your Italian is improving, Giovedì, as your driving is not. But I am glad you are not learning Italian anymore from my cousin. He is from the Veneto, and the men there have a particular way of talking. Very high and musical like a songbird." She did a fluty imitation of her cousin: "Vabon! Vabon!"

She could hear Giacomo's voice echoing in my own? I began to check myself, as a hypochondriac does when hearing of a new disease. I told my employer that she found fault with all of my teachers. How was I expected to learn? "Simple," she said. "As you will learn to steal. From me."

The drive was only three hours or so, passing Florence and the charming walled town of Lucca and, as the Baronessa pointed out, the famous marble quarries of Carrara, cut like rice paddies into the mountainside. "The Certosa di Pavia is all of Carrara marble," she told me. "They did a circumnavigazione of Italy to bring it! Today you could drive there in an hour." I had no idea what a certosa might be, but I did know Pavia, and the idea of circumnavigating the country appealed to me. The drive also skirts Pisa, which my passenger found delightful; Florentines have an innate aversion to Pisa. I am told it comes from a medieval siege the Pisans waged against Florence, and it is said this time of privation is why the local bread has no salt. This is of course absurd; that was centuries ago. They have had plenty of time to change the recipe. But the animosity evidently continues and is, in fact, mutual. "A friend of mine was once in a car accident near Pisa," my employer told me. "The Pisa driver was clearly in the wrong, and the carabinieri agreed and told the man to pay a fine. He pointed to my friend's Florentine license plate and declared, 'But this bastard is not even supposed to *be* here!' "

I must not have laughed as I was meant to, because she turned to me and said:

"You seem distracted, Giovedì. Perhaps it is Oscar on your mind?"

I told her it was not, in fact, just Oscar. I was in a state of confusion, but she would not let this rest, either, and kept prodding me. I don't know why—I assume she was anxious about our trip, terrified by how Oscar's death left her in the roiling sea of old age all alone, and so clung to the closest railing at hand: myself.

I said, "Giacomo invited me to go to Milan at Christmas. When I leave here. Go live with him in the house there."

"And his new baby?"

I said, "We would have a separate flat, but yes. Yes, with his new baby."

She looked over at me. "An unconventional arrangement."

I smiled. "I thought it was rather in your style."

"HO HO HO! You think me like our Venetian courtesan!"

I told her I thought of her in no such way and said the decision was causing me great turmoil. "I don't know what I'm going to do," I said. I glanced over to see her reaction. I imagined I might have summoned up memories of her own struggles, of which I was sure there were many. She took a long time before responding, and when she did it was not in the tone I was used to.

"Well," she said, looking out the window. "We all have our problems."

I say the drive is only three hours, but not if you have a certain passenger aboard. We were making good time, and I could see the sea gleaming between the hillsides on the left, when the Baronessa intimated that she would love to visit a local toilet. "I am reminded of my time in Manaus, you recall." I replied as best I could that I felt similarly; the morning coffee I'd needed to brace myself for Nimali's Italian was working its way through me. My employer turned to me and said, "I may be able to offer us some relief at the next exit. You know, I was thinking about the Tetrarch's toe." I could not follow the path her mind was taking. She clarified: "From the four Tetrarchs of Rome."

"Oh yes!" I said. "The statue."

"Technically it is a sculpture group. Carved in AD 300 for Diocletian. It was in Constantinople for almost a thousand years! Imagine that! And then the Venetians went and sacked the city and brought it back as plunder. They placed it on a corner of the basilica of San Marco, right there in the piazza. Only they left little bits behind. You know they found a heel in Istanbul in 1960? Well, I went not long after, and there it was on the ground, where I suppose it had lain for centuries. The toe. Only Oscar was a witness. So I popped it in my purse. And it has been in my house ever since. The treasure you didn't guess!"

I said something about how I was shocked, though of course I was not at all shocked; I had learned enough at Villa Coco to find one must measure a theft before judging it. Still, to me, to steal a priceless artifact seemed like going too far.

Irritation clouded her face. "You disapprove?"

"It's like stealing something from the Louvre."

"What makes you think I haven't stolen something from the Louvre?" she replied sharply, and I did not know how to respond. Had she? "No, of course I haven't. That's sticky business. This was like taking a pebble from the beach. We went there on a particularly memorable occasion, and I wanted to mark it. Which I have."

I suggested she should make it a gift to the city of Venice.

"They stole the whole group themselves!" she countered. "From the Byzantines! Like your empress Theodora. To whom should I return it? Nimali?"

"That doesn't make—"

"And yet," she said in a mysterious tone, "you've made me think. I cannot keep it at the villa. Don't put it on your list."

I took this as a sign of my own influence: "I won't. I'm glad you'll consider it."

She seemed suddenly serious. "It depends upon a great decision." She rapped me with her cane. "Turn here! Here!"

A few harrowing turns later and we were in the bustling downtown of a fairly modern, unprepossessing seaside town. What joy to exit the car and be relieved of the Italian language, like a tie you can remove at the end of the evening (my tie was still in place). But it turned out she had not made me exit for a toilet; it was for the focaccia.

"It is here," she told me, taking my arm to struggle across the uneven pavement. The street ran along a dry canal, covered in weeds, and the buildings on the other side were the typical five-story palazzi of most small towns. I noticed that these, instead of having actual stone cornices decorating the windows, had theirs painted on. One building had a side whose windows were entirely painted on. It was a remarkable effect. But we were not there to admire the local art of false window painting; we were there to enter under the rather grubby green awning of a focacceria. Inside, the Baronessa flashed that smile of hers and asked to use the bathroom. I was left standing before a glass counter displaying what looked like a single cheese pizza. Behind the register stood a woman with an auburn wig rather like a faina. Behind her was a wood oven, and all around her a dusty chaos of liquor bottles and framed photographs too small to make out. I thought the bathroom might not be up to the Baronessa's standards. But then I thought of Manaus . . .

Soon it was my turn, and by the time I returned, the Baronessa had in her hand two paper plates nearly transparent with grease. "It is focaccia. Filled with cheese." She handed me one.

"But," I insisted quietly, "but we're about to have a *luncheon*."

"And so?"

"A memorial *luncheon*. That Oscar *planned*."

Her watery eyes had the exasperation of someone forced to explain to Americans not to use a spoon with their spaghetti: "Giovedì, we are here in Liguria, we are here in Recco. The focaccia is in our hands, we want it." Her chin shivered with irritation. "And we won't be back."

I was facing, once again, her fury. But I understood it was not about Liguria, or Recco, or the focaccia in our hands. Of course she's right, I thought as Oscar's smile came to mind. All that is for certain is we won't be back. Not at this place, this moment. Not ever.

We arrived at the luncheon slightly in ritardo, due to our focaccia detour, but this meant we could slip into the party unseen, as the cat burglars we were. Instead of the black-clad Anglo crowd of mourning I had expected (and for which I had dressed), I found a brightly colored and chattering flock, drinking prosecco and taking food from trays passed around (cries of "Buono!"). Of course, I knew nothing of what to expect; I had attended only the funerals of my grandparents, dreary New England affairs with just neighbors and the postman in the pews, followed by a diner lunch of coffee and Denver omelets; I did not know how loved ones would celebrate a life, especially the life of someone who shone so brilliantly, who made of friendship an art. But I was also utterly unprepared for how to dress for this scene which I was entering, for here it was at last, the world that had terrified Giacomo into marriage and bored the Baronessa into fleeing to Capri, here it was before me: the aristocracy.

There were elderly white-haired ladies in woolen suits and pearls, holding glasses of white wine as they chatted; more bohemian types together on the sofa, their hair dyed the same deep black as their Pomeranians, wearing large costume jewelry and pleated Japanese fabrics; and others by the window with shoulder-length blond hair and long coats or capes in deep green (who I later came to know as the "sciuras" or signoras of Milan). One woman, her bouffant gloriously blond in contrast to her deeply tanned and furrowed face, wore a long white tunic trimmed in gold, as if she were Athena herself come to visit a favored mortal. I half expected to see Princess Pippa in the crowd, with her pajama robes and artificial flower, looking around as anxiously as her beloved monkey back in Zanzibar, but perhaps she was too eccentric a character to be seen at such a gathering. I saw perhaps half as many men as women, all in tailored suits of windowpane check with open collars, almost identically bronzed from recent vacations, all of them clean-shaven but just two or three with full heads of silver or white hair, grown in wild locks as if to taunt their bald companions. I tried to imagine the Baronessa among them in her younger days, but while she seemed to be from them, she was no longer of them. A world left behind when she ran to Capri.

And we were there to steal from under their aristocratic noses.

I had always imagined Oscar as living in a great windowed room, bare except for his canvases; perhaps I got the idea from a production of *La Bohème*. But his actual living quarters could not have been more different. They were five or six rooms, all white with white furniture, but with elaborately designed ceilings, laid out in hexagons and rectangles, each painted with a monk or saint or figure surely every Italian recognized, though I could not. Some held sheaves of wheat. Others led donkeys. But it dazzled the eye, as did the crowd gathered in the foyer, whose center was filled by a set of free-standing bookcases arranged in a cross. There was a table set into the bookcase, and on it were an open book that I assumed was for visitors to write their names, a small lamp of translucent glass, and a red metal urn. My eye settled on the urn meaningfully, and I turned to my companion . . . but found she had vanished. A woman in a maid's uniform appeared with a prosecco, which I took gratefully, then offered a tray of focaccia. Which I declined. I looked back at the urn. I noticed this time that hanging on the bookshelf above it was a handwritten sign reading CERCHI DI DORMIRE. I assumed this to be the Italian version of rest in peace. Or, perhaps, a wish for a troubled soul to rest at last.

I began a hunt for my employer, who with her scarlet suit could not easily hide herself, and found only her camel coat draped across a side chair. An American man stood alone in the corridor, staring at the artwork. He was enormously tall, somewhere handsomely in his seventies, and I knew he was American by the business suit he wore: crisp and dull. Beneath it, the white shirt and yellow tie typical of the American man abroad. I understood, because before Formica I had dressed the same way. Then his eyes caught mine; something in them flashed. I don't know why, but I turned and fled into another room.

Oscar's bedroom, it seemed. And I was alone. Framed charcoal drawings lined the walls below a plasterwork ceiling, all in white this time, and in the middle of the room stood a small brass bed with a coverlet of abstract orange suns or flowers, I couldn't tell. A lamp was on beside the bed. It was the cell of a monk. A wooden valet stand held a single tie and, below it, a pair of red velvet slippers. They were the precise ones Oscar had promised me from Venice but never had the opportunity to deliver. Maybe it was the influence of so many weeks at Villa Coco, but I felt an urge within myself to nab them. I took a step closer, reached out my hand—

"Ah am so glad to see you and Lisabetta made it."

I turned and it was the Baronessa's old nonfriend, the prince's paramour. Pullman . . . no, Furman Childress, the man who had appeared in my first weeks, wearing a fedora like a meringue. All in black today, like myself, but with a purple scarf around his neck. His bald head was glazed with lamplight like a morning bun. Or perhaps like the diamond my employer said he got out of her friend. That single blond lock on his forehead was its flaw. "Mr. Childress!" I said in surprise.

He bowed and purred in his Southern accent, "Oscar will be greatly missed."

I said, "I heard you knew him from Capri."

He giggled and adjusted his glasses, looking around the room. "Oh yes. Lisabetta introduced us. Long, long ago. Ah later bought some works from him."

"I've never seen his paintings."

"His? Oscar?" He stared at me and his smooth face puckered in surprise. "Ah think you're mistaken, darlin'. He wasn't an artist. He was an art dealer. He specialized in French and

Spanish Cubists. Mostly he dealt through Lisabetta; she had all the connections. They were quite a team. But Ah always preferred Oscar, if Ah can be candid. Our . . . baronessa was always a bit . . . nasty."

She was many things, but I never thought of her as "nasty." Either time had diluted that aspect of her, or else she never had any need to use it on me. Or else: I had never caught on. "You were with them both on Capri?"

"Oh yes." He got that dreamy look that older people get, looking back on the past. I tried to picture him at twenty, seducing a jewel out of someone, and the Baronessa staring daggers at him across a sun-drenched terrace. "You know Ah met Lisabetta, oh, maybe fifty years ago. She was a looker at forty. But you know what she was most known for?"

I braced myself. "What's that?"

He put a hand to his scarf. "She was a thief."

My heart jumped its rails. I thought only of the present tense; I wondered if he was talking about the toe or the ashes. But he was speaking of something else entirely.

He leaned against the doorway with his hand still on his scarf. "That's how she started, you know." I thought I saw a ripple of rage cross his placid face. "Charming lady at all the parties, always in red. You would never guess. She stole from my friend the prince. Mariano. She stole a diamond and told everybody it was me." Then he smiled. "Isn't that interesting?"

Strange, how I had become such a part of Villa Coco that I felt immediately defensive of my employer. His snarling portrayal of her held no charm for me, and he seemed hardly an innocent himself. Yet wasn't the story of accusing him precisely the story she had told to me? He must have been very young when all this happened, and it was possible an older adversary might have bested him with this prince, this Mariano. It seemed unthinkable to hold grudges for fifty years, but perhaps when it comes to diamonds there is no statute of limitations. For either party. "I haven't heard that story" was all I said.

He fairly shimmered with pleasure at retelling it: "She turned the diamond into a boat and the boat into that house of hers in Tuscany, where you are, Ah understand, busily tallyin' up everythin' inside." He released the scarf and unbuttoned his jacket to put his hand in his trouser pocket. He was every bit the foreigner who had tried to make himself into an Italian. He seemed to see some kinship in me, saying, "Ah'm glad she found an American. She turned her old career into the more proper one of an art dealer."

Our friend Pullman tells many stories about me, she had said. *Only some of them are true.*

"And do you know what else Lisabetta bought?" Furman went on. "She bought the very thing you call her. Her title. She's no more a baronessa than Ah." He noticed my expression. "Oh, did Ah disappoint you?"

I found myself sifting through his words, trying to sense what could be a lie and what could be the truth, weighing them against the words of my employer, that great exaggerator. It fit too neatly: that she was a thief. Hadn't she and Oscar joked about being caught? About admiring someone who stole? Weren't we on a caper this very moment? And what was that credo of hers, that if you like it and you want it, take it, since we won't be back? Was it not the very philosophy of a buccaneer?

I managed my confusion with a smile. I said he did not disappoint me at all. I was leaving her service very soon, in fact.

"Her service?" he asked, seeming confused. "You mean the catalog you are makin'."

"Of course."

He smiled, not at me but at a painting beside me. "Villa Coco is a very beautiful place. Full of beautiful things. What a wonderful thought, to live there." Then his attention came back to the young American in the room and he nodded to me formally. "Ah'll slip away now, if you don't mind; Ah don't enjoy these crowds. Work well." He tipped an invisible hat. "And give my best to Lisabetta."

I found my little pirate queen in the hallway, with her purse and her cane, looking at a painting of a brown and muscular bearded man, almost entirely naked, with his ear being pulled mischievously by a pale and equally naked woman. It seemed like something from a museum. Was it possible I had seen it before? She saw me and gestured for me to come quickly. "Koo-koo!" I began telling her I had been chatting with her old friend Furman but did not quite know how to phrase it, or how to put to her the many questions he had raised in my mind; anyway, she was already in her own discorso: "I have been unable to do the wicked thing," she whispered. "I have not found the moment. And I admit I have been overcome, being here without him. Look at this, do you see the Tyrian purple he went to jail for?" I looked again at the painting, at the expression of anguish on the face of the muscled man. Hercules. The painting for which he had risked prison (in his telling, he was set free). She changed topics: "To have all these awful people is sadder than . . . Oh! Buona!" She had turned and plucked a piece of food from a passing tray, and her expression went quite gold with grief. "La cima! You'll never get it anywhere else. I wonder if they have the baccalà?"

"What were you and Oscar up to on Capri?"

"What a strange question."

"I wonder if it was something more than art."

She said nothing. I looked from her stern gaze to the painting and back again, and I think it was at that moment that I understood.

She gazed out at the crowd. "I don't know anybody anymore."

I followed her cue; her silence had satisfied my curiosity. "I never thought Oscar had so many friends."

She brushed this away with a gesture. "Friends! They are his clients. I thought there would be some of mine. But all of them strangers . . ."

I was surprised to feel her leaning heavily against my arm. I saw that the day was not a mere frolic after all; of course it wasn't. "While in my seventies I could pinch anything I liked, now with the cane and the vertigo, I'm finding I'm not the cambrioleuse I once was. We need an unsentimental party—" I understood her immediately.

"I will not—"

"You give up too quickly," she snapped, clearly annoyed. "Remember, Oscar was a thief, and an honest one."

"But—"

But I was interrupted. The music suddenly ceased and a man began clapping in the main room, calling us all to gather there. The Baronessa headed over with the others, leaving me beside the painting; I could see a little of the scene from where I stood in the hall. People had made a space where stood a small, thin man, his head a bald globe except for continents of gray hair on either side, and he wore a set of wire reading glasses I suppose a globe also might wear. He seemed to have a letter Oscar had left with his maid to be read aloud at this event. Oscar had planned everything.

The crowd left me no room to enter, and I could hardly hear anything. Only a few snippets came through:

"I gave my heart to the wrong . . ."

". . . the last years of my . . ."

But I could make out little more. I bided my time by wandering into the foyer, looking over the various books and considering the task at hand. I thought of Oscar and my employer and their life together in Capri, a pair of thieves, according to Pullman. The thrill of the grift. Something that I, as a good American boy, had never felt. But perhaps there are no limits to what a person might become if he were corrupted by a figure such as the Baronessa, whom it seemed I did not know at all. What might I become? I was never moral, only organized. I gazed on Oscar's urn and thought of what to do. The man went on for some time reading Oscar's letter, and again a few phrases floated over the crowd:

"I did not know . . . in store for me . . ."

". . . not ever get those years back . . ."

And once I had done what was necessary, I wandered back to the hallway, carrying my employer's bag and coat, and saw that the reading had finished. Nearby, I heard the sound of weeping, and to my astonishment saw it came from the enormously tall American, his face now in his hands as he sobbed inconsolably. The Baronessa appeared, looking wide-eyed. "This is a very surprising thing our friend has written—"

"We have to go!" I whispered, taking her arm.

"Now you are impatient? There is still—"

"We have to *go*!"

"But Oscar—"

"Oscar," I said, looking her clearly in the eye, "*is with us.*"

I regarded her frail little figure in the hall and saw something curious in her expression, something akin to that of our very first meeting on the staircase, when she regarded me as through a lorgnette across an opera box, only this time it was with distinct recognition—as if she had at last perceived on me (a rogue pretender) the port wine stain that proved my claim. A smile broke across her lined face. "Sacré bleu! How did you do it?"

"I thought of you and the toe!" I said. I lifted her purse with both hands, and it was visibly heavy with our dear friend's ashes. "I just popped it in!"

She clapped her hands in glee.

Later it would be said of the luncheon that everybody enjoyed it but the host. I take their word for it; we missed the end of the event, forwent the traditional endless arrivederci (I have always said Italians would be trapped in a burning building because of the length of their farewells) and vanished down the stone staircase of the building. Soon we were in a small piazza in the shadow of great green-shuttered buildings, decorated with graffiti and one single sundial, which must have been in sunlight when someone placed it there long ago but now sat in the perpetual shadow of its neighbors. It seemed a fitting metaphor somehow. The Baronessa was all abuzz from my criminal activity and, even with her vertigo, had no problem navigating the narrow streets, crowded with scaffolding and public works, with great rapidity. I barely listened to her excited words, and it was only when we were in the car that I could relax.

"I feel very jolly!" she informed me. "Our friend is coming home."

"I'm worried someone will mind."

"No time for second thoughts. I told Maria we are driving to Torino. You see how I can stick to a plan. By the time the lawyer finds us, Oscar will already be in bed, and nobody is going to do anything then."

"The lawyer. What was the letter he read?"

"Ah! You missed a wonderful scene! Oscar revealed he had only truly given his heart one time, but to the wrong person."

"Who was that?"

"You must have seen the tall man crying, just when you found me."

I said indeed I had.

"This was the American he lived with in London. He had come all this way and Oscar had one arrow left in his quiver for him! Oh, you should have seen it. It was marvelous."

"Did the letter say he had been lazy in love?"

She pulled her coat closer around her. "Lazy in love? Those years in London were terrible for him. They often are when each person wants something different. It was Oscar who suffered."

"That's awful. But the American must have known Oscar was unhappy."

"Sad that it makes no difference. Nous sommes de mauvais tailleurs." She smiled and looked out the window, perhaps still in the glow of brigandage.

The news of Oscar's words shocked me a little. He had said he was a harmless old man, well liked. That was how he always described himself; it is how I have described him in these pages. But there was more to him. Another lesson, if the young would have the heart to listen. *I did not think another life was possible*, he had told me. *But it is always possible*. Lazy in love—that was Oscar himself, years ago, in giving his heart to the American, in giving the years he had not known would be his last for romance before he decided to forswear it all. He had not known what time would bring. *You take what comes*, he had said to me. How I wished he were there to tell me what one should take instead.

She turned to me now and said, "I was too short with you

before when you talked of your story. I can sometimes be impatient. And I have had my mind on Oscar all day."

I mumbled some kind of thanks; I was too surprised by such a thing as an apology coming from her lips.

We moved along the sea again, in and out of tunnels through the rock, and passed the signs for Recco and its glorious focaccia. She was right, of course; we would not be back. The sun hid behind the furniture of the sky and made the afternoon dimmer than our outward journey had been; even the white marble grandeur of Carrara seemed like loaves of unsalted Tuscan bread. We moved inland, between what must have been tree farms: ornamental plants arranged by species, growing in unnatural rows along the highway. We were nearing Lucca.

"You know, I have had many 'stories' in my life." I could hear she was choosing her words carefully despite her blithe delivery. "Some of the short ones meant more than the long ones. And of course we have all been with a married man." She cleared her throat; I was listening carefully now and glanced over to her. She looked directly at the road ahead. "With a married man. You know what you are in for. You know that he is with the other person because of a promise. About finances and inheritance and a house and friends, and he will keep that promise. But he is in love with *you*." She gestured around her. "So you get all the wonderful parts. The time in bed, the adventures and dinners, the wonder and love, they are all ahead of you! What more could you want from someone? But you must be funny, and be clear, and say you don't want him to leave his marriage. You just want to be with him. It is enough." I saw her glance over at me briefly, perhaps to see how I was hearing this. "Decide. Enough, or not enough. The decision is yours and you cannot say later that you expected more. If not enough, then you must let him go."

We came upon the Arno, flooded beneath the gray sky, the tops of trees poking out of it, an autumnal sight. Dark in the distance were mountains, looking like the fur racks of Formica. Ahead were the first signs for Pontassieve, Forlì, our little town, and as we rode up from the floodplain the sun flashed the last of its rays.

"Make a wish just before the sun sets," she said, and sat quietly beside me as the light faded. She glanced at me, then added: "I have made a very modest one."

Mine was considerably less so.

She went on: "I wonder if my wish will come true. Oscar cannot travel with me. That is a great loss."

"Yes?"

She patted her handbag, where her friend resided. "We made great plans, great plans. And now he will not see them come to fruition."

"Was Oscar an art forger?"

She did not answer me but followed some private will-o'-the-wisp: "We were going to Venice, and from there . . ."

"Lisabetta, he was, wasn't he?"

She brought herself up straight in her seat, in a show of her irritation. She opened her mouth, then closed it. I wondered what was going on in her mind. Then, at last, with a little shake of her chin, she said: "He was a gentleman."

Before I could delve further, we hit a pothole and I switched into a lower gear on the worn Tuscan road. It was a moment later that the sun appeared again.

"Look!" she cried out. "He's back! Have you ever seen the sun do that?"

I explained it was because we were gaining altitude. Yet I was surprised; there it was, a fiery wedge between two peaks. It seemed impossible I had never seen this before, but more impossible still for a woman four times my age.

"Ci rivediamo! And now he's setting again!" She laughed. "It's an actor coming out for a second bow!"

"Wow!" I said in my Americanese. "What's happening?!"

We watched as, a second time, "he" quivered on the horizon, a blazing, molten droplet, before the road descended and the light vanished once again behind the range's black scenery.

But . . .

"Look!" she cried again moments later, when we rose up another incline and the sun sat there, waiting for us, ardent, fiercely shining, above the mountain. "He is a bit of a 'ham,' as you say," she said, and grabbed my arm, laughing and laughing. We rode along quietly until the sun, one final time, spread its arms and nodded and went offstage, and the twilit countryside sat still and expectant, waiting impatiently for an encore and yet eager to be home.

She took my hand on the gearshift and squeezed it. I had not thought a woman as indomitable as the Baronessa would ever have need of someone as trivial as I.

Or I of someone as capricious as she.

"I will always say, Giovedì, this is the day I saw three sunsets." She added: "And the day you learned to steal."

Perhaps that was the day she ceased being, for me, the Baronessa. What did it matter if her title were "real"? What would it even mean? From then on I simply thought of her as "my baronessa."

The next morning, I went over the catalog of Villa Coco. It was nearly complete; I had gone through the entire upstairs and had only the captain's cabin to finish. Looking over what I had done, what a strange list it seemed: hundreds of items of cutlery found (so she said) over the years at Formica, along with plates and platters and a pewter tea set engraved with the name Leona that caused my baronessa to cackle whenever she saw it; serving spoons in wood and silver, corkscrews in brass and steel, antique coffee dispensers, cups, glasses, trays; stools, chairs, tables; pillows with designs of birds or pugs or medieval creatures or Arabic words (I never asked the meaning); bowls and urns and amphorae; mirrors with frames painted blue and white and others made of wrought iron or of tin stamped with designs of nettles and flowers; figurines of angels and marching soldiers and stiff pilgrim-looking men and every description of animal, some of them impossible; a metal ball divided in two for holding ice on one side and ice cream on the other (for picnics); a chair and coatrack made of deer antlers; and the art: marble sculptures of abstracted figures that joined together and glazed pottery of a woman's breast, dioramas of some kind of dream or haunted house with wire birds flying overhead, and paintings by the dozen, few of whose creators I recognized besides, of course, the Picasso. A life in objects—a life of junk, she would have said. And the final object on the list: *Sculpture of boat, in bronze: CAPRICE.*

"Koo-koo!" came the familiar cry from down the hall. "Lunch is pronto! We are having the truffle!"

"With eggs?" I shouted, walking out to find her. I knew she claimed it might be her last.

She stood there in a turquoise kimono, one finger raised into the air. "NOT with eggs!" she said.

"With anchovies?"

She nodded.

"A jump into the abyss!" I said, laughing.

She shrugged. "I am ashamed to have shown fear of an anchovy." Then turned away and went down the stairs with her pugs.

We had entered December and I had not made a decision about Giacomo and Milan. I asked him not to call me and certainly not to visit; my mind was confused by Oscar's death, by the few words I'd overheard from his letter, by the words my employer had spoken, by all that had happened at Villa Coco, and of course by my own uncertainty about my future. Without Giacomo around, I discovered, time expanded greatly, so that my personal hours seemed to double, a fact my employer noticed, as she subsequently doubled her expectations of me, just as I was going over the final catalog. Grocery duty and postage duty and oddball tasks around the house. I managed to buy some private time when she said my hair needed cutting and gave me leave to visit her salon in the village. I accepted the time off but not the venue; instead, I took Estelle up on her offer to give me a trim.

But it came with a price.

"I want you to pose for me," she said when I asked her assistance one day in the upstairs hall. I asked what she meant. "For a painting, stupid American. And," she added, "you will be nude."

It is pleasant to look back on one's younger self and the joy one took in one's body; when I reached her house the next day, I happily shucked off my clothes and lay on the white linen pillows of her couch. She instructed me on how to position myself, and in the end I was a male Olympia, with even a black cat sleeping by my feet. All this confidence and ease, and yet my heart fell slightly when I saw Estelle bring out the canvas she meant to work with: about the size of a hardcover book. I would be captured in miniature.

"Um," I said, "is that the painting?"

"I can't make any more large work. I'm moving, you know."

"You decided?"

She nodded and told me to stop talking or at least lose

that foolish expression on my face. "I'm going to have to pack up the rest of my work. Or burn it. I was thinking of a great bonfire one night!"

"You can't do that! Why not store them with Coco?"

She shrugged and brought out her pencil to begin her sketch. I understood the subject was somehow closed. And yet, with my days so few, I wanted to sketch a little more myself. To get down in my mind what was soon to be out of view.

"Estelle, how did you come from Algeria?"

"I came with my mother," she said without looking up. "On a boat."

"What kind of boat?"

"Put your arm back where it was."

"I just want to understand you better."

"I don't remember the boat," she said. "I remember the water. How terrifying it was. I remember staying with two aunts in Rome who wore nothing but black. They were terrifying too. But beautiful! They would pour me tea and dote on me and dress me up." Estelle put down her pencil and brought out her paints; we were getting to the real work now. "I started to dress myself up. I got to know artists, and I posed for them and was in their world. I made some hard choices. Maybe when I was your age, yes."

I lay there trying to hold my pose while letting all her words run through my mind. I saw her lean forward to look more closely at me.

"I do not envy you your youth. I think it is a terrible time. But Visconti found me and brought me to Milan, which was a piece of luck. Better, though, Coco found me."

"Ah!"

"The best thing that ever happened to me was coming here."

"So why are you leaving?"

"I wonder what you will think of coming here? Later, when you're old?" A dab of her brush onto the palette and she held it out before her, then she lowered her chin. "Stay perfectly still. I'm about to commit you to eternity . . ."

Christmas was on the horizon and, with it, my impending departure. I had expected my baronessa to be readying Villa Coco for the holiday (it seemed an occasion for her favorite activity: decoration), but her response to my questions was that Natale would not be celebrated in the traditional way this year. A tree was apparently out of the question. I had noticed one in the village square, but to my baronessa this was an abomination. "A tree? I had enough of Germans in the war. No, I think the house is fire hazard enough." Nonetheless, I noticed she had Vinsanda cut pine boughs and place them in every room, a far more flammable arrangement, to my way of thinking.

St. Nicholas's Day—December the sixth—arrived. I came to talk with my baronessa before dinner. I had heard presents arrived on St. Nicholas's Day, but when I brought up the subject, she looked at me curiously. She wore an apricot sweater and matching scarf and sat on her white sofa, a pug on either side of her like guardian lions. "For small children," she answered, "not us." I asked about Santa Claus. "HO HO HO!" she laughed. "San Nicola was a Turkish bishop who never went north of Puglia. You may visit his tomb in Bari! But I don't think he's bringing any present for you. You must wait for La Befana." Who was this? Another look of surprise from her. "It is the old witch who brings presents on January the sixth!" Well, of course it was. Two weeks after my departure.

She had turned off the volume on the television when I

entered, but from the corner of my eye I could see the visual was still on (it was her detective show), and her gaze was now and then drawn to its watery movements. Outside, I heard Ghazel and Vinsanda wrestling with a metal ladder.

"This invitation from my cousin to Milan," she began, to my surprise. "It seems like a trip that can be delayed."

I stood above her, hands in pockets, trying to understand. From the yard came the disastrous sound of metal falling and then familiar voices shouting.

"Why would I delay it?"

She took a deep breath but still did not meet my eye. "Oscar was to come with me on this rather important trip to Venice. But he is no longer able."

"Are you asking me to go with you?"

"I don't see how it changes your plans," she said. "On the twenty-third. It's just overnight."

Yallah, I heard out the window, *Yallah!* I tried to forestall answering. "I have to think about it. I have a ticket home for Christmas. My mother said she knows of a job for me in Washington. A college friend invited me to London."

So here it was, the moment the man with the green scarab pin had foretold.

She looked up at me again; she seemed determined. "You can as easily go to Washington or London from Venice as from here."

"Maybe another time," I said. "I'm a bit . . . eh, ahem, overwhelmed, to be honest."

"You are picking up my cousin's habits again. A night in Venice will let you think. As it did for Hemingway."

"I have too much to do. I have to pack—"

"It is all the same," she said, "to pack for one place or another. And think of Oscar. We leave two weeks from Friday by train."

She'll come to you and say, I have an important trip.

"I cannot, I'm sorry."

"Eh?"

"I CAN'T!"

I saw her left hand shake slightly until she put it in her lap and covered it with the right. "I wonder what I will do." I walked to the doorway, unsure whether to leave her there. She seemed so uncertain. Ghazel shouted again outside, and without lifting her head, she said to me: "Gazelle has failed again with the faina. Vinsanto is helping him with a . . . a snare, I think you call it. As in an adventure movie. Poof!" She made a gesture of something flying upward into a tree. Then I heard her sigh. "Let us be honest. This faina will outlive us all."

About a week later, I found myself deep in her closet, searching for a missing shoe: a Chinese slipper in blue and gold. All around me hung the dresses and robes of her long life, and below, the tangled city of her shoes, some tied in pairs with ribbon but most heaped to the side in a mass. "I bought these shoes in New York City," I could hear her saying to Nimali from beyond the closet doors. "I was with Allen Ginsberg and he was very, very high." She was in "high spirits" herself that day, in her own words, and I had a sense she had achieved some secret goal; certainly she walked about in dreamy thought and giggled like a girl in love, and I felt it did not suit her. On she went with her story about Allen Ginsberg as my fingers felt the crinkle of paper; I pulled it to me and found pink tissue and, looped within it, a triple strand of pearls. The Marie Antoinette pearls! Of course the words came to me, from my doppelgänger at the café. I could sell them whole or in parts and secure a bit of my future. I had only to pop them in my pocket, like a Tetrarch's toe, and perhaps if what Furman told me was true, it would be a kind of karmic justice . . .

But do you know what? I could not do it.

I was never moral, only organized. And of course my baronessa herself had taught me how to steal, how to "just pop it in" my pocket. But if I had lived long enough at Villa Coco to absorb its lessons, it also strangely made theft impossible. Selling the pearls would be like selling the floor or furniture on which I depended. For she was going to talk me into staying. A year, another, until a dozen years would pass. I would become so much a part of this world that I would be no longer a separate person but a character in its story, as much as the mouse that ran across the counter. What would a mouse like me do with a triple strand of pearls? Nothing; it would live always in the kitchen walls, as I would live always in the room of animals. I would grow old like the man in the café; I would wear a purple scarf and a scarab pin. I would take up smoking. I would forget my homeland as had the flamingos of Comacchio. If I stayed, my life would become as obvious as one of the soap operas my baronessa watched late into the night . . .

I heard someone shouting from the other room.

I feared the worst and pulled myself from the closet to find Nimali standing over a startled Baronessa, who was sitting in a rocking chair. Nimali's hands were in the air as if about to cast a spell. "ENOUGH!" she was shouting. "ENOUGH! ENOUGH!" Then she stomped out of the room.

I asked what on earth had happened. My employer turned to me and said she had no idea. She had been in the middle of listing precisely what Nimali was to pack, and in what manner, and was telling an amusing story about Salazar in Portugal, who had once—

"No, no, what did you say to her?"

She paused and looked out the window. "I suggested she put on one of the maid's outfits I find at Formica."

"You know she hates those."

"Where did she learn that rude word? 'Enough'?"

I stood there and wondered if anyone had ever said it to her before. "From me."

And she began to laugh.

I held out my hand. "I've found your pearls."

"Thanks God!" She clapped her hands together. "You have betrayed me with Nimali! But this has put you in my list of favorite people. You will see me wear them in Venice."

Holding the pearls, I almost regretted my decision. *There may come a point when you want to leave*, Oscar had said. *But do not go. As a favor to me and to yourself. It will be worth whatever trouble you have to go through.* I wondered if he had seen this side of her many times. It seemed impossible someone could be so stubborn. "I told you, I'm not going—"

"We leave a week from Friday by train."

Estelle drove her Ape to the villa to show me my finished painting; it was too cold for me to walk to her, and the cars were once more in the shop. My baronessa was taking a rest in her bedroom, so we sat in her parlor with its ceiling-high shelves filled with books, every one of which I had cataloged. Estelle wore a knit wool dress in forest green that made her look somehow elven. From her bag she brought out the little canvas.

"Estelle, you made me better-looking than I am."

Smudges for feet, long noble legs, a generous depiction of my midsection, the torso twisted into triangles with my arms akimbo like the handles of an urn, and careful delineation of my face into angles, the kind of flattering depiction a patron might ask an artist to make of a lover, idealized. And yet, I realized, much more mature than my years. Not a college boy at all. The arm muscles and jaw and stern erotic gaze: a man.

She smiled. "It's how I see you."

"May I keep it?"

"I'll bring it to Venice. Maybe it will tempt you to come," she said, standing. "Otherwise, this is goodbye, Giovedì."

"You know my name was never Giovedì."

"It suits you, though."

"I don't know about Venice. But I do know I can't stay here. And I know," I said, looking carefully at her face, ". . . I know the painting in her bedroom is not a Picasso."

She stood motionless, the portrait in her hands.

I asked, "What were they up to?"

"He wasn't—"

"I assume he sold the real ones for her. Did she just want to keep up appearances?"

"You've misunderstood something," she said.

"I'm sure I have. It's probably none of my business."

For someone I had always thought of as cool and unworried, having passed the hard exams of youth and entered the tenure of middle age, Estelle looked at me with surprising emotion. She put her hand on my arm. I did not understand what was going on around me, and no more did I understand this woman. "Giovedì!" she said in a low voice. "Please don't give anything away. Just make the list as before. Please. For Oscar."

"The package we drove to Ferrara. It was the Picasso, wasn't it? Oscar was supposed to handle the sale and she had to do it without him."

Estelle swallowed heavily. "Don't worry, nothing terrible is going on."

"As I said, it's none of my—"

"It's nothing, it's silliness. You'll laugh." She grinned, and whatever worry I had seen in her face was gone. "And something else . . ."

I asked what that might be. I was wary of her, in this newly emotional form.

"Go to Venice with our friend. She has her reasons for wanting you there. Trust me. And so do I."

When one has resolved to leave a place, the days approach like a slow tide coming in to sweep one's boat out to sea, and it can be a torture for the impatient. The arrival of a new cover of snow helped divert my attention from the advancing foam. Improbably, I was put to work in the dormant vegetable garden with Ghazel, who explained, in his usual dreamlike Italian, about planting by the phases of the moon. But everything was dreamlike in the days before my planned departure, and I touched each corner of the property knowing I might never see it again.

One afternoon, I came across my baronessa and Pushkin and Gorky in the little grove of olives, the ones with roses trained throughout them, which of course were pruned and bare. The world was colorless, the sky scudding with oblong clouds like a slide of paramecia. When she heard me, she turned and said nothing. She was dressed in absurd English tweeds. Her hand with garden shears fell by her side; I recognized them, at last, as the ones I had seen on my first day, lying in a basket in the sun.

"I was thinking of a dear friend of ours," she said.

I felt a tenderness I tried to push away. "Oscar . . ."

"Oscar? No," she said, looking once more at the pruned roses, "I was thinking of our Cesare and the pen. Do you remember? When his face was all blue?" Of course I remembered; it was my very first morning, when so many details of the place imprinted themselves on me. "He ate the pen. Many dream, but he *acted*! And look—it did not kill him." She glanced back at me and raised the garden shears. "So why not eat a pen every now and then?"

I shrugged and laughed. I said, "You told me everything was new to him. Just like me. That he was afraid of everything."

She seemed affronted. "Cesare is afraid of nothing!"

I considered how different I was from the dog. "I've finished my cataloging," I said.

"Eh?"

I held out the collated set of papers: the "longhand ledger" she had requested. "I said I've finished my cataloging—"

"Oh! May I see it?" She seemed suddenly full of intensity and grabbed the papers from my hands. I saw her tongue emerge from between her lips as a sign of concentration (a habit she shared with Pushkin and Gorky), and, with a finger, she went over every item I had so painstakingly elucidated.

I told her to notice I had not put down the toe.

"I thank you." And then she came across an item described as *Braque, red and black*. "What is this?"

"You know," I said. "The one in the parlor beside the courtesan."

Her manner was firm. "That's not a Braque! It's a Gleizes."

I laughed. "The signature—"

"I suppose," she said, catching my eye, "I could be wrong."

"I believe Oscar," I said meaningfully, "would say it was a Braque."

She put her hand on my arm. "Look at that tree," she said in a quiet voice. The angle of afternoon sun was such that it filled a chestnut tree as a fountain is filled with water, its ice-coated branches tilting in the spill of light. But what amazed me more than this moment of beauty was the woman beside me. A woman who seemed, to me, jaded about so much of life—small talk, fashion, music on the radio—but who was not at all jaded about the light in this tree. She had seen this tree every day for forty years, had in all probability planted it, known it in spring and fall and winter, and here it stood before her: as fresh as that first day. She was moved by its beauty. I could see that. So little appeared to move her—she had developed either armor or immunity against all manner of insult, sentiment, or nostalgia—but she was defenseless before this simple being. Something that had nothing, after all, to do with her. Something she could not control, could not *make* beautiful. And yet was beautiful.

"We must take this list to a notaio," she said at last. "So it is official. Will you do that?"

"A notary?"

"There is a female notary in Rignano. She looks like a murderess." The way she said it, it sounded like a compliment. A notary would make me officially an accomplice to whatever chicanery she and Oscar had been up to, endangering my reputation with my very first position out of college. Something I might have cared about deeply three months before, arriving with Ghazel in the Mitsu-bitchy.

"Of course," I said.

A quick smile. "So now your work for me is done. But I have a temptation for you. If you do the simple favor of accompanying me to Venice, I will follow your suggestion."

As she had never followed any of my suggestions before, I asked what it might be.

"The toe," she said. "Perhaps you are right that it belongs with the Tetrarch once again."

"I'm proud of you," I said.

"Ah! So the toe has tempted you!"

I could hear a car making its way down our road.

"I told you," I said firmly, "I have not decided—"

"Eh?"

I took a deep breath. "I HAVE NOT DECIDED." Although, to tell the truth, I had indeed decided something important.

Once again, she pretended she had not heard me. "We leave this Friday by train."

"I cannot promise," I insisted, "to leave this Friday by—"

"Sacré bleu!" she said, staring behind me. "What is my cousin doing here?"

"I need to talk with you!"

Giacomo and I stood on the road, by the little outbuilding that housed mysteries of water and electricity; my baronessa had been brought inside by Nimali after a terse greeting for her cousin. The cousin himself, dressed in a thin houndstooth coat and a scarf the same purplish brown as the dead-leaf landscape, hugged himself for warmth. His ears, nostrils, and cheeks were highlighted in red—a technique we had seen in the mosaics of Ravenna.

"We do need to talk," I said.

A light came on in the kitchen: a sign that Nimali had begun dinner preparations. An elaborate wrought-iron-ivy shadow fell across the road. Giacomo, so tall and broad, looked somehow smaller as he rubbed his hands together in the cold before me.

I said, "She has asked me to join her in Venice."

"What's in Venice?"

"I don't know. She leaves Friday by train."

"Two days before Christmas," he said.

I nodded.

"Come to Milan instead. We have everything ready for you."

I could hear the words that Oscar wrote to be read at his memorial—*I gave my heart to the wrong . . . I did not know . . . not ever get those years back . . .* —and I struggled over how to tell Giacomo, that beautiful man who had treasured me and offered me a whole world in Milan, what was gradually becoming clear. I was younger than he, and barely more experienced, but I had gradually assimilated the mistakes of a much older gentleman, gaining knowledge by proximity and observation as I had gained the new language I now spoke daily. The cold air made my eyes tear up. Was I wrong? How to know? The flush on his cheeks brought on by the chill, so like that flush in bed when he would tease me about my way of speaking ("Wow! What's happening?!"); the cloud on the lower rims of his glasses, fogged by his breath, so like how they would steam up after the bath; the stutter, the slow blink—these echoes confused my resolve. And yet Oscar's words came to me. *I gave my heart . . .* What could I say to him? What honesty would not cause more pain? Because I was seeking to decide not just for myself but also for him, to relieve him of the years that he would spend on a mistake. For, as I have said, all we had heard was the overture—the first chords of our affection—and to stake a life on those, to build a home and family and invest the years of youth seemed, I am sure, precisely the brand of boldness his cousin had taught him: we were here, after all, and would not be back! But she always implied the following: *If it is what you want.*

How hard to sort: what we are flattered to believe, what we hope is true, what is really true . . . and what we want. For all my training, I struggled to organize the muddle in my heart.

And yet I knew, though it meant choosing the unknown. I knew it was not enough.

What was the price again, a heavy price, for seeing things as they really are?

"You can't stay here," he said.

"No, I can't stay here. And, Giacomo," I said, taking his hand. "Giacomo . . ."

He stood shivering in the twilight, hope in his eyes, waiting for my decision.

The price for seeing things as they really are. It is our youth.

We left that Friday by train.

At our little station, brown shutters on yellow with Christmas wreaths above the door, I bid a silent goodbye to San Drogo. I had already made my farewells to Ghazel and Vinsanda and Nimali ("Enough!" she shouted merrily), to Cesare and the animals in my room and, finally, to Giacomo's ancestor beside my bed. I packed some of Tonino's wardrobe in my duffel for whatever life awaited me, and when my baronessa discovered how much I had left behind, I merely explained that it belonged better to that charmed place than out in the real world. She seemed irritated, looking me up and down. "You are mistaken about the real world." As for my employer, there was, to my mind, an inordinate amount of preparation for what she claimed would be a one-night stay: a raiding of her closets, including the one in my room, and hours of careful study and conversation with Estelle, robes and dresses and trousers laid out on the bed and analyzed, after which the result was a number of steamer trunks packed into Duccio's truck and sent away like naughty children. Apparently

Estelle went with them, along with Pushkin and Gorky, or at least this was what my employer alluded to as we stood in the courtyard with our luggage. I took Estelle at her word that I would still get to say goodbye to her in Venice. The morning of our departure, my baronessa looked for a long time at the rose-twined olives, the monuments to pugs and loved ones, the tangled forest hiding the old entrance, the olive groves and wisteria and petunias in their pots, and, at last, at the ivy-covered wall that hid Villa Coco from the world. "Avanti!" she said briskly, and went into the car where Vinsanda was waiting, and so we left.

We spoke little on the train from Florence to Bologna, enduring the long dark tunnels in silence. We had chosen facing seats with a table between and I had fallen asleep soon after picking up my book; she had given me Goldoni to read in preparation for my first trip to Venice, and while I found the eighteenth-century jokes amusing, it was a bit like preparing for London by reading Chaucer. *The Servant of Two Masters* was the title, a comedy about a man too greedy for life. I awakened to find my employer seated primly with her purse on her lap, staring directly at me. I took a moment to look out the window and saw a river sparkling below. Not a river, I realized: white butterflies in a deep valley. I thought of my tearful goodbye with Giacomo.

Lazy in love. Oscar had not meant that I must grab what came and hold tight, but the opposite—that I must let go of what I did not want. Let go of an offer that to anyone else might seem the height of glamour, this flat in Milan with a shared affection, perhaps even a shared child, a man to trouble himself over me, support me, adore me for who knew how long? Long enough, for most. But not for me. I could not have told you why; I understood only that it was not what I wanted, that it was not, in my baronessa's term, enough. Let go of Giacomo-Giacomo. And now? Off to the unknown, a servant of no master.

My employer coughed, and I turned my attention to her, sitting in her leather seat beside the window. "So you have ended things with my cousin."

I said I had.

"You are like the lady with the pitchfork," she said.

"What?"

She turned her face to the window. "The lady who fixed your mattress. To end a story at the proper time. It takes an inner will not everybody has."

I said I thought I was unlike the lady with the pitchfork.

"I think we are both in a rather poignant mood. I, too, have had a sad adieu. Perhaps you can tell me a funny story."

"I'm not sure I can think of one right now."

"Tell me about Porta Rossa."

I asked what she was referring to.

"With my cousin and his wife," she said brightly. "Estelle intimated it was like a Feydeau farce!"

Tell me a funny story. She had said this before, on our journey to Ferrara, but I had not previously understood. That day on the train to Venice, however, I did. Of course I was full of sorrow and confusion, but I took the details of the evening in Florence and made of them a funny story. Not just for her; for me. Sitting with her as the landscape raced by, and perhaps inspired by Goldoni, I told her of Laurine's conspicuous pregnancy and her arrival from the train with her girlfriend, Carlotta ("In a hunting jacket? Was she off to hunt lions? Oh, I like this very much!"), and how Giacomo had arranged two rooms at the Porta Rossa. As we came aboveground and passed by Ferrara, I told her of our meal of too much wine and bistecca alla fiorentina ("Buona!") and the lion-hunter girlfriend who spoke only Italian ("This was good practice for you"). How the four of us walked into the lobby, ready to pair off to our rooms, when all of a sudden we heard Laurine's name being called in two high, piercing, harmonizing voices: her aunts, staying on the very same floor ("Disastro!"). I told her of being introduced as the husband of the lion hunter and, in the confusion of us all in the hallway, being forced to enter our room as man and wife while Giacomo and Laurine entered theirs, bidding the aunts good night. Carlotta phoned her girlfriend; a lot of Italian yelling; another phone call and she ordered prosecco, which we shared. The timid knock on the door; Laurine bearing Carlotta's rage, Giacomo bearing mine. How we did not talk until the next morning, and of course then had come the call from Ghazel . . .

I put my hand on her arm: "I forgot to tell you something you would like about her. She is a dog breeder."

"The lion tamer?" She had become a lion tamer in my baronessa's telling.

"And more," I said, then paused. "She breeds pugs!"

She laughed.

I saw so clearly on the train to Venice what I could not see earlier. Not that we were to tell only of silliness and frivolity, not at all; she herself had touched on war and death several times in a dinner conversation. She meant the *story* was not funny—that I had no control over it, or had not reined it in like a wild horse to the course of my choosing, that the comedy I heard so often in her own stories was not at all the shallowness of a rich woman with nothing to worry her but the fierce gaiety of a woman who would not let tragedy bend her. Yes, I had cried in my room after leaving Giacomo: confused, unsure, perhaps a little in love. She was urging me to share that, but not unprocessed, unfiltered so that it remained in its crude, original form of pain and sorrow, plunked down like a bottle of homemade wine. *You must tell it again another time*, she had said on our way to Ferrara. Made better, not just for the sake of the listener but for the sake of the teller. To have mastered the story. It is the work of the metallurgist to extract the gold from a clump of earth, and so it was the work of the speaker, I understood at last, to extract and refine, from the admixed events of love and life, the comedy.

"Lift the shade higher, if you can," she said. "I'd like to watch as we arrive."

I did so, and asked if she could tell me what we were up to in Venice.

"Oh, it's best not to tell until a thing is half accomplished," she said mysteriously. "You have pointed out yourself how superstitious I am. Look, the first seagull! By train is the best way for your first arrival. Many prefer by plane, where you then take a water taxi, but for me it is too modern, and the taxi makes one feel like a whaling vessel. No, it is best to arrive . . . like this."

And so we did.

The arrival in Venice by train is quite famous, and yet it seemed impossible that I was stepping from an ordinary train station into this fantasy of water and stone—a vision covered, as if by a fire curtain before a performance, by a thick layer of fog. I could see lights glowing through the mist, but the city I had heard and read about was not yet visible to me as I followed my baronessa down the steps and to the vaporetto stop. There, she insisted on a "piccolo sconto" (a discount) and, playing the little old lady, she was granted one. A boat came out of the fog, long and narrow, and once a worker had tied it to the dock, we boarded. Again I wondered where Venice was, for all I saw was a blanketing whiteness and churning water. Then the worker closed the gate, unlooped the rope from its mooring, and with a rumble of the engine we were off.

The vaporetto took us onto what my employer told me was the Grand Canal, though to me it was a misty passage from which phantoms appeared—of pilings, rusted gates, lampposts, once the carved head of some drowned god—like the morning's remembered fragments of a lost, elaborate dream. Soon we passed into the lagoon and entered the wider, choppier Giudecca Canal. Here, nothing could be seen. Our boat sounded its foghorn, and from somewhere in the whiteness, another boat signaled back. I heard the clang of a bell. We made a number of stops along the way, disgorging most of the tourists on board, leaving just my baronessa, myself, and a woman with dyed red hair and a tiny dog seated on her enormous bosom. Our boat sounded its foghorn again. "Eccoci," my employer announced, taking my arm to keep her balance, and I wondered how she knew our stop had arrived. I could see nothing. Then, from within the fog, I caught a glow. As we approached, I began to make out the stern gray form of a church emerging as if from a cloud and, set upon it, a light in the shape of a shooting Star of Bethlehem. And then Venice itself came into view, alive with merchants hauling crates, a tourist crowd in red and blue, nuns and sailors and baby strollers and that star reflected on the water like an angel rising there. Of course! How had I missed it? The paintings in the captain's cabin, whose varying weather and costumes had me take them for different harbor towns, were in fact one and the same: They were all Venice. Different moments in time, different facets—like a person you have known all your life.

Soon we were ashore, and I had barely glimpsed the great gray churches and Moorish castle walls of the palazzos before my employer led me to the interior of the city. We turned into an extraordinarily narrow alley ("This street is not for our friend on the boat!" she commented) that emerged onto a small piazza, a kind of compass rose with alleys leading in all directions, some with signs PER RIALTO and PER SAN MARCO in curious U.S. Army stenciling. "Never follow these," my employer warned me, "they are the tourist routes." A bakery displayed domes of Christmas panettone in dark blue paper and plain pandoro wrapped in clear plastic, ready to be shaken with powdered sugar, and some other cake labeled FOCACCIA NATALE that looked nothing like what we had eaten in Recco. We plunged into another dark crevasse, above which hung bedsheets in butterfly patterns and strings of electric lights, then crossed a canal and stopped before an ornate building. The doorbell was a brass circle set inside a concrete one, in which a series of holes were punctured as in an old phone receiver. My baronessa pushed the button, a woman's voice came through, and we were buzzed inside. There was a terrifying, clattering, windowless elevator, and soon we found ourselves being let into a dim room lined with bookshelves. An elderly woman in a shawl kissed my employer on both cheeks. Her stooped figure and bonnet of brown hair reminded me of my aunt Gwen.

"This is Benedetta," my baronessa explained to me. "She speaks no English, but it is not necessary. She is the caretaker while Pippa is away."

"This belongs to the principessa?"

"I always stay with her. Come to the terrace. The view is the same as when I was very young."

I said I had not known her to be sentimental about the past.

She seemed insulted. "Me? Sentimental? Have you ever heard me talk about my childhood home? Not far from here, you know, but I never visit. Too much has changed. But this is something that does not change."

We moved onto the terrace, and I was surprised; the fog was clearing, and the view seemed cluttered with television antennas and satellite disks and various pipes and cables festooning the spaces between the buildings. But I cannot deny that the expression on her face was one of pleasure. Perhaps the mess of things had always been there, the chimneys built in bell shapes or cubes or inverted cones, the terraces so clearly added on later, resting precariously on a few brick pillars, the laundry hanging everywhere to dry. I could not see the canals, or the lagoon. Just one church tower rising above, and a foreboding of storm clouds behind it. She saw something else there that I did not.

"I must rest a little, and then I have a rendezvous at Florian." She pointed to the stone clock in the tower. "Wake me when it points to six."

I did not mention that the clock was hours, if not centuries, out of sync with the world.

When I came to wake her, I found she had already changed into her red silk suit and wore, as she had promised, her famous pearls. I asked if I should change as well, and she said while it was always nice to be elegant, it would not be necessary. "I am meeting someone; you are not. You will take me to San Marco, it is not so far, and then you will leave me. Come now, I am in need of your arm."

Down we went and out into the little piazza like a compass, where green metal streetlamps hung from the corners of buildings, then crossed a canal over a twisted bridge, past little bars opening for the evening and workers already taking advantage of them, drinking wine in plastic cups along the water, smoking, laughing, and a shop of Neapolitan delights that drew me until I felt the pull of my baronessa's hand on my arm. There had been a storm while she rested, erasing the fog, and the stones were black and shining with rain. Christmas lights glittered in the evening air. We came to a street that was signed PER SAN MARCO and, to my surprise, my baronessa led us there. I suppose there was no helping it—that was where we were headed. Here we met the crowds of tourists with gelato. "The only thing tourists can think to do is have gelato," my employer commented, then grinned up at me. "They would never make it down our alley." Impatient with the couples walking slowly hand in hand, blocking the way, and families trying to walk four abreast in a narrow street, and Germans marching along with backpacks and walking poles, she raised her cane in a feint of striking them. "Venice is full of alpinisti this year. Are they heading for the Dolomiti? I can see no other reason for such enormous rucksacks!" She went into a litany of complaints but then added: "The only thing worse is old ladies like me." From some radio above floated music that I recognized as Giacomo's beloved Nina.

A crowd of teenagers, under siege by seagulls for their gelato cones, screamed all out of proportion to the danger, and I thought this would also irritate my employer, but she merely said: "High spirits!" She murmured it again—"High spirits . . ."—and I can only imagine she was remembering her own with Oscar in Istanbul and Capri. "And here for you is San Marco." As she said it, she pushed me slightly out into the open, then looked up at me like someone offering you a syringe of a narcotic, one they have taken many times themselves and developed a tolerance for, so their only pleasure is watching the ecstasy of your first time.

"It is best to enter from here," she said quietly. "From the side. Then you can see the water, look."

A flock of pigeons flew before us—I was reminded of Ghazel's chickens, loosed from his arms and making a chaos of feathers—a flock of pigeons mixed with gulls like a concert of birds, and then the birds departed, revealing the long avenue to the water, which lay still darkened in places beneath storm clouds, in others shining from the sun like a bronze rubbed of its patina. A tower stood erect before us, all in brick with a greenish pyramidal spire, on top of which some gilt archangel trumpeted. Below and to the right, colonnades surrounded a piazza, wet with rain, and to the left the great basilica itself, like the window of a viennoiserie displaying iced domes and sugared biscuits trimmed in gold. The scattered storm clouds caused shadows to lap against the stone and brickwork, but far away the clouds parted, and in that distant sun-glitter a masted ship stood in silhouette. Gull shrieks and water-taxi growls. I walked in awe as she led me to San Marco's southwest corner and from there along the more modest marble walls to a corner that seemed of interest to no tourists or guards.

"You will recognize this," my baronessa said, holding her purse before her.

Nothing more than a rough purplish carving fitted into the wall of the basilica, forming an angle, and it was almost as if some heavenly creature had come down with a cake knife and taken a portion from the great building, revealing a cherry baked in by a tipsy chef. It seemed to portray four nearly identical rulers with swords . . .

"Wait—"

"Such an ancient thing. I'm always surprised nobody notices."

"Wait, is this . . . ?"

I looked up at the Four Tetrarchs, older than anything in the city, standing in this forgotten corner of the piazza, unprotected, like four men waiting for a bus. Their swords were curiously parrot-headed and so, in a way, were their faces: the blank everyman expression of medieval tapestries.

My baronessa pointed with her cane. "See how it has been hacked away. And of course the missing heel . . ."

Indeed, one poor man's foot was made entirely of white stone, making him look like a high school track star in a cast. I wondered that no tourist had cared to sign it. Seagulls tilted above us and moved on to more promising targets. I looked back in wonder at my employer, who wore a grim expression. From her purse she pulled a purple stone and silently stepped forward and fit it into the base. She stood back to judge the effect. "There, I hope you are less ashamed of me now."

I looked upon the source of so much trouble as it sat there, nestled in the white stone of the missing foot. It seemed so insignificant now. "Is that it?"

"I am not sure what you are referring to."

"You had it in your purse? And you're just going to leave it there? Maybe we should . . . is there a mayor or something? A doge?"

"A doge! Napoleon would be amused to hear this."

"It should be presented to the city."

"It belongs to nobody but the Tetrarch himself. He has been reunited with his toe after eight hundred years. I should think this would be enough for anybody."

Strangely, I felt she had a point. I said, "I'm very proud of you." I asked if she felt a weight lifted from her.

I saw her considering this, looking back at the four grave men. "I feel like Casanova forced to pay for something he used to get for free."

Without sentiment, she turned and had me take her past the piazzetta toward the colonnaded piazza, where an orchestra was tuning up its instruments. To my surprise, we headed directly for the orchestra, and I could see there was a café set within the imposing building, and that it seemed to glow a golden color from within. Each wall, I saw, was painted elaborately and protected by a pane of glass; it seemed less like a café than a chapel, and the long table set with goblets and plates, draped with white cloth, its altar. There was no one seated inside, and the tuxedoed waiters looked at us expectantly. I now understood her formal suit.

Seeing my expression, she said, "This is the café Casanova frequented. Also Goldoni. Sometimes a bit of theater is necessary. Here you will leave me."

"Here? How will you get back to the apartment?"

"I am not completely gaga! I will not get as lost as you will."

"But—"

"This part, which is difficult, I must do alone." Then she nodded to me and I watched the figure in red silk, my employer, make her slow way to the café across the cobblestones. I imagined her wearing the clogs of her painted courtesan, stepping gingerly through high water. The waiters went to her at once and brought her within the glass enclosure, and she seemed to have stepped into a living painting.

My baronessa predicted I would become lost, which I promptly did. I found myself almost immediately back at the water, where a bride and groom had been taking wedding photos; it was high tide and the water kept splashing on the walkway stones, and so the bottom of her dress was irredeemably stained with mud. She appeared to be resigned to this and lifted her ruined skirt as they made their way to a bar, where already friends seemed to have ordered her a spritz.

Across the canal, the island of Giudecca had its own pastry shop of domed churches and temples on display, shining in the reflections on the water, along which sped boats like the one that had brought us here. Candied poles stuck out from the water, striped in yellow, red, and pale blue, and along the canals I saw "streetlamps" to light the watery roads. Down an alley I plunged, hoping it was the right direction. SILENTIUM read the sign at the entrance to a church. And indeed, in the wood-beamed passages I took, so low I had to duck my head, all was silent except the lapping of the waves. I began to feel ill at ease; the sound of the rising water was too much like the tide of the past I could feel already dampening my feet, and the low passages too much like the future pressing down from above. With shaking breath, I knew my old life would soon return to me, with its foolish terrors, and all I could do was remain on the perch of the present as long as it would support me.

I passed a shop with an angled window display of slippers. And all of a sudden, as something Oscar once said to me returned, a mouse ran across my heart.

I mentally felt my way back through the streets until I came again upon the store of Neapolitan delights. There, in the window, were displayed two kinds of sfogliatelle: riccia and frolla. It seemed strange to find them here, so far from Naples, and I considered letting this whim vanish, as Oscar had made it clear it was a treat only to be had in Naples, but then another voice came to me, and I decided I was here, the pastry was here, I wanted it, and I would not be back. Behind the pastries stood a middle-aged woman, blond and wearing a pink paper hat; she smiled in anticipation. And yet the choice seemed so obvious; I could not understand how anyone could choose the other. I did not even want to know anyone who would. I stood for a long time before I spoke my choice aloud, then headed into the street to enjoy it, and it is possible that in that moment, without even knowing it, the course of my life was set.

By the intervention of some saint, I found the princess's door again, and, after some discussion with a moaning intercom, was let into the building and then the apartment by the maid, so remarkably like my aunt Gwen, with the same bowed head and backward way of exiting a room. I was left alone in the dim parlor. Potted palms were lined up against each wall, and two red tufted couches sat opposite each other, at a somewhat hostile distance, and on one of them lay Pushkin and Gorky, snoring and seeming hardly to have heads. So they had made it, presumably along with her trunks. There I stood, lit only by the chandelier's sphere of radiance, contemplating the great decisions I had before me—when I heard a rustling from the southward palms, like that of a creature about to emerge from a jungle, and indeed a form did appear from among the leaves, first hard to make out in the dim light, then seeming to take the shape of a great parrot clambering along its perch, turning its beak this way and that so as to get a bilateral view of the situation, and I recognized the personage atop whose head quivered one single artificial flower.

"So good . . . to *see* you," pronounced the Princess Maria Augusta, holding out her hand into the chandelier glow, where it was lit as by spotlight. I took her hand (barnacled with rings) and kissed it. "And how is your life in *Italy*?"

I stepped back to give Pippa room to enter. "It has come to an end, I'm afraid. I'm only here to deliver your friend the baronessa."

She cocked her head. "And what will you *do* now?"

"I may go back to the States," I said. "Or to London."

Her pause remained. "To learn *English*?"

I nearly laughed and stuttered, trying to find a response, but it turned out one was not called for:

"Isn't it *wonderful*?" she said, striding now completely into view. I saw she was draped in shawls. "Lisabetta has her *Caprice* at last." I nodded as if I understood a word of what this meant. "I am glad to have been of service to my *friend*. It was *I* who found her, you know!"

I blinked and kept a smile performing on my face.

She tapped my shoulder with a finger. "The boat," she said. "The boat!"

I remembered my first days at Villa Coco, when my employer explained my role—*I have put something in motion from which there will soon be no returning*—and when she told me about the Tetrarch's toe—*it depends upon a great decision.*

I said, "The *Caprice* . . ."

The smile was like a curtain festooning as it is pulled up, laying bare the stage furniture of the principessa's bright, beautiful teeth, stained slightly blue from the red wine I saw now she held in her hand. She nodded to see my comprehension.

I released the courtliness of my speech. "That's ridiculous!" I said, somehow infuriated by this extravagance. "She bought back her boat? How much could she use it? She's ninety-two. She barely leaves the villa."

I watched as the principessa crossed the room to pull the tassel of a lamp, whose delayed glow seemed like a slightly off lighting cue. She turned to face me with that same smile:

"You know she's not going *back* to the villa!"

I said simply: "What?"

"Your English has *greatly improved*!"

"What do you mean, she's not going back?"

"She *sold it*."

"Sold it?"

The principessa gestured to the entirety of her own apartment. "Sold the house *and* . . . everything in it!"

This revelation shook me. I hardly knew where to begin, or whether to believe her. "But Villa Coco is her home! It's her—" I did not want to say *masterpiece*. "It can't be."

"To Pullman!"

This also took me a moment. "Furman Childress."

"Yes, Pullman."

"She sold her house to Furman Childress." It seemed impossible my baronessa would dispose of her collection, sell off the fruits of her talent, her "eye," as Oscar had put it, to someone she so clearly despised.

The princess raised a finger, and there was a twinkle in her eye. "*And* . . . everything in it!"

She had to say it twice for me to understand.

The princess fairly glittered with excitement. "You know . . . that it was all *my idea*? When she told me of Oscar's illness, and said that she was selling everything and getting the boat. I said, *Lisabetta!* You can't sell Pullman . . . your *treasures*! There's a funnier way to do it! Remember . . . the Queen!"

"The Queen," I said, trying to follow.

She gestured wildly with one hand. "Do what I did with the Queen and my sofa. Give him . . . *copies*!"

I recalled my employer saying the princess was an inspiration to others—they must have cooked up this plan long before my arrival. "And Oscar?"

"Oh, my dear," said the princess. "She did it *all* . . . for *Oscar*."

Of course. My baronessa had known of Oscar's illness and, with Pippa's help, created this final diversion. Perhaps to cling to the past or perhaps in the belief that "high spirits" might yet keep him alive. To fool their old nemesis one last time. Sell him all of her remaining "treasures," each one meticulously copied and replaced. The originals sold from Oscar's apartment to fund a grand adventure for the two of them, one last caprice! Except that Oscar had not made it to the end.

The principessa was eager to ask: "Tell me, did Pullman accept . . . *the list*?"

"It was notarized," I said.

"Excellent. That was his . . . *stipulation*. An expert American archivist."

"I see," I said. And so at last I knew my job description.

"Yes, yes, it was all . . . *my idea*!"

I tried to stifle a laugh but failed, and it came out in an unbecoming snort. The princess drew herself up augustly. I was about to point out how ridiculous her "idea" was, the kind of thing a group of schoolboys would come up with to taunt a rival, and full of holes such as . . . But I stopped myself. Because of course that's exactly what it was, and what was the point of telling her? Children. Elderly, larger-than-life children, such as Oscar and my employer and Pippa herself, operating in their cartoon world of cartoon logic, cooking up a scheme that would never work except against someone as childish as themselves. Some enemy from their youth. They lived in a sealed world of comic-strip logic, and within that world, all schemes ended as happily as a monkey's life in Zanzibar.

Do you know? I had become so used to the whims and chaos of that villa, the walls of dogs and elephant graveyards, that it made a kind of mad sense. I had auditioned for a role—that of the wide-eyed American scholar—and I had been a triumph. I was, in a strange way, honored now to be in a story that my employer would tell around her dinner table . . .

And then it hit me that my parting from Villa Coco was not, as I had somehow imagined, an arrivederci to a place to which I would surely return, this time not as a servant but as a guest. I thought of my baronessa's thoughtful look back. It had been goodbye forever.

I asked, "And what is her plan, I'd like to know?"

"To live her days at *sea*."

I must admit that I laughed. "Our baronessa? Is going to live on some boat? I don't believe it."

"You don't?"

"People don't do things like that."

And then the old princess, tottering from one spotlight to the next like some aged chanteuse, in her shawls and her jiggling flower, spilling wine onto the wavering terrazzo floor, said something to me that was so strange—and yet so important—that I have made it the epigraph of this tale:

"Lisabetta knows the trick to life," she said, "is knowing what you want."

At the time, I stood back, baffled by such a statement from her. I had taken her for a vain, foolish, morally myopic species of flightless bird, but here, suddenly, were words to ponder. I had considered life to be a matter of knowing what was needed, what was necessary, what was crucial to each circumstance—the mindset, I suppose, of a servant to life and not a princess or a baronessa, someone who has never bought off the rack—and so I shook my head in confusion.

But I was asking the wrong questions. And I was asking the wrong person.

My baronessa did not return until late. I had made myself a makeshift dinner from cheese and prosciutto in the "frigo" and broken off a piece of panettone on the counter; I found

I could not stop myself, and was ashamed to realize I'd eaten half the cake. Pippa herself had cheerfully bid me good night, which I took to mean she was off to bed; instead, she put on a shimmering golden cloak and headed out the door, presumably to a party or merely to walk the streets of Venice as if it were Carnevale. I sat and drank and amused myself with a book I found on her shelves, Graham Greene in Italian; I had read it before in English and so could keep up with the plot. A bell rang the hour from some distant tower. I sat very still as Pushkin and Gorky mumbled to each other in their sleep. A few minutes later, another bell rang the hour. Who knew which one to believe? Sound of the buzzer; the maid pattered into the hall (as Aunt Gwen would have), dressed now in a flannel housecoat. Through the intercom I heard my employer's crackling soprano. The maid and I waited as the elevator chugged to life, then clanked to a stop. The maid opened the door. Somehow my employer had managed the streets of Venice without wrinkling her red suit, though her lipstick was worn away and she seemed weary beyond measure. Beneath the veil of weariness, though, a glimmer of triumph.

"I am glad to see you found your way. I will have a glass of your wine," my employer said, taking the sofa with Pushkin and Gorky. "I have abstained all night to keep my wits, but my wits are no longer needed."

I poured her some wine, and she appraised it before taking a sip. I sat down opposite her and observed her for a moment. "Why didn't you tell me?" I asked.

She smiled. "Ah, you talked to Pippa."

"Why didn't you tell me why you hired me?"

"Are you referring to Pullman and the house? Pippa's wine is always awful."

"No, no, the reason you hired *me*," I said. "Me in particular."

"I don't know what you mean."

"You hired me because I'm American."

"Eh?"

"All this time making fun of me for not knowing Italian, not knowing history or art. But in fact that's exactly why you hired me. A young, stupid American. Who wouldn't figure out—"

"I have nothing against the young."

"It's just the most ridiculous plan! Just to . . . stick it to Pullman for something that happened fifty years ago. I'm ashamed of you, honestly."

"Ashamed!"

"Why didn't you tell me?"

"I don't enjoy explanations," she said without looking up. She sipped her wine and sighed deeply. "Besides, you would have played fair. It would have spoiled everything for Oscar. Are you very furious with me?"

There was a racket of someone across the courtyard battling with their shutters, a clanking, then a creaking of rusty hinges like the sound of geese. A rushing noise was perhaps a boat going by on the canal below.

"I am," I said. "I should call your friend Pullman—Furman—right now."

"HO HO HO! Hardly a friend. I suppose it is foolish. One last time with Oscar, I thought. One last trick on that cretino. Why not? Though there is a poetry to the latest I heard from Nimali, which is that they have found the second pozzo at last! You recall, from our first day." She snickered very wickedly. "It has overflowed onto Pullman's new property."

I was not to be distracted by her scatological humor. "Nimali and Vinsanda! Ghazel! What happens to them?"

"Gazelle is to join his son, who is a great success. As for

Nimali. You think she learned nothing in my household? Embezzling. Embezzling all along! I am told she bought herself and Vinsanto a little house by a river."

They had also taken Cesare. I was surprised and delighted and relieved. I was reminded of the diviner who had told my baronessa that she was not to die in that house. Villa Coco was a great treasure for her to give up. But by giving it up, she had shaped destiny to her liking.

"You were a strict young man when you arrived," she said, lowering her chin. "But you will not call Pullman."

"Why not?"

"Because you are not that young man anymore."

I regarded her, sitting crookedly in her red suit and camel coat with Pushkin and Gorky asleep around her. Was this, from her, the highest form of praise? That I, too, had lost my sense of morals? But, as I have said, I never really had them. I thought of Estelle's portrait of me, so much older than I saw myself.

"I misjudged you," she said. "That is the truth of it. Estelle was always your advocate, but I would not listen to her, I said we could not tell you under any circumstance. You are too American to trust. She is, by the way, a wonderful painter but terrible at forgery. That was a disappointment. You see how hard it was to lose Oscar. We had to hand over to Pullman a number of my best works. And Oscar meant to sail with us . . ."

"Yes. You did misjudge me."

"You must forgive me," she said. "I will need you tomorrow. We will have to be up very early. The arrangement is Schiavoni at dawn. The harborage is not entirely legal, but I am advised the carabinieri are not early risers, thanks God. I am not as nimble as in my seventies, but with luck, we may elude them! I will need your assistance to board, as Estelle will meet us there with my luggage and Pushkin and Gorky."

I understood this was to be my final duty as her assistant. Or adjutant or maggiordomo or man Thursday or archivist or whatever I had been to her. I said I would be up early to wake her before our goodbyes. My baronessa turned to me and said:

"Do you think it is a great folly?"

I leaned forward, hands on my knees. "Since you ask, I do."

She seemed serious. "I'm a foolish old woman, you think."

"No, no, of course not."

Her chin lifted. "But still you don't approve."

"It's not something I would do."

"Live a life at sea?"

I exhaled with frustration. "I mean forge art and lie and sell everything on a whim. *And* live on a boat! It's ridiculous!"

"You don't see the humor?" she asked. So this was the why: simply because it was funny. "Think on it for a moment. Surely a life at sea has an appeal!"

"But to choose this? At your age?"

She was half in shadow now on the sofa, the red wine trembling in her hand, but Pippa's strange lamp gleamed in her eyes, and I could see how pleased she was.

"We have to choose something," she said at last. "The wrong choice, maybe, but we have to choose."

I went to bed and could not sleep. Too many images floated across the walls of my mind, like those headlights from when I was a boy that seemed like enchanted figures, or portents, when they moved around the confines of my ordinary bedroom. I was so afraid. I had made a choice without knowing what came next, like staying on a train after your stop has passed. What was ahead? I almost panicked and picked up the phone to call Giacomo. And then the strangest occurrence: like those crossed phone wires that allow one, at ghostly moments, to listen to some stranger's conversation, my baronessa's words from earlier began to play in my head—*we have to choose*—over and over, loudly—*the wrong choice, maybe, but we have to choose*—and it was almost as if I were trying to silence the sound, but I could not stop it before my heart overheard. The images remained, a celestial globe of constellations turning in my skull. Somewhere in those moments, sleep flowed into my mind and my thoughts dissolved there, turning into dreams.

I was awakened hours later by the sounds of whispering and of people moving heavy things; I must have left my dream-door unlatched because, at one point, my bedroom door opened and a menace, silhouetted in the dim hall light, seemed to have walked into my room. He fumbled in darkness but departed with a thump of the door. Minutes later, another thump and then no more; my dream intruder was gone.

How easily I can picture the wetted stones of the campo that Christmas Eve, the topos delivering fresh rolls or vegetables or foodstuffs; the garbage scows; the boats bringing bales of fresh linens to hotels, lifting them onto the walk with red-painted cranes; the ducks sleeping head under wing in the gondola shipyards; the pink-tinted glass of the lamps along the Schiavoni, precisely the same color as the morning sky; the waves crashing against the walkway as we arrived at the appointed spot. I had awakened blearily that morning and found, for the first time, my employer dressed before me. I put on clothes from the night before and barely got a coffee in me before we were on the streets. I was to deliver her here and then return to the principessa's, grab my duffel, and head to Florence for my flight home. I wondered what awaited me there. I looked around. Not a single boat was berthed; perhaps they were elsewhere for Christmas. My baronessa saw a red wooden bench nearby, and we waited there, watching the sun (behind us) begin to catch the green bell tower of San Giorgio, the sky behind it lightening to reveal the dark angel standing at its peak, then catching the golden globe held up by two Atlases at the foot of the Dogana, a statue that swiveled in the wind. Between, the water was striped wine red and black.

"I had some news from the villa last night," she said at last. She sat with her cane upright between her feet, her hands balanced on its silver handle. "Our enemy is vanquished."

"Pullman?" I said. "My God! What have you done to him now?" I wondered if the murder mysteries had given her too many ideas.

"The faina!" she said, turning to me with a smile. "She has died at last!"

I sighed with relief. "How did Ghazel accomplish it?"

"He did not accomplish it. She died," my employer said, "of an overdose! She made her way into the house and found the fish oil. What a party she must have had! They found her curled up . . . on your mattress." I saw both her admiration of her foe and her delight in having outlived her.

"I apologize," I said quietly, "for calling you ridiculous last night."

But she did not seem to hear; her mood was too merry: "You know I am worried for Estelle. That she will fall in love with the skipper I've hired. I would fall in love if I were still in my seventies, and as you know, she and I have the same taste in men. And the *Caprice*! I was pleased to discover they had not renamed her. I've been through that once; it is an ordeal. You have to give the old name to Poseidon, who it seems is still out there, and hail the gods of the wind. All sorts of things."

I shook my head. No apology was necessary, apparently. "Where will you travel first?"

"To Split, I think. That is the closest city, and Croatia is quite beautiful. But I am thinking of returning to Jaipur, which I have not visited in many years."

I went to a mental map of India. "Isn't that . . . isn't that landlocked?"

She considered this. "They were always speaking of building a canal. I'm sure they've finished it by now."

We sat in silence after this bit of absurdity, watching as the water lost its blackness, as if dissolving the effects of night, becoming first striped in mauve and blue and then, as the sun rose fully into the sky, turning the streaked whiteness of mother-of-pearl.

She took the cane in one hand. "You are still thinking of America?"

"I have a ticket."

She was saying: "We both know what would become of you."

I snapped to attention. "And what is that?"

"You would go back to old habits," she told me, tapping one of my slippers with the tip of her cane.

"Such as?"

"You would start thinking again that literature began with Hemingway and art with Warhol. That the fate of the world depends upon your presidential election. That a proper dinner conversation is to discuss your favorite television shows. Like every American, you would lose—"

"Really?" I broke in, irritated. "What would I lose?"

She looked at me at last. "Your sense of humor."

I sighed and found myself chuckling, shaking my head. It was true I would miss the ridiculousness of life at Villa Coco, her errant tales, and even more stories I had not heard and would now not be part of. A passing boat sent waves that splashed over the seawall, and we pulled our feet back to avoid getting soaked.

"I have a funny story," she began, this time without her usual verve for storytelling. She seemed to be saying it not to me but to the sea. "I lost the *Caprice* to a man! Of all things! He was a Ukrainian toothpaste magnate. Isn't that absurd? But very handsome and very charming. I met him at a party in Capri, and we took off our shoes to dip our feet in the pool, and tout à coup he grabbed my shoe and threw it far into the sea! 'Now you can never leave me,' he said. The most charming thing a man had ever done. I think you know a little about love."

I said nothing as she looked out across the water. Concern creased her face; the hour had come and gone for her beloved boat to arrive. But she kept on with her story:

"Later I cheated him and was caught out. A little jewel. It is simply my nature. I could not give it back because I had already sold it to buy the *Caprice* and so on and time had passed. I told you Oscar and I had sailed her all the way to Istanbul! So the Ukrainian said, 'Darling, I will save you from prison. I will take your boat and we will part as friends.' I had no choice. Perhaps I loved him, but I loved my boat more and I have only my own bad character to blame."

"Was he who you met at Florian?"

"No," she said quietly. "He is long dead. That was his grandson."

We sat for a moment as the morning sun lit the building across the canal.

"I see you have bought the slippers Oscar suggested," she said. I lifted them into view. "Do you feel like the pope?" she asked.

"Not very," I said, then added: "I guess this is goodbye."

She sniffed and kept looking out to sea.

"I will always think," I added, "of the most glamorous shit in Southern Europe."

She let out a yelp of laughter and briefly touched my hand; I knew this was as close to goodbye as I was likely to get from her. I looked out again to the empty horizon.

"Do you think they are coming?" she asked briskly.

"Of course," I said. "Isn't that what you agreed?"

"I wonder if I should not have paid them in full last night. As you see, I can be foolish when I want something so dearly."

I turned to face her. "Have you seen the boat?"

She seemed startled. "Not in many years."

A feeling of dread overcame me. "How do you know he even has your boat? And you paid him already. That wasn't wise."

"You think not?" she asked. "I am becoming unsure."

I put my hand on hers, and I could feel it trembling. "Oh no," I said, "what if you've been fooled?"

The old larcenist, the old pirate queen, my baronessa—her eyes were wide, her mouth hanging slightly open as she looked far out across the Giudecca Canal at the brick Fortuny building. A bit of sun broke through, hit the waters, and darted across her features, scribbling as if leaving its signature there. She looked very old at that moment. Perhaps the years were flashing before her, not in sequential order like a train passing a village station, but in the strange associations of her mind in which all the nights in Jaipur, all the lovers' words in French, all the Venetian childhood winters linked together and floated, in groups of two or three or more, like wreaths on Dal Lake. A finale for the woman in the fourteenth row. Perhaps it was occurring to her that this could be the end of her lucky streak; she had cast the shoe of fortune into the sea and now there was no leaving. A cold wind came across the wintry canal and sent a shiver first through me, then through her. Then through whatever ghosts attended us.

"Coco . . . ," I began.

I heard her sharp intake of breath, and just then I saw it, coming from the east and partially disguised by the darkness of the barrier island, a silhouette of two lugsails against the sunrise, the boat I recognized from the bronze sculpture far away in Tuscany, which I now realized I would never see again. But what was the need to see it? For here it was, beyond all doubt: the *Caprice*.

Burning on the waters of the lagoon: a burnished throne of purple sails, the sun like beaten gold upon her deck, like silver on her fittings! Twenty meters from bow to stern and crafted after the old two-masted trabàccolos that used to ply the waters of the Venetian lagoon, painted black but decorated, at the stern, with gods and sea maidens in white and red. Her name was done in gold leaf—*CAPRICE*—and as soon as she pulled up, the skipper waved to my employer to come aboard. He was a strongly built man, deeply brown, with a gray-streaked beard and a white kerchief tied on his head. Around the boat I saw a crew of five or six. Estelle appeared suddenly from the cabin, waving frantically. I think I had never seen her so happy. The skipper threw a board down to the stones at our feet.

"You see how attractive he is," my employer said, standing now with a smile on her face.

Estelle yelled to us in Italian but I could not make it out. She was holding something in her arms, and now I could see it was those able-bodied seamen Pushkin and Gorky.

"My trunks are all on board," my baronessa said. "Along with your bag, I'm afraid. A misunderstanding with the porters."

I thought of my visitor in the night. "Maybe they could bring mine ashore—"

She leaned toward me with a whisper, "This skipper will be trouble. Mark my words."

"So we can say goodbye—"

"And our dear Oscar," she said, patting her bulky purse, "will make the voyage after all! Along, I am afraid, with a disappointment."

She opened the purse, and within I could see, beside the tin that must have contained our friend's ashes, the purple toe of a Tetrarch.

"You will forgive me, but it lived so long with me, I thought it could live a little longer." She sighed. "A last caprice! Now help me with this difficult part of going aboard the barca."

I assisted her, as best I could, in traversing the board, which seemed none too stable. I would have to grab my bag and return across this board in velvet slippers. It was a slippery endeavor. My employer struggled along with her cane, a hand on my arm, until one of the crew took her hand and brought her on board. I looked around; my duffel was nowhere to be seen. The skipper approached my employer, kissed her on both cheeks, and she exclaimed:

"The vertigo! It is gone!"

She threw down her cane in triumph, then turned to me:

"You see? I am only really myself when I am at sea."

She was in her place in the world. And I began to think, quite suddenly, of my own. For it was as if I had delivered an important message to a remote king, who had read it and sighed his understanding, and now I would be out of the story and on my own to return from this foreign land to my home, which months or years of travel had made to me a distant place, or else continue on my journeys, somehow, in hopes of keeping in my veins this strangeness, this incongruity, which had become my ordinary life.

Estelle ran up to me and kissed me on each cheek.

"You're going?" I asked.

"Yes, I'm going!" she said, grinning. She wore a gray padded down vest over an oilskin coat, a white scarf and hat; she was certainly dressed for a life at sea.

I shook my head. "You're crazy! Both of you are crazy!"

She shrugged. "I have your painting aboard."

"Thanks, I'll take my bag and say goodbye."

My baronessa's mind was elsewhere: "Oh, we must be quick, the carabinieri are up early. We don't want questions."

And indeed two men in white sashes and red-striped pants were already walking down toward the water, for my employer had, unwisely but perhaps typically, made her arrangements within meters of their headquarters. I saw them catch sight of us and hasten their walk. Luckily, they were hefty fellows unused to great exertions, and so they were not making much headway toward our illegal berthing.

"Quickly now, time is made of gold," my employer was saying. "They must pull up the board."

"Hey!" I said. The sun had appeared again, like an actress peeking between the curtains to gauge the crowd, and light silvered the water all around us. Gulls were fighting above. The two policemen were lolling toward us like characters from a Pulcinella show. I felt dizzy. "What's happening?! I have to—"

"Fate has placed your bag here, Giovedì. It seems to me one should follow fate."

I looked around foolishly, as if my duffel would suddenly appear. "What? What?"

My former employer pulled her camel coat closer about her. "We will leave any moment and I think you should remain."

"What?" I asked one final time, comprehending. "I can't live on a . . . on a . . ."

"Why not?" Estelle asked, and my employer's eyes asked the same.

"I have other plans, I have—"

"What are these plans?" my baronessa insisted. "You must consider how difficult it will be for us, only two women at dinner."

Estelle said, "We do have the skipper."

My employer countered, "It is always best to have an even number."

It seems to me, even now, with the long expanse of years, impossible that she could have arranged the arrival of carabinieri to make the boat's departure so urgent, but then again, her genius was in making life do her bidding. For I understood that this very moment had been under discussion for a long time between the two of them. I remembered the gleam of recognition in her eye the day I stole Oscar's ashes.

"I can't," I said. "I can't."

Estelle took my hand and held it.

My baronessa startled me by calling me by my true name: "Geoffrey," she said firmly. "Here we are in Venice. You are already aboard. Here we are, Geoffrey." She paused a moment and looked me carefully in the eye.

I said, "And we won't be back."

She seemed surprised. "What are you talking about? It's Venice!" she said. "Of course we'll be back!"

I turned and watched the carabinieri making their absurd stride along the walkway, as slowly as if they were treading in high water. It is hard to peer through the midnight ocean of time to see myself glimmering down there, so small and young and unformed, and understand I am somehow still that same person who came to those choices, the choices that have made me who I am. What were my thoughts at that moment? What were my fears?

All I know is I turned to my baronessa and said—

"Mollate gli ormeggi!" shouted the skipper, and "Aye, aye, capitano!" called the crew, and the board was swept onto the ship, the motor started, and we were headed off into the lagoon with the police ashore, waving their hands. My employer, as she said, seemed free at last of her dizziness and withstood the movement without a tremor. It was some moments before I realized that I had chosen to join the voyage, although perhaps if I had asked Estelle (positioned now beside one of the furled sails, grinning into the breeze), she would have said I had made my choice long before. I wondered what I had packed that might suffice for our first stop in Croatia, perhaps, where I would surely leave the party and find my own road, or for Greece or Egypt or Aden, for undoubtedly at some port I would step ashore, like a well-used crewmember, to find my own particular fate. We sailed toward the sunrise, toward the barrier island of the Lido and the Adriatic beyond. On the horizon, I could see three stars still clinging to the glowing sky.

"We will have to live frugally aboard," I heard my employer saying. "There will be privations of persons and of pleasures. Here on the barca we are living off the sales of my property and art. There is enough, but no more! Let's hope I don't live too long."

"Nonsense!" Estelle shouted in the wind.

My baronessa clapped her hands. "In barca," she said, "italiano!"

Our young man, switching to Italian, laughing, said, "Coco, you will live forever!"

And so she did.

* * *

ABOUT THE AUTHOR

Andrew Sean Greer is the bestselling author of seven previous works of fiction, including the Pulitzer Prize winner *Less* and its companion, *Less Is Lost*. He lives in San Francisco and Venice, Italy.